ROM ~~ANCE~~

# THE
# UNDERCOVER
# MILLIONAIRE

## CLARE LONDON

JOCULaR PRESS

Can poverty and privilege find a loving compromise?

Alexandre Bonfils, a rich and spoiled second son, is tired of being ignored and decides to help when the family's exclusive wine business is in trouble. Going undercover in the warehouse, he loves the adventure—and the chance to be close to the sassy and sexy manager, Tate Somerton.

Tate is hardworking and financially struggling, bringing up his siblings on his own. A suspected saboteur at work is his latest challenge, but now he also has a clueless, though very attractive, new intern. There's an immediate spark between the ill-matched couple, until a shocking accident cuts short Alex's amateur sleuthing.

While recovering in the generous care of Tate and his family, will Alex realise what belonging really means? Passion and pride come together to fight for the company they're both committed to preserving, but can a personal bond remain when the dust settles?

## DEDICATION

To my readers, in the hope they have as much
fun reading the story as I did writing it!.

# CONTENTS

# CHAPTER 1

"Alexandre, good morning." Charles Bonfils, the patriarch of Bonfils Bibendum, the highly prestigious London wine merchants, a cousin of an English baronet, and a personal multimillionaire—if he ever had the poor manners to share actual financials with anyone other than his personal advisors—inclined his distinguished, salt-and-pepper-haired head at the young man sitting on the other side of his desk. "Good of you to turn up on time."

Alex Bonfils inwardly winced. His father was one of the few people who could, without fail, make him feel four years old again. He resisted rubbing his palms dry on his designer slacks, but only just, and nodded in reply. "Papa, when you call, I come. Of course."

Charles lifted one eyebrow; that was all.

It was enough.

"Father." Alex took a deep breath and ran his hand through his blond hair, inevitably destroying the artful work of his personal stylist. "Okay, so I know I haven't been your most reliable son—"

"I only have two," Charles murmured. "And all I ask is that they are both full participants in the family business. Or any legitimate business, for that matter." He sounded calm, but his fingers

1

tightened dangerously around his antique ink pen.

"Yeah." Alex assumed this summons was something to do with him missing the latest Bonfils management meeting. Or maybe it was because of those embarrassing paparazzi pictures taken in the nightclub last weekend with the twin male models. Or when he gate-crashed the Queen's garden party last summer, or the fact that Alex had never bothered to finish his university business management course, preferring to go backpacking in Ibiza, or... or... oh, many more examples of how he continued to disappoint his august Papa.

"I think the time has come to face facts," Charles said.

"Yes? I mean, it has? What about?"

Charles grimaced, obviously struggling to keep his temper. "You have shown little enthusiasm in the business to date, whereas Henri...."

Alex bit back a snort. *Henri.* His revered, very sober and sensible elder brother, with a gorgeous aristocratic wife and two precocious children to carry on the Bonfils family line. Henri was their father's chosen heir to the business dynasty. Henri was brighter, smarter, more reliable, more respectable, more predictable—

"Alexandre? Are you listening to me?"

Alex jolted back to attention. "Sure. Go on. You were talking about Henri. How does that affect me?" He hadn't meant to sound snappy, but constant comparison to a preferred sibling would do that to a guy.

"He's Bonfils's CEO for a reason, Alex. He's

committed to the company, a fierce supporter of the industry. He listens, and he learns. Then he works hard."

The implication was there—Henri was and did all the things Alex wasn't and didn't.

"I can work hard." Alex wished he sounded less defensive. He *could* work hard. He was just so rarely inspired to. Or rather, he was distracted by things more exciting, more dramatic, more intriguing than profit and loss accounts, stock turnover ratios, and five-year operational budgets.

He hid his shudder at the mere thought.

Surprisingly, his father didn't scorn his protest. Instead, his gaze almost softened. "Believe me, I know you can. And you do, for the things you love. You have many excellent qualities, and the good intention of using them. But I can't rely on mere intention for the continuing, successful management of this company. It needs to be your life's work."

Alex blinked hard. What was Charles saying? "Jesus, Papa. Are you *firing* me?"

Charles blew out a tight breath. "I cannot fire you, as you so quaintly put it, when you have a unique position as my son. However, I see no reason to burden you with an operational role any longer." His tone hardened. "Alexandre, I think you should find yourself a new, personally satisfying project. You will no longer be needed at the monthly management meetings. Your personal allowance will continue—it was your mother's last wish that all members of the family are supported, regardless of their role in the business—but I think it best for both our expectations if you distance yourself for a while from Bonfils's Bibendum." He placed his pen down on the desk blotter with exaggerated care.

Alex was speechless. It was an unfamiliar status.

For a long moment, Charles was still. Then he stood and half lifted his hand from his side, as if he was about to shake Alex's hand or maybe—just maybe—pat him on the shoulder. Instead, he sighed deeply and gestured gently toward the door for Alex to leave. "And now, if you'll excuse me, I have an appointment elsewhere."

Alex was still in a state of shock a half hour later. He sat in one of the luxurious chairs in the office reception area, nursing a cup of coffee that had gradually gone cold. Just for a while, he wasn't sure where else to be. He'd put aside most of the day to meet his father, assuming his periodic hauling over the coals would take its usual thorough and teeth-clenching time. However, it had taken Papa less than fifteen minutes to *dump* his own son. Okay, so that was melodramatic, maybe, and Papa had dressed it up in a civil way, but that was the gist of it. His father had probably assumed that Alex would be relieved to step away from daily management, to leave the hassle and complexity to Papa and Henri. After all, that's what Alex usually did, wasn't it?

But it still hurt, and in a rather perplexing way. He'd never really worked anywhere else but

Bonfils. During school vacations, he'd helped out with menial tasks in the office or one of the warehouses, though he realised now he'd never given work the same attention that Henri did. He didn't *need* to work, was the issue at the heart of everything. He had family money, excellent schooling, the youthful confidence of a well-bred English man in his late twenties, and—no point in being coy—natural good looks. That had sufficed him through life so far. His lovely French mother had died when he was only thirteen, his bereaved father continued to work all hours God sent, and Henri was already working toward his position at Papa's side in the business. So there was little rein on Alex's behaviour. What was he meant to do, with such minimal supervision? They were damned lucky he hadn't gone completely off the rails. As it was, he'd spent most of the time enjoying every opportunity his position and wealth made available. He sighed rather theatrically, though no one paused in their scurrying past him, to and from the meeting rooms. Everyone knew their place here, and their duty to the Bonfils family.

*Except me, apparently.*

"Mr. Alexandre? Would you like some more coffee?" The two beautifully groomed assistants on reception were very polite, but maybe a little nervous as well. People weren't used to seeing Alex in the office. And when he did pass through, it was always in a rush of laughter, impatience, and widely dispensed flattery. Not this unfamiliar introspection in the guest seating of his own family's domain.

"I'm fine, thanks." He didn't miss the quick glance between the young man and his female companion. He might have been introspective but he wasn't blind. From their shared expression, they were wondering whom to call on his behalf. His father? A doctor? *Security?* Alex bit back another sigh. He seemed to remember confidently flattering both of the lovely young things in the past. No wonder they were bemused.

His gaze drifted to the large windows beside the reception desk. Here on the eighth floor of an exclusive building in the heart of the financial district, they maximised a superb view over London. Birds wheeled around the top of the tower blocks, the late October sun glinting off their myriad windows. Black cabs trundled along the road, so far below Alex that they looked like Matchbox toys. Homegoing office workers scurried onto double-decker buses and down into the Tube system, swarming and swerving around each other with the same innate sense of purpose and direction as soldier ants. Souvenir shops splashed the red, white, and blue colours of the British flag in their merchandise, coffee chains tempted passersby into their premises with seductive menus, the occasional, select fashion stores displayed the latest glamourous styles on androgynous models. On the Embankment, the London Eye loomed over everything, its pods revolving so slowly, so soporifically, that Alex wondered if he should just sit here another hour or so, watching them as meditation. It reminded him of that vacation he took in the Himalayas one year, on the quest for life advice from that grizzled old guru—

Yet it was the memory of another place that struck him now with a rush of joy, peace, and some bittersweet memories. The Fairweather Vineyard in England's West Country, where the grapes for Bonfils's sparkling wines were grown, had been part of Alex's life from when he was a child, from when... Mama was still alive. He found himself yearning for that now, for the quiet yet vibrant fields enclosing the site, the lush grass under his often bare feet, the rustle of the vines on their supports. He and Henri had played there as kids, and even in Alex's later years, he would visit there when he needed to break away from the hectic city life he led. They'd helped with the harvest until their late teens—well, as much as youngsters could help who didn't depend on the crop for their wages and got caught eating the too-sharp grapes too often to be efficient. The managers were grimly tolerant of him, Papa had rolled his eyes, and Mama...? While she lived, she always smiled even after she chastised him, even though the smile was sometimes sad. She'd loved the vineyard too and had helped plan the hospitality suite they ran there for guests and tourists. She'd chosen the warmest side of the building to build a luxurious patio, where she herself could sit and enjoy the view across the Devon hills at any time of day or night, gazing over the heads of the vines and the surrounding hedgerows, sipping a glass of her family's best wine.

It was one of his most vivid memories of her.

A well-dressed, attractive woman in her early thirties sat down abruptly in the chair beside him. "Alexandre? Good to see you here. We need to talk."

*Good God.* One of the grimmest phrases in the English language, in Alex's honest opinion. He could remember more than a few exes starting off their final conversations with him with just those words. "Tina, ma chère! Hello to you too. Are you bringing a message from my father?"

"No. What were you expecting?"

A grovelling apology from Papa for ever doubting him? A plea for Alex to come back to the board, to bring his unique blend of charm and wit to the stuffy old agenda? *Not gonna happen.* Alex knew it as certainly as he knew the young man at reception—quickly replacing the handset of the telephone, having called in his reinforcements— was now very obviously blushing at him, and could be tumbled into a compromising position within the hour, if Alex wished it. He couldn't remember the last time anyone had refused him anything. Well, until today's meeting with Papa.

"You heard I'd been brutally sacked? Told to keep out of the damned way?"

"Oh, I'm sure it wasn't like that at all, Alex. Heavens, everything's so melodramatic with you." Tina graciously thanked the young woman who brought them fresh coffee, as if magically conjured up. Tina Archer was his father's PA, and a dear family friend. She was unflaggingly professional and always discreet, but she also took no nonsense.

"I've been fired. Discarded. Abandoned." Alex was working himself well into the role of victim. "I've never wanted to be anything but a Bonfils."

"You always will be. But did you think that was a one-way street? That you wouldn't have to offer your time and effort in return?"

"I am family. That should be enough."

Tina snorted in a very unladylike manner. "Yes, like I said. You make everything a performance."

Alex opened his mouth to protest angrily, then rethought. If he were honest with himself—and he almost always was—she was right. But dramatic effect made life more exciting, didn't it? His life, anyway. His hedonistic, rather empty, purposeless life. *Dammit.* He couldn't help but recall his father's earlier sigh of disappointment and frustration. Maybe it was merited, after all.

Tina sipped her coffee and her expression became more sympathetic. "You are so lucky, Alex. You have looks, charm, access to almost limitless money. Yet what do you do with it?"

He was pretty sure *have fun* wasn't the right answer.

Her gaze softened. "I love you dearly, Alex. We've been friends since you were a teenager and I first came to work for the company, remember?"

He did indeed. Tina had arrived in the London office with the glowing references that Alex would have matched to a much older, more serious, and extremely dull person. Instead, he'd met a witty, pretty, perceptive young woman who, over the years, had paid as much care and attention to the Bonfils family members as to the company's smooth operation.

"Back then, you and Henri were enthusiastic, caring, fun-loving young men. I know what he grew up to be—"

Alex tried hard to keep his expression neutral, he really did.

"—and yes, I know you think that's boredom personified. But what about you? You've swung so totally the opposite way, I sometimes don't recognise you. You've created this frivolous, careless playboy image, then take every opportunity to thrust it in everyone's face. Your timekeeping is appalling, you chase after every latest fad, you serially date any and all young men who take your fancy, you habitually waste money, and above all, you show little business interest in the company. Is it any wonder Mr. Charles has grown tired of trying to engage with you? It must seem to him that whatever you're given, you expect more. That you really do think everything is yours for the taking."

Wow. No holding back there, then. Yet her words reverberated in his mind. *Am I really like that?* He knew exactly how well and enjoyably he lived, yet he didn't want to believe that was the whole story of his life. An unfamiliar flush heated the back of his neck.

"Wait." Tina reached out to take his hand, shaking her head. "I haven't finished."

"Good God, really? Well, don't feel you have to hold back on my account—"

"No, you idiot." Tina laughed at his aggrieved tone. "I know very well that isn't the sum of Alex Bonfils. You have far more to offer, you're intelligent and compassionate, and care for far more than entertainment. You just hide it too well! For example, who really knows it was your idea to start a Bonfils sommelier internship, open to all applicants?"

"Well, no one outside the board, but that was so obviously a good initiative—"

"And that you've been mentoring Liam, the new assistant in HR, developing the training programme?"

"I mean, yes, but that's no hardship, when he's got great potential and is so very enthusiastic—"

Tina pressed on, more firmly. "And when the company budget wasn't adequate, you paid personally for all the staff in Packaging to attend training in the new inventory system?"

Alex was silent for a few moments. *Busted.* "We needed to take more notice of their feedback and enthusiasm. I didn't do it for the praise. It's just the right thing to do."

"Exactly. It's good work, and perfect for the company. Your heart and loyalty are in the right place, Alex. You just need to master the rest of it."

He grimaced at the smirk on her face. "You mean foreswear the relaxed timekeeping, the delight in every change of fashion, the joy of spending money?"

"Oh, but yes. Maybe you should consider monogamy, too, as a gesture towards showing your maturity…? Well, okay, from the look on your face, maybe that one's a step too far."

They both laughed and Alex hugged her. That should set the office gossip cat among the pigeons, the wayward son clutching the very prim PA in full view of London's business district!

"I worry about you," Tina murmured into his shoulder.

"Me?"

Flushed, she lifted her face up to his. "You make people think you have so much fun. But I think... maybe you don't. Maybe you're a little lost."

Alex didn't want to parrot again, but he did. "Lost?"

"Forget it." She shook her head.

"I have grown up, Tina, whatever people may think. And I dearly want to contribute. I just haven't found... well, the right opportunity so far." An aimless daydream skittered into his head, featuring his father asking him to help steer the company through challenging times ahead, in a warmer voice than Alex had heard for several years. And Henri, clasping his brother's shoulder in gratitude for his help and companionship in decision-making. Alex brightened. "You think I should call Papa and talk this through?"

"Um. No. You need to give it more time." Tina looked alarmed. "To be honest, he was very disturbed by that rumour about a reality show with you and the circus performer. And so soon after the garden party debacle. The Palace was most displeased."

"Look, the show was never going to be made,

right? And the Palace? I had an open invitation from the underbutler. In writing." *Almost.*

Tina's rueful smile confirmed none of his excuses were working on her. "I'm sure, after a few months, Mr. Charles will welcome you back into the fold, and then you can prove your worth, can't you?"

*A few months?* Alex's dreams of immediate board appointment as joint CEO with Henri began to deflate.

"I know you're not the most patient of men," Tina continued, correctly reading his chagrin. "But just make sure you keep in touch with your father in the meantime." She looked earnest. "Maybe I could see about getting you on the occasional guest list for his monthly industry dinners."

Alex's dreams popped with a loud farting noise. "No way," he said shortly. *Industry dinners?* Boredom #101, to say nothing of the implied insult in "occasional guest." How mortifying for a Bonfils son! "If I'm to prove my worth, it should be with something much more important."

Tina looked genuinely shocked. "But that's not going to happen overnight, is it? I don't mean any offense, but you know so much less about the business than either your father or Henri."

"I can learn. I can catch up."

"Of course you can. Just not in the middle of this troublesome period."

"Now you're patronising me." *And wait a moment...* he forced his gaze away from the smoochy-eyed looks the man on reception was giving him and glared at Tina. "What do you mean, a troublesome period? What trouble is there at Bonfils's?"

Tina's eyes widened and she went very red. *A-ha.* So she obviously shouldn't have said that. Jesus, was Papa keeping everything from him?

"There have been... worrying events," she said slowly, lowering her voice. "Breakages in the warehouse beyond usual tolerance levels, an increase in customer complaints about deliveries. There's a certain amount of tension at work because these are the months leading up to the UK Heritage Wines Awards and we need everything to run smoothly. Your father is relying on that event to launch our new Angel's Breath sparkling wine. It will be a magnificent triumph."

English sparkling wine was growing in worldwide prestige and popularity, and Bonfils Bibendum had always excelled in their selections. Even though he hadn't attended all the management meetings, Alex knew that Angel's Breath was something special. Unlike French producers, Bonfils had decided not to whole bunch press the English grapes but to crush them first. This wouldn't work well in a hot climate but in Britain's cooler climate, it boosted the flavour. It was a masterstroke.

Alex leaned forward, eager for more detail. "Is that the Bristol warehouse?" It was the nearest to the vineyard. "You suspect industrial sabotage?"

Tina rolled her eyes. "Remember what I said about reining in the melodrama? No, I'm sure they were just mistakes. But while Charles and

Henri are sorting all that out, they don't want.... Oh, hell. You know what I mean."

Yes, Alex did, and he bit back his dismay. They didn't want bad publicity from the profligate lifestyle of the second son. They didn't want *Alex* associated with a serious business with serious problems, despite it being as much his inheritance as Henri's. Dammit! He'd have to show them he could be trusted, after all. He could contribute to strategy; his passion could be of invaluable use to the company's future. Couldn't it?

*I'll prove my worth before Papa even has to ask for it.*

Inspiration came suddenly: a weird, amazing, bizarre idea that had just popped into his mind. "Tina? This thing about me not knowing the business...."

"Hm?" Tina glanced at her watch; she must be due back on duty with his slave driver of a father.

"Wouldn't it be better...."

"Alex," Tina said warningly, her eyes widening as if she dreaded what he'd say next.

"...if I started right now, at the beginning? If I got a job and learned about the business from the shop floor?"

Tina's pretty jaw nearly hit her chest. "What are you talking about? You've never actually worked anywhere! And anyway, your father would never let you take a staff job. You're a Bonfils son, after all."

Alex blithely ignored the jibe about him never having actually worked anywhere. How unfair! After all, he'd run a disco one night in Ibiza, erected yurts in a Himalayan village, held a "Golf Sale" sign in the middle of Trafalgar Square for an old school friend one afternoon.... "But I won't *be* a Bonfils."

"Sorry?"

"I could go undercover. You know, like that TV programme? Where the boss goes into the business in disguise to see how it's really being run." Oh my God, what a laugh that'd be! "I can join up using another name. I may even find out where these problems are starting. Your special spy!"

Tina started to laugh, then bit it off at the look on his face. "Alex, no. That's a daft idea. Why can't you just show a little patience? Your father will come around and find you a new role."

He barely heard her: the plans were already spinning in his mind. A new project always brought out the best in him, especially if it involved some risk. He'd need a new hair colour, a set of appropriate clothes—he always used his personal account at Harvey Nichols for his clothing, did they *do* workwear?—and a necessary distance from his family for a few weeks. That could be the sweetest advantage: a whole new life with no one interested in his financial worth or harassing him about his alleged flakiness. "You'll help me, right?"

"I'll—?" Tina nearly choked and, for a few seconds, the woman behind reception looked genuinely concerned for her health. "No I won't! What would Mr. Charles say?"

Alex waved his hand airily. "He won't know."

"What?"

"I'd be going undercover from him, too. If he knows, it'll ruin the whole thing. It'll blow my cover." He was even starting to sound like a secret agent.

"Blow your cover? Good God. You're sounding like James Bond."

"It would be like a detective novel—"

And then Tina just snapped. "The business is not a novel, Alexandre! Not a spy movie, nor some kind of game. It's been in existence for nearly a century, and both of our families have served it loyally. Two of my siblings work in the warehouse, and before the death of my parents, my mother was a buyer for the London office. Its reputation is terribly important to your family."

He blinked hard. "Tina, ma chère, I'm sorry. I didn't mean to upset you. I know it's where our millions come from."

"It's not just that. It's the reason your family thrives as it does. We've produced a wide range of extremely superior wines, developing a rewarding relationship with many of the best European vineyards. The prestige, the superior quality, the Bonfils reputation known throughout the world? That's been your grandfather's and your father's life's work. And Henri's."

"I know."

"And it should be yours." She sighed. "Forgive me, I'm overstepping the mark again."

"It's fine." It was Alex's turn to put his hand on hers in reassurance. "You have every right to say it." *Just as Papa did.*

"Your honesty does you credit." Tina smiled gratefully. "Now I really must get back to work. I have duties to pass to my assistant before I go on annual vacation next Saturday. I'm really looking forward to three whole weeks of relaxation, and no contact from the office." They chatted briefly about the remote Greek island she was going to with her husband, and then Alex stood as she took her leave.

"Look after yourself," she said, kissing him on the cheek. "You're not a bad boy at heart, I know."

"Is there a *but* hovering there?"

"You know your real problem?"

"That I hate that sentence?" Alex said wryly.

Tina grinned. "You've always been too rich for your own good. And, to be honest, that's not really your fault." She glanced briefly and perceptively at the man on reception, who began busying himself with shifting papers. "And try to avoid corrupting our staff, will you?"

Alex scoffed. "You're the one said I'm not a bad boy at heart, remember? You can rely on me."

Tina paused, halfway between the chairs and the corridor leading to the meeting rooms. "When you say I can rely on you...."

"Yes, ma chère?"

She almost whispered, but he heard her clearly enough. "Can I rely on you to drop this silly undercover scheme?"

"Of course."

"Alex? I know you, remember."

"I said so, didn't I?" He laughed brightly and waved as she passed out of view. Then he brought his other hand forward: he'd been hiding the crossed fingers behind his back. A silly childish superstition, maybe, but as he had no intention of dropping the *silly undercover scheme*, it seemed sensible to have something on his side. He moved toward the elevators, on his way out of the building, but had already pressed a direct dial button on his phone.

"Good morning, this is the HR department of Bonfils Bibendum" came a young, bright voice. "How may I help you?"

"Come for lunch, Liam," Alex said, confident that Liam would recognise his mentor's voice. "And I'll explain exactly how!"

# CHAPTER 2

Tate Somerton usually liked breakfast time: not just the food itself, but the bustle of the family all gathered together, discussing plans for the day, catching up on problems and news. Gran was usually still in her pajamas, but the kids would be up and dressed for school, and Tate's best friend Louise would drop in on her way to work to join them all. Another pair of hands was always gratefully welcomed, with so many bodies to feed and organise. The kitchen would be warm and aromatic from cooking bacon and bubbling tea, spoons clattered in cereal bowls, knives scraped over burnt toast, and inevitably someone would have lost their backpack or books. It was loud, frantic, and fun.

But today was proving to be a bloody challenge.

Everyone had overslept, for a start. Gran's arthritis was bad and she wasn't able to help with the kids' breakfast as usual. It made her unusually tetchy, refusing to put in her teeth, and dropping the chewier toast crusts onto the floor for her pet dachshund Freddie, whom Tate had expressly asked Gran *not* to overfeed. The kids didn't help much with his mood, either. Twelve-year-old twins Hugo and Hattie—the H's, as Tate affectionately referred to them—were arguing fiercely over some character in a sexy reality TV program that Tate wasn't sure either of them had even watched, and their little sister, seven-year-old Amy, was sniffling. She wouldn't tell anyone why, just sat at the kitchen table with the occasional sigh over her bowl of cereal. Tate just hoped it was one of her frequent, imaginary concerns rather than anything seriously wrong.

He swung past the breakfast table, scooping up a piece of buttered toast as he went. One bite, and it slipped from his greasy fingers and landed— butter side down, inevitably—on the front of his shirt. *Shit.* He'd have to change, and he couldn't remember if he had another suitable work shirt that was both clean and ironed. Turning on his heel, he nearly tripped over Freddie and, as he flung out a hand to steady himself, he knocked Gran's set of upper teeth off the counter and into the dog's water bowl. *Double shit.*

"Hugo hasn't finished his muesli," Hattie announced loudly.

"Hattie's wearing my favorite red socks," Hugo added.

That was the twins for you. One minute they'd speak as one, then the next they'd be arguing or telling tales on each other. Tate would have to leave them to sort their preferences out on their own behalf this morning, but he ruffled Amy's hair as he passed.

"You okay?"

She lifted soulful eyes up to him. "The dinosaurs have been 'pletely wiped out."

Tate blinked. "Um. Yes. But it was a very long time ago, love."

"Before you were born," Hattie contributed cheerfully.

Tate could see that only adding to the grief and gave Amy a quick hug. "Cheer up. We can go and see the remains of one at the Natural History Museum, in the school holidays."

"We can?" Amy was brightening up.

"No. It's gone," Hugo announced.

"Hugo, for heaven's sake!" Tate tensed for protest from the startled Amy.

"Don't talk with your mouth full," Gran admonished both Hugo and Tate, totally ignoring the irony of talking toothless herself. Soft food obviously hadn't been enough for her—her prodigious appetite was usually the talk of the senior citizen's café—because she was currently gumming her way through a cornflake sandwich.

"They replaced the dinosaur skeleton with a whale's," Hugo explained to Amy, though after a wary glance at Gran, he'd swallowed his mouthful of cereal first.

To Tate's relief, that was a plus for Amy, and she started quoting facts about whales instead. Tate had no idea whether they were true or not, but Amy was never happier than when she had a new topic to investigate. The teachers at school had explained to him that Amy was extremely able, academically speaking, and would need extra support and encouragement at both school and home. While Tate was burstingly proud of his sister, in his experience there was a wide range of subjects Amy already knew more about than he did.

"Late today?" Gran gave Tate a gummy grin as he picked up her teeth to wash them off at the sink.

"Nope," he said blithely, knowing full well he was. "Is that Louise at the door?" With Gran distracted, he grabbed his coat off the back of the chair and darted up the narrow corridor to the front door. He opened it to his best friend's yawning face.

"Looks like we're both slow to get going today," he said with a smile. They both worked at Bonfils Bibendum's main warehouse in Bristol, and as Tate didn't have a car of his own, Louise often gave Tate a lift when they were working similar shifts.

Louise smiled back at him, pushing her habitually unruly hair off her face. "I was partying with the girls from Packaging. What's your excuse?"

Tate wasn't offended: Louise and he had a healthy banter going most of the time. "I offered you the after-hours meeting on the new Health and Safety directive for warehouse security, but you turned me down. Your loss, eh?"

"Oh, sorry, should I have been crying over lost chances, rather than dancing the night away at that new club by the harbor?" Louise laughed heartily. She was three years older than Tate— they'd celebrated her thirtieth birthday together last month with giant pizza, much beer, and increasingly bizarre reports of their respective, unsuccessful dating experiences—and she'd been a cherished constant in Tate's life ever since his parents were killed.

As the oldest child, Tate did his best for the orphaned Somerton family, he really did. He adored them all—they were his reason for living. But with three young siblings to look after, his live-in gran, and trying to keep down a responsible full-time job? There was no time for dancing, let alone anything more romantic. He was knackered most of the time. "Are we ready to go?" he asked, and Louise nodded, jiggling the car keys in her hand.

"Twins?" Tate turned in the doorway to call back to the kitchen. The H's were casually bickering between themselves, and deliberately ignoring him. "Sally's mum is picking you and Amy up for school this morning, okay? Make sure you're ready."

The H's didn't pause their insults, but Tate knew they'd heard him. Amy was singing a popular song but in a strange, high-pitched wail. He paused, unsure whether she was ill or just out of tune, but then Gran poked her head around the kitchen doorframe and grinned at him.

"You get off now, kids," she replied. "I'll get them all ready in time. Once Amy's finished her exploration of whale song, that is."

Tate rolled his eyes. "I'm going to uninstall the internet on your laptop, Gran, if Amy's spending time on it at breakfast."

Gran pursed her lips. Was she laughing at Tate? And he thought he was acting so stern. "And if Hugo can't find his backpack—"

"It's under my knitting box," Gran interrupted. "I know." She waved her hand as if brushing him away. "Go, I said. And my aches will have eased by tonight, so I'm in charge of supper, okay? I know you've got another meeting after work."

Tate blew her a kiss and dashed quickly out of the door before the kids realised the latest meal plan. As it was, he'd probably hear the groan from miles away. Gran's cooking was so very far from gourmet, it could be from Mars.

When Louise paused her Mini at the traffic lights at the end of the road, she murmured to Tate, "I thought you had a date tonight? That guy from the pet shop?"

Tate grimaced. "I told him I couldn't make this week."

"Tate, you idiot. That's twice you've done that. He won't ask again, you know."

"So? Then it wasn't meant to be." He sounded defensive, he knew. But Louise was always trying to set him up when he could least pay attention to it. "I can get a date another time, when there isn't all this trouble at work."

"Yeah?" She raised her eyebrows. "That easy, you reckon?"

What the hell did she mean? "Why not?"

"Take that scowl off your face. I'm telling you this for your own good. You could cut your hair, for one. Dress more smartly."

"I shower daily, don't I? I'm over twenty-one,

right? Run down your checklist. I'm employed, in my own house, single, free—"

Louise coughed.

"Well, almost. With a family like mine, we come as a package, you know that. But what more could the guy of my dreams want?"

Louise grinned, still keeping her attention on the road ahead. "I think a lot of them want you, Tate, honey. That's not the problem. It's whether you're willing to open up sufficiently to give the poor buggers a chance."

He paused a moment. No, that was crap. *Surely?* "It's just a matter of finding the time. I have a lot of stuff going on in my life."

"But you invite a lot of that, don't you? Filling up the hours so you don't have to risk inviting anyone else in."

"I don't—"

"Tate, you collect commitments like I collect pairs of Doc Martens!" She laughed a little sadly. "At work, there's the Health and Safety committee, supervision of the intern program, and union representation on the annual pay rise negotiation. To say nothing of organising repairs to the library car park, your ongoing membership of the PTA committee, running the local shelter Christmas appeal, and campaigning against the closure of the local independent grocer." She sighed. "And that's just this year. When are you going to allow time for your own causes, Tate Somerton?"

"Someone needs to take on these issues, Lou. Else we're all taken advantage of."

"Yes, Tate. Of course, Tate."

Okay, so he was scowling again, but she really shouldn't provoke him on this already hectic morning. "Look, I'm fine. And I date plenty."

"No, you don't."

"Do so."

Louise was still watching the road but she stuck out her tongue. "Don't, so."

He had to laugh. After all, Louise already *knew*. He'd told enough late-night, bittersweet stories to amuse them both. "Hey, get off my case. What about Mark? That lasted—"

"Bare weeks, Tate. You went to the movies. You had an evening at the pub. You wouldn't return his calls."

He shifted awkwardly in his seat. "Irreconcilable differences."

Louise raised her eyebrows.

"Lou, he thought gay marriage wasn't a cause worth fighting for."

"And that tall guy…, Nigel, was it?"

"He thought what this country needs is another prime minister like Maggie Thatcher. He admitted he found her quite sexually stirring." Tate winced. "No way."

Louise chuckled. "And Owen?"

"He supported fox hunting." They were both laughing by now, but Tate was grateful this was only a short car journey. "Anyway, we'll talk about it another time. Tonight's meeting is about the new forklift safety regulations. Can't have the company shirking those, it's our lives and limbs at risk. I'll get the bus home, but we'll probably have a swift pint at the Queens Head first, if you want to join us."

Louise turned the car into the industrial estate. "Anyone interesting going to be there?"

"No cute gals for you, if that's what you're angling for," he said. "But for me?" He grinned to himself when her shoulders straightened and her eyes widened with hopeful anticipation. "Jeff Miller from HR is joining us—"

"Married. With four kids," Louise interrupted with disappointment.

"And Penny from Packaging."

Louise blushed, rather suspiciously. "A busty, *gay* blonde is not your demographic, Tate!"

"And that unmarried, male hunk—"

"Yes?" Louise sucked in a breath with excitement.

"—from Accounts Payable."

Louise snorted so loudly, Tate jumped on his seat. "The only person who meets that description," she said, "is Archie and he's three months off retirement."

"Don't knock maturity and experience!"

They were in fits of laughter by the time Louise pulled the car into one of the vacant spaces behind the warehouse. "Okay, I'll back off," she said. "But I'm just saying. You need to let go sometimes, have some fun rather than always trying to set the world to rights. Not everyone is out for all they can get, you know. You have to trust someone, some time."

"It's not just that." Tate hadn't meant to share, but it just slipped out.

Louise nodded, quiet for a moment. "They don't all leave, either," she said softly.

Tate swallowed hard. "I know." He didn't want to talk about this, he really didn't. Yet if he didn't trust Lou with it, who else did he have?

She patted him gently on the hand. "It was a horrible accident. You lost your mum and dad."

Tate shook his head. His damned eyes still pricked when he thought of it. "It was so unfair."

Louise nodded. "No one can argue with that. But thank God you have the kids."

"Bloody kids," he said, but with a grin.

"You love 'em." Louise thumped him on the arm, so hard he winced. "And Gran helps out around the house, doesn't she?"

Tate loved his gran, and she was devoted to them all. She was a godsend: if he didn't have her love and support, he'd never have been able to keep a steady job. But when her arthritis flared up, the help she could give was very limited. He hated seeing her suffering, too.

Louise was still talking. "... and now they're at the age you can take some time for yourself. Like I said."

"Like you keep saying, you old nag."

She stuck out her tongue at him again. "Less of the *old*, young Jedi. Romance just needs a little compromise."

*Compromise?* Tate couldn't remember a day when he didn't live that word. But yeah, he'd really like someone special. He just couldn't... well, it wasn't top of his To-Do list, that was all. "We need to get inside before we're really late."

"Sure." Louise had twisted in her seat and was looking at him fondly. "As soon as you tell me about the troubles."

"Huh?"

"You said, you'd date when there isn't all this trouble at work."

Jeez, Lou was sharp. She worked in Accounts, so she probably hadn't heard about the latest upset in the warehouse. He should watch his mouth, though he knew he could trust her not to spread gossip. "Some berk accidentally spilled hot liquid over a whole pallet full of bottles, ruining the labels. We'll have to send for replacements from the vineyard."

"Who the hell did that?"

"No idea." Tate shrugged. "It happened either late at night or very early morning. I just came into work to find it that way. And no one's fessed up so far."

Louise frowned. "Remember last month? I told you how an invoice from a major supplier got lost, and they put our deliveries on stop for two weeks. Caused all sorts of hassle with the inventory system. But it was an odd thing to happen, because I can say with total conviction, we've never lost any of their paperwork before. We were trying to get things straight in the office, in readiness for the rush of customer orders after the Awards, and I was sure I'd seen that invoice when it arrived. But we turned the place upside down, and no sign of it."

Tate frowned too. There'd been a noticeable spate of accidents in the last six months, and

Louise's experience was only confirming his own suspicions. "Too much going on to be coincidence, I'd say."

"What are you saying? You mean, it may be deliberate sabotage?"

For a moment, they just sat there, staring wide-eyed at each other. Tate wondered if his expression matched the worry on Lou's face.

"What should we do?" she asked quietly.

"What *can* we do? Except keep an eye out for any more trouble. At least, that's what I'm going to do."

Louise grimaced. "Another cause for Tate Somerton?"

He shrugged but didn't deny it. It was worth his time, wasn't it? He was proud of his work, proud of the company's reputation. That didn't mean he'd let them take advantage of the workers—after all, everyone knew that management couldn't always be trusted when profits were in the mix—but it had been a good career for him so far. He'd left school at sixteen with only basic exam results, but a contact at Bonfils had recommended Tate for a job in the warehouse. Every employee was expected to work their hardest, and Mr. Charles Bonfils was a fierce old bird when he walked the shop floor. No one dared be caught shirking. But if you were seen to be loyal and determined, as Tate had been, you were rewarded. Tate had been made a supervisor by the time he was twenty, and manager a couple of years after that. Yeah, he reckoned he had both duty and incentive to save the company from trouble.

Louise pushed open the car door. "Anyway, come on. You're the one worried about being late."

As Tate followed her out, his phone rang with a call from Percy Grove, one of the warehouse supervisors who reported directly to Tate. "Percy? I've just arrived—"

"Get here as fast as y' can, Tate."

"What's up?"

Percy swore colourfully. He never minced his words, in front of fellow workers and management alike. "The shipment of the new Merlot has been seized at the bonded warehouse in Calais."

"What the hell?" Tate caught Louise's worried look over the roof of the car, but waved her into the building ahead of him. He leaned against the car, the breeze lifting his unevenly cropped curls, the noise of distant traffic in his ears. "Percy, we need that for the Awards event program." The run-up to the Awards was full of social and marketing events, where Bonfils provided the liquid refreshment from their own ranges.

"You're telling me. Some shit about the wrong paperwork. It's just another fuckup." Percy's grizzled old voice almost growled. "Feels like someone's out to get us, boy." His voice dropped as if he didn't want to be overheard. "Y' know what's even bloody worse?"

*What could be?* "Tell me."

"The new intern has arrived, some uppity young kid. On time, admittedly, but if he had the sense he was born with, he'd still be in the negative. Better get here soon before I lose him in bay twelve." Which, as Tate well knew, was where the giant refuse bins were.

Tate shook his head, smiling grimly. "On my way," he said, and sighed to himself.

Looked like it was going to be one of those days.

# CHAPTER 3

Arriving in the warehouse at ten past nine, Tate took up position just outside his office, watching through the open door as Percy interviewed the new intern inside. Or, at least, that's how it was meant to go. The company had regular intern programs, in several disciplines, and a few weeks in the warehouse was a critical part of every schedule.

Percy glanced at the paper in front of him. "So. Goodson."

"You may call me Alex."

Percy pointedly ignored that.

"Excuse me, but is this the right place? They told me I had to report in to the manager, Mr. Somerton, for training." The guy in the chair peered at Percy's name tag. "Mr. Grove, is it?"

"I'm doin' the interview, boy."

Alex Goodson raised his eyebrows. "Ah. Okay. As you wish."

Tate could see it took Percy a lot of effort not to roll his eyes. He didn't suffer fools gladly. This was possibly why Tate did many of the interviews and was official liaison for the interns. But no one could better Percy in sizing up a new guy within a matter of minutes, and he'd rarely been proved wrong.

At the moment, the new kid was concentrating on Percy and unaware of Tate's scrutiny. Well, he was no kid really, which was the first surprise. They usually got school leavers or university graduates, whereas this man looked a similar age to Tate. Maybe he was making a career change or coming back into the workplace after a break. Watching the way Alex Goodson twirled the temporary security pass on its lanyard like a novelty toy he'd never seen before, Tate reckoned it was the latter.

And, shit, but he was good-looking. Tate could see enough of the guy's face from his angled viewpoint and couldn't resist taking a longer look than his role as training supervisor merited. Alex had lovely gray eyes, a strong jaw, and fine mahogany-brown hair with a slight curl. It was ridiculously shiny, like those heads on hair product adverts, and so evenly shaded Tate wondered for a random moment if he dyed it. Even more randomly, Tate's fingers all but itched to run through it. *What the hell?* He shoved his hands into his pockets to try to redirect his attention. He hadn't felt such an immediate, physical response to someone for a long time.

The second surprise was how confident Alex looked: no sign of the usual nervous desire to make a good impression common to most interns. He wore a pair of dark-rimmed spectacles, which he awkwardly pushed back up his nose a couple of times, but his gaze was bright and fixed steadily on Percy as if he were his equal. Not that Tate didn't believe in equality for all, at heart, but there was a certain respect you were expected to show your supervisor. And definitely toward Percy, who had a whole bunch of opinions about how anyone younger than him—which included almost all the warehouse and probably Mr. Charles himself—should behave toward their elders.

Tate bit back a smile. He could see Percy was resisting glancing at Tate over Alex's shoulder. Well, if that was Percy's game, to ignore Tate's presence for the moment, this could turn into quite an entertainment.

"Thank God," Alex said cheerfully, with a nod at Percy's chest.

"I'm sorry?" Percy's tone was at its deepest, most no-nonsense best.

"No ghastly nylon overalls," Alex said. "You're wearing a branded polo shirt. I assume they do it in slim fit as well?"

Tate blinked, trying desperately not to laugh. Percy's shirt strained over his broad chest and ever-increasing stomach. Percy's favorite snack was donuts, and even he knew that was beginning to show.

Percy cleared his throat in what Tate knew—but this poor sap Goodson had no idea—was a menacing way. "Where's y' employee manual?"

"Sorry?"

Percy gestured dismissively at Alex's empty hands, resting casually in his lap. "Y' pick it up in HR *before* y' start. Plenty of youngsters have already read through it before I meet them." The disapproval was strongly implied. "Y' don't think y' need to swot up on it, boy?"

Alex stared at him as if something hadn't yet connected mentally. "What's that word you keep calling me? *Bye?* Oh....." He nodded, as if praising himself for being so perceptive. "You mean *boy.* Is that a true Bristolian accent? That lilt at the end of a sentence—"

"Manual!" Percy snapped. "Y' hear me?"

Alex seemed at last to pick up on the seriousness of Percy's tone. "Sorry. I mean, yes, I have one. I picked it up before the weekend and have already perused it fully."

"Perooosed it, have y'?"

Alex raised one rather well-groomed eyebrow. "I signed all the necessary forms, too. Did HR's confirmation get lost in transit?" He glanced quickly over the messy pile of papers on the desk—filing was going to have been Tate's first job this morning—and for a moment, his lips pursed. Then he glanced up again and caught the look in Percy's eye. He had the grace to colour slightly. "Never mind. I'm sure you have it all in hand."

Percy's raised eyebrows spoke far more eloquently than his words. "So now we've cleared that up to y'r satisfaction, y' can get on with the work. Y'll shadow Jamie today, under my close supervision."

Tate knew that look of Percy's. It was the one that made new staff feel twelve years old, caught with an illicit smoke behind the bike shed. Alex Goodson, intriguingly, just smiled. Was he brave, or genuinely clueless?

"And when will I meet Mr. Somerton?" he asked.

Percy stood, straightening his shoulders. "Mr. Somerton is busy elsewhere."

*I am?* Tate assumed this was another of Percy's games. It seemed Alex Goodson had really rubbed the old man up the wrong way.

Alex stood as well. He looked a bit bemused. Percy leaned forward on the desk and spoke more slowly to him. "They told y' about the trainin' program, right?"

"Right. Training. Of course. Is that before or after lunch?"

Percy's swallow of disgust was audible. "The program will extend over several weeks. Mr. Somerton insists on it."

"He does?"

"He does. Jamie's only a new boy himself, but I can't spare anyone else to keep an eye on y' today. We're expecting deliveries. I suppose if y' pick up any bad habits today..." Percy's resigned expression showed just how very certain he was of that. "... Mr. Somerton'll have to retrain y', however inconvenient that'll be for him."

"Mr. Somerton sounds a pain in the arse, right?" Alex grinned.

Tate bit his lower lip, the chuckle inside him begging to be let out.

Percy scowled. "Better watch y'r p's and q's, Goodson. We respect management around here."

To give Alex his due, he realised his mistake quickly. "Of course. I'm totally sure I'll soon pick it all up, Mr. Grove."

Percy paused, probably just long enough for Alex to start wondering what he'd done wrong now, then he nodded. "Percy."

"Uh... sorry?"

"Call me Percy, for God's sake. Mr. Grove sounds like y're talking to my old dad."

To Tate's surprise—again—Alex grinned. "I know the feeling." He stuck out his hand and firmly shook Percy's. "Thanks, Percy. I look forward to working with you."

Percy growled in the back of his throat. "*For* me, boy."

"Yes, that's what I meant. *For* you." Alex nodded, but nothing in his tone suggested he was apologetic.

Tate couldn't help it—he laughed softly.

Alex spun around. From the startled look on his face, he'd only just realised someone else was behind him. "Sorry, who are you?"

Tate gave his most cheesy smile and took Alex's hand in a formal shake. "I'm Tate Somerton, Percy's manager. Percy's just been keeping my seat warm."

Alex gaped. "Mr. Somerton? But you're...."

*Too young?* Tate mentally filled in the gap as Alex's sentence trailed off. It wasn't the first time he'd been mistaken for nothing more than the tea boy. He knew he could look younger than his age, and—yes, Lou was right—he could have had a smarter haircut and worn more professional clothes. But he spent his days driving forklifts and climbing over and under pallets, and as long as he did a good job with the warehouse staff, no one minded him dressing in the same smart casual wear.

"Um. What I said earlier?" Alex looked a little disturbed, obviously not sure how much Tate might have overheard. "I suppose I may have been a tad out of line."

Tate shrugged. It was an apology of sorts. "What matters to me is that everyone does their best in the job. If you shirk, or cause trouble, well... that's a different matter."

Alex was still staring at him. He also hadn't let go of Tate's hand. For one long, pregnant moment, their gazes locked.

Tate knew he shouldn't be devouring Alex's attention like he was—it was rude, he didn't behave like this, at least he hadn't before, he didn't even know if the guy was gay, and he'd never thought about dating a fellow employee before, that would be unprofessional, right? And oh God, even his mind was rambling—but he couldn't seem to look away.

Alex's hand shifted very slightly, but enough for his thumb to brush the palm of Tate's hand as he let go, almost reluctantly. A small smile teased the edge of his handsome mouth. "Mr. Somerton, may I say—?"

"No, y' bloody may not!" Percy snapped into his ear, having borne down on him without either Tate or Alex noticing.

Alex gave a small, embarrassing yelp.

Tate bit his lip to stop from laughing. "Welcome to the firm, Alex," he said briskly, and turned away.

Alex stood rooted to the spot for a few minutes as Tate and Percy paused in the doorway ahead of him, discussing in a low voice something about a delayed shipment.

What a bloody idiot he'd been! Challenging the supervisor; calling the manager a pain in the arse. He'd hijacked a temporary space on the general intern scheme with his fake name and his friend Liam's help, but he needed to remember his menial place. Laughable, really, if his mission weren't so serious.

Maybe Tina had been wrong, and he hadn't grown up enough yet. One of the first, and hardest, lessons his parents had tried to teach him had been to know when to hold his tongue. Truth was all very well but, in his experience, people tended to want *their* truth, not his spontaneous, unvarnished version.

*Dammit.* He'd have to keep his head down if this plan was to work. He'd only persisted about meeting Mr. Somerton because he wanted to make contact with the warehouse manager as soon as possible, so he could investigate the troubles there'd been. Data and observation were needed for any good investigator to get started. But he wouldn't get anywhere if he annoyed everyone on the first day and got fired.

*Fired.* Jesus. That'd be a new experience for him, wouldn't it?

But then he *had* met Mr. Somerton—and what a delight that had been. He glanced quickly and surreptitiously at Tate. What an attractive man he was! Alex was used to appraising men as potential dates, but the spark he'd felt when he shook hands with Tate Somerton—that was something at an instinctive level. Wiry, and less well-groomed than Alex's usual type, but with glorious, messy auburn hair, tanned skin, and such an angry, passionate fire in his eyes. As Alex had turned in his chair to see Tate for the first time, he'd caught the tail end of Tate's smile. It had been heart-stoppingly delicious. Pity it was so quickly covered with the managerial scowl. Tate wasn't model-type handsome but had something very special Alex couldn't immediately put his finger on.

*Heavens.*

And that was what he wanted to do, wasn't it? Put not just his finger on Tate, but his hands and his lips, and all places in between. Alex's cock stirred gently beneath his jeans. He was bemused by such a visceral reaction toward a man he'd only just met. Tate may not even be gay, though Alex suspected from that long, warm, startled handshake that Tate had been interested in him in return. But even Alex's easygoing attitude toward dating didn't usually encourage him to pursue someone he wasn't even sure *liked* him.

"Alex? Are you ready to get started?"

"Yes. Right now." *Damn.* He focused on the two men—his bosses—who were calling him. How long had he been ignoring them, off in his reverie?

Tate had a last word for Percy. "You'll look into the paperwork? We must get that Merlot delivery back on schedule."

"Leave it to me," Percy grunted back. "Looks

like they had the wrong signature, though fuck knows how that happened. We submitted it with y'rs on, as usual."

Tate sucked in an almost imperceptible breath. "Get them to send through a copy of that document."

Percy frowned. "What, the wrong one?"

"Yeah."

"Okay. Can't see why, though. No good to man nor beast, in my opinion, but if y' say so...."

"Which I do," Tate said.

Alex's ears pricked up. There was assertiveness in that low, sharp tone. Alex felt it all the way through to his toes.

Tate's alert gaze met Alex's again. "This way, please. I'll show you where you'll be working today."

Alex was torn between following that cute arse, and the innate difficulty of being obedient to anyone. But he could be, couldn't he, if he concentrated?

If this was how employment went, he'd better get used to it damned quickly."

# CHAPTER 4

Alex had never, *ever* imagined what a working day in a wine warehouse could be like. Well—any structured working day, really. When he was in the Bonfils office to see Papa or Tina, he spent his considerable spare time surfing supercar sites or chatting to the staff about any celebrities he'd met recently. His whole life had been run largely to his own timetable. No one had ever presumed to tell him what to do, and when to have it done by.

Until today.

What the hell had he done with all his hours before now? Every damned minute of this day had been crammed full of activity: both muscle-straining physical work and mind-whirling instructions. Alex felt like he was running just to stay in the same place. Yet none of the guys around him seemed to pause or question it all. They groused, they laughed, they pitched appallingly rude insults at each other, and then they knuckled down to the work as if their lives depended on it. Was this really how people spent every working day?

Trucks pulled up at the warehouse continuously during the morning, and the forklifts trundled past again and again. It only took a couple of nudges at Alex's arse from the front prongs to cue him into recognising the approaching noise in time to get out of the way. He might have been mistaken those first few times, when the smirking driver appeared to be driving straight at him—very amusing, *not*—but Alex soon cottoned on.

But his learning curve was steep. It didn't take him long after starting his training to discover how very *little* he knew. It was sobering. No, actually, it was bloody embarrassing. He understood and appreciated wine, how to grow and nurture it. He'd been all but brought up at vineyards and tastings. But the subsequent storage, transport, and selling of that wine? In that, he was—what did they call it?—a newbie. Plenty of times he had to bite back a protest at the lack of time to absorb barked, half-alien instructions, the uncomfortably sparse conditions he had to operate in, and, worst of all, the disrespectful way they treated him.

But of course, he had to. He was meant to be one of them, wasn't he? And in a weird way, it was hardly personal, just endemic to the whole atmosphere. Almost *flattering*, really.

His first mistake had been to ask the way to the cellar. Jamie—a tall, skinny man in his early twenties, who apparently had failed in a sales career at Fenchurch's, Bonfils's major competitor, and was probably being given stewardship of Alex as some kind of karmic punishment—just stared at him. Another, burlier employee called Stuart, who was older and drove one of the forklifts with the arrogance and panache of a Formula 1 racer, had roared with laughter and slapped Alex so hard on the shoulder he nearly toppled over.

"Take a look around, kid. What d'you think is on all these damned shelves? We don't use a cellar any longer, at least not for the regular retail deliveries. The only specialist storage is where we keep the expensive stuff, and that's locked away, around by the manager's office. Otherwise, everything's out there on the pallets."

Alex took another look around the warehouse. Huge, high shelves surrounded him, in a row of aisles stretching as far as he could see, stacked with pallets wrapped tightly in plastic. Stuart roared with laughter again, Jamie had a sly grin on his face, and now Percy was on his way over.

"What the fuck?" Percy said brusquely. He stood in front of them, hands on hips, feet planted securely. "We got deliveries stacked up, gentlemen, and y're discussing y'r manicures or somethin'."

"Prince Harry here thought we were still fermenting the stuff in the dark, one bottle at a time," Stuart chortled.

"No, I didn't," Alex snapped but, he suspected, too late to save his credibility. "And my name's Alex. Not Harry."

"Nob's accent like yours could slice through cheese." Stuart snorted. "Looking for royal privileges with the bosses, I bet?" He gave an obscenely exaggerated wink, and Jamie sniggered.

"Oh, for God's sake," Alex muttered. He'd noticed that Jamie and Stuart hung around together almost all the time, like a pair of mismatched, smirking bookends. "I'm not a *nob*, as you put it. And as for the wine, I just didn't think it through." He wasn't used to watching himself so closely, to worrying about what he said or what people thought of him. So why the hell was he worrying now? This whole mission of his was having a weird psychological effect.

Percy turned a thoughtful gaze on Alex and sighed. "Boys, take him out the back to the grape barrels. Couple of hours stamping on 'em should see him right."

Alex gaped. He wasn't dressed for that! And, God, when had he last been to the gym? His abdominals and glutes had never been that resilient, and if he was expected to crush grapes for an hour at a time—

They were laughing again. At him.

"Ah. You're joking." Alex was ludicrously relieved, while the catcalls bounced back and forth around him. Then he was angry too. "To hell with you."

Stuart and Jamie were laughing too much to take offense.

"Your face!"

"Prince Harry to a tee!"

Alex found Percy's steady gaze on him. Percy was also grinning, but his eyes glinted with a more quizzical look. "Our idea of a joke, boy, nothin' more. Y'll cope, I'm sure. We don't make wine here, even the English labels. A lot of the catalog is bottled and imported, mainly from France. Do y' know anythin' about this business?"

Alex flushed more deeply than he'd have liked.

"A little," he said through gritted teeth. *Yeah, yeah. Let's all make a fool of the new kid.* But he had to admit, it wasn't that different from his first year at Eton, and he'd managed to get through that, hadn't he?

"Y' can go and collect a couple of pallets of the premier cabernet. They're needed for a tastin' at the Waldorf on Friday."

"Great!" Alex was much cheered up at the thought of taking his turn on the forklift—

"Stuart will drive," Percy said sharply.

Chastened, Alex turned to follow the still chuckling Stuart. He couldn't help but hear Percy's words to Jamie, just before the younger man turned to scuttle after Stuart like a little shadow.

"Tate is gonna eat that boy for breakfast. He doesn't have patience for anyone who can't keep up."

Alex gritted his teeth. *"Y'll cope,"* Percy had said to him.

Looked like he'd have to!

Tea breaks were another eye-opener. Alex had given up on waiting for drinks either to appear from a kitchen somewhere, or for someone to offer to run to the nearest quality coffee shop. After a few false starts, he'd learned to stand behind everyone else at the vending machine at the back of a small staff seating area. What he hadn't learned was how to extract a cup of coffee from it without squeezing the plastic cup too hard and spilling it either over his crotch or back into the machine's tray. Not that that was an ongoing problem. By the time the afternoon break came along, he'd suffered through several half-full cups during the day, and had determined he would rather drink his own urine than that bitter concoction. Maybe tomorrow he could smuggle in his own personal blend from his Soho supplier. Also, maybe, a decent china cup rather than those plastic death traps....

"Wotcha waiting for?" Jamie asked him, appearing at his side with a disarming silence, at least until he took a noisy slurp from his tea. "We only got fifteen minutes, and there's anovver stack by the door to move."

"Is there any food?" God forbid he should ask for cake, but surely there'd be something offered to keep their strength up toward the end of the working day? All he'd managed at lunch had been something from a trolley wrapped in plastic that purported to be an egg sandwich, but with filling the same colour as the bread and barely a difference in taste between them. If he had his way, things would change around here on the culinary front. Like, right now, he was just about ready for some of those little cinnamon biscuits, or a couple of summer fruit and fresh cream pastries—

"No way," Jamie interrupted Alex's thoughts quite cheerily. "No food trolley in the afternoon. Cutbacks, y'know."

Alex didn't, but he understood the impact.

"You coulda brought some wiv you. But Tate doesn't allow open food on the main floor, so you have to keep to the seats. And you better not leave litter. He goes mad about it."

*Tate this, Tate that.* Damned man wasn't even around, but his bloody rules hung over everything. Alex was beginning to revise his initial intention of getting to know Tate Somerton better. "So, how long have you been here, Jamie?"

Jamie stared at him for so long, Alex began to think the young man had lost his previous job at Fenchurch's due to an inability to express English. Then Jamie took another slurp of tea and answered. "Six monfs."

"So you know most of the chaps—I mean, the guys here, and what they're like?"

"Sorta."

"And I bet you know who takes liberties, eh?"

"Huh?"

This conversation was going to be like pulling teeth. "You know what I mean. Who cuts corners, who's open to any offers *on the side.*" Alex was proud of his command of shady idiom, but Jamie still looked at him blankly. "On the take," Alex said bluntly. "Putting the odd spanner in the works. Out for what they can get, even if it harms the company."

"Your Highness!" came a yell from the other side of the warehouse. "Mop-up duty, aisle twelve!"

Alex bit back the snap of irritation at being interrupted and both he and Jamie turned to go back to work. But Alex didn't mistake the almost guilty glance Jamie darted toward the office as he scuttled away. And when Alex also looked that way he saw a man leaning against the door, arms crossed, chewing gum, and obviously waiting for Percy.

It was Stuart.

Alex changed direction abruptly and strode toward the office, but before he got there, Stuart peeled away and darted into one of the bays. Alex paused, unsure what to do next. *What would James Bond do?*

Then Percy appeared from inside the office with a clipboard in his hand and three pens perched behind one ear. He raised an interrogative eyebrow at Alex. Alex was beginning to hate that expression with a rare passion.

"You want somethin', boy?"

"I was just wondering...." Dammit, he'd started now, Alex supposed he had to create some kind of cover story. "When my shift will be over?"

Percy continued to look steadily at him.

"Not yet, then?" Alex said weakly.

"Well. Y' can go when y' like," Percy said slowly. He smiled, but there wasn't much amusement in it. "I'll send y'r pay on to the Palace."

In other words, don't come back. Alex bit back a sigh. "Guess we're all here for the duration, right?"

"Delivery day," Percy gave a curt nod. "We all pitch in until it's done. Y'll learn."

"Yes," Alex said spiritedly. "I suspect I will."

Percy's other eyebrow popped up, which was a

surprising variation. All Alex could hope was that it showed some tolerance for him, rather than further ignominy.

"Mop-up in bay twelve, I heard," Percy said, deceptively calmly.

"I know. I'm on my way," Alex said quickly, turned, and walked away with more haste than usual.

The forklift whirred past him just as he reached the first bin.

"Hey, Your Highness!" Stuart called over. "You gotcha personal helicopter? There's another three pallets to shift." The vehicle trundled on up the aisle, Stuart's laughter ringing in Alex's ears, and Jamie trotting after the truck like a loyal puppy.

*Jesus.* That nickname would give Alex nightmares. And he hadn't been called kid or boy so many times since he left school. He wondered if that was because these guys were less politically correct—or his family and friends had never had the balls?

Either way, it was bloody wearing.

# CHAPTER 5

At afternoon break time, Tate thought he should check up on the new guy. He always monitored new staff, didn't he? Nothing to do with wanting to check out Alex Goodson for personal reasons, take another look at the man's good looks and that strange mixture of naivety and confidence. That cool, sensual handshake, the mischievous twinkle in his eyes, the flicker of sexual interest in his expression.

As Lou would say, "Yeah. Right."

He decided to check in with Percy first, who was using Tate's office to chase up the shipment that was being held by customs. Tate dropped into the chair on the visitor side of the desk, and asked with deliberate casualness, "How's the new intern doing? Goodson, isn't it?"

Percy didn't look up from the pile of manifests he was checking. "His Royal Highness, Prince Harry?"

Tate snorted a laugh. "Really? That's what you're calling him?" It was inevitable, he supposed—Alex Goodson spoke like a toff, and exuded an unfortunate sense of entitlement in every move he made. Unfortunate for a newbie worker in the Bonfils warehouse, that is. But Percy proceeded to surprise Tate.

"The kid's okay." Percy grunted, licked his finger, and flicked through another few pages.

"Yeah? You think we should keep him on?"

Percy paused and looked up. "That's y'r call, isn't it?"

"I... yes, it is. If he's pulling his weight."

Percy took a long moment before replying. "Boy's a fool who says the wrong thing at the wrong time. I'd say he's never had a proper job in his life. But from what I've seen today, he learns fast and he's a hard worker. And y' know how I know that?"

"Because you've thrown everything in his way?" Tate said shrewdly. He knew from past experience how mercilessly Percy tested the new recruits.

"Best way. Sink or swim, that's my way." Percy shrugged. "He'll learn to keep his head down. Don't know if he'll learn to stop oglin' y', though."

"Me?" Tate blinked hard. *Ogling?*

Percy turned his attention back to his paperwork. If Tate hadn't known better, he'd have taken the twist of Percy's mouth to be a small smile. "Undressin' y' every step of his way, boy, and making a poor job of hidin' it. Y've made a conquest there."

"Don't be daft. And I'm not looking for a conquest, like you say."

Percy's expressive eyebrow twitched, nothing more.

Tate left the office more disturbed than he wanted to be. He concentrated on projecting nothing but objective professionalism when he found Alex sitting by the water cooler, sipping gingerly at a plastic cup of water. "No tea or coffee?" Tate asked, opening out another folding chair to join Alex.

"Are you kidding me? People choose voluntarily to drink that stuff?" Alex then seemed to realise who he was talking to. "That's their choice, of course. Mine is to avoid stripping out the lining of my small intestine if it can be avoided."

Tate gave a wry smile and glanced over at the few other staff still gathered around the vending machine. One of the guys waved to Tate, another gave a mock bow in Alex's direction. A few of them laughed.

"Having trouble with the other guys?" Tate asked carefully. He didn't condone bullying in the workplace, but he couldn't have oversensitivity either.

"The Highness thing?" Alex grimaced. "No problem. I just call them ignorant peasants and we agree to rub along within the archaic British class system." Then, when Tate stared at him, he laughed. "I'm joking. I can take the teasing, I'm not *that* thin-skinned. I know I'm the new *boy*—" He mischievously added a West Country burr to the word, in mimicry of Percy's broad accent, "—and I have to stake my place in the hierarchy. They'll soon get tired of it."

Tate nodded, but he'd lost most of his concentration as soon as Alex smiled. What a change! It wasn't the sardonic smirk he'd given when he originally took Tate's hand, but a genuine grin of amusement. It seemed that the warehouse banter, rather than sending Alex Goodson off with his tail between his legs, had spurred him to stand up for himself. Tate felt rather sentimentally proud of the guy. "Percy says you've worked hard today."

"Good of him to notice." Alex tutted as if that should never have been in doubt. "From the way he's been barking at me, I rather thought he was planning my public flogging."

Tate shook his head with mild irritation. Alex should learn to take praise. Neither Percy nor Tate gave it out that often.

"Does that mean you agree with Percy? About the flogging?" Alex peered at Tate in a very unsettling way, then grinned. "I should warn you, I may like it. You never know, right?"

"What—? I don't want.... I mean, of course I don't agree." Tate hoped to God he wasn't blushing. What a bizarre bloke Alex was. It was as if he just opened his mouth and let any old wild words off their leads. Hadn't anyone ever told him to watch himself?

"So you'll keep me?" Alex said, more softly.

"In the job, you mean?" Tate wasn't falling for that seductive tone again.

"Yes indeed."

They gazed at each other for another of those charged moments. Tate's skin felt uncomfortable: his fingertips itched and his throat dried. He knew, without any doubt or hesitation that he wanted to be out of all his clothing and pressed against Alex Goodson. The thought was both shocking and terribly, wonderfully exciting.

"...won't you?"

*Shit.* Alex had been talking to him. "I'm sorry?"

Alex's smile turned down at the corners. "Wrong answer, Tate. You should have said, yes, I'd love to, Alex."

"What?" God, he was being so bloody rude, but something about Alex had him in a state of complete confusion.

"I said, now you're happy with my performance—I mean in the warehouse, of course—you'll have a drink with me after work tonight, won't you?"

*Good God.* The man's arrogance was astounding. "That's not appropriate. I'm your manager."

Alex shrugged. "It happens. And this will be outside of work. You have a life outside, don't you, Tate?"

"Yeah, I do, thanks very much." *What a nerve.*

"I can pick you up, I'll get a cab. Where do you live?"

"Forget it," Tate said sharply. This was getting out of hand. "Anyway, I have a meeting after work." Hell's bells, was that an *excuse*, like he thought he owed Alex one? Like he was actually, genuinely tempted to go for a drink with him?

Those twinkling eyes, that half-arrogant, half-self-deprecating smile....

It was the first time in a long time that Tate regretted being on call for one of his obligations. Despite Lou's disgust, he hadn't felt any guilt at dumping the pet shop guy for tonight's work meeting. But Alex Goodson? Tate found he was leaning forward in his seat, his head too close to Alex's for comfort. When Alex let out a long breath, Tate felt the warmth on his cheek. He instinctively lifted a hand, as if to touch Alex's arm. Alex's eyes widened slightly, entrancingly.

*Watch out!*

Tate reared back in his seat, hands safely back by his sides. "So where do *you* live?" he threw back. "Are you a local lad?"

Alex looked disconcerted. Tate suspected the man was rarely refused. Well, Tate Somerton wasn't going to be another notch on anyone's bedpost, however attractive. Funny, though, how it didn't give Tate any great sense of satisfaction to turn Alex down.

When Alex spoke again, his tone had flattened. "I just moved here. I... um, well I don't have a permanent place yet."

Tate nodded sympathetically. "Staying in rented rooms is no fun. Or is it a hotel?" God, he was being rude yet again. "I'm sorry, it's none of my business."

Alex was looking at him with a strange, soft expression. "No problem. I appreciate your concern. I'm staying at...." He paused as if trying to remember. "The Crown."

"Wow. That's a smart place." Tate was startled. If Alex could afford to stay in a posh hotel, why was he chasing a basic intern's job at Bonfils Bibendum?

"Is there anywhere to go, in that part of town?" Alex asked. He sipped his water absentmindedly.

"Nightlife, bars, you know the thing."

Tate knew exactly what kind of things, but he couldn't call himself an expert on the social scene. When was the last time he'd been to a club? Oh hell, yeah, there'd been that night with the guy who said he worked for Amnesty International, but who seemed to have no problem with trying to curtail Tate's personal freedom with a chokehold when Tate told the guy he wasn't interested in sadomasochism....

"What's that sigh for?" Alex asked, his head tilted sideways, his dark eyes quizzical.

"Nothing." Tate needed to keep better control of his expressions, or he'd be sharing his disaster of a love life with everyone in the warehouse. "I'm fine."

"Good. You can show me around the sights tonight, if you like."

Alex smiled as if he was fully aware of how cheeky he was being. Tate had to admire his persistence.

"See? You're smiling too, now." Alex sounded gleeful. "You should do that more often, even if it's at my expense. You're irresistible. We'll have a hell of a lot of fun together."

The joke should end right here, Tate decided. He stood brusquely. "I think I made it clear enough. We're not going out."

Alex stood too. "Don't be angry. I'm provocative, I know. But you can call the pace."

"You are. And I'm not. Calling the pace, that is. Or anything. I'm not interested."

"Oh, Tate." Alex just looked at him with a

rueful, I-sorta-hope-you're-lying expression.

*Dammit.* Because Tate was.

Alex finished his water, and placed the plastic cup carefully, almost fastidiously, in the nearby bin. "I'm totally free tonight. I'll wait around for you after work, in case you change your mind."

"I told you, I've got a meeting—"

"Tate?" The small voice interrupted them. Neither of them had seen Jamie shuffle over. Kid was like a ghost sometimes.

"Percy told me to tell you, the forklift meeting tonight's been postponed. They just rang down from HR."

"It's fate!" Alex said to Tate with obvious delight. "So what time will you finish work?"

Jamie's eyes opened wide.

"Jamie, haven't you got somewhere to be?" Tate said sharply. He waited until Jamie scurried away to where Stuart was backing up with some pallets, ready for the top shelf of a nearby bay, before turning on Alex. "What are you playing at?" he growled. "I'm not going on a date with you. Keep your mind on your work. Jesus, you only started today!"

"What has that to do with anything?" Alex was unfazed. "My approach is to strike while the iron is hot."

"I'm not an iron," Tate snapped.

"But you're hot," Alex shot back, the light of triumph sparking in his eyes.

Tate shouldn't laugh at such a cheesy line—he really shouldn't, however strong the temptation.

"But not for a date with you! That's my final

word on it." Tate knew he'd won that exchange when Alex's face fell. "Now we'd better both get back to work." He folded up his chair and looked toward the office. He ought to give Percy a hand with that paperwork. They were still confirming the wine deliveries for the entertainment planned on the lead-up to the Heritage Awards, and this issue with the seized Merlot was disturbing. They'd never had any problem at the docks or with customs in all the time Tate had worked there.

"Are there problems with the warehouse equipment?" Alex asked, inches from Tate's left ear.

"What?" Tate jumped, distracted as Alex crowded up against him. Alex's cologne smelled surprisingly expensive, from what Tate knew of perfumes. Personally, he was more used to basic soap and water, plus the delicate layering of sweat after a day's work.

"A meeting about forklifts, I think you said. I just wondered."

Tate felt frozen in place. His body's reactions warred with his brain's caution. *His Highness, Price Harry.* That's what the other guys were calling Alex. *Not hot for a date with you*, Tate had replied with spirit.

Was that the problem? Tate wouldn't consider going on a date with Alex because he talked like posh totty? *Have I got such a chip on my shoulder?* Tate had a natural suspicion of people who were—or acted—his superior. Tate's family had worked for Bonfils's for a long, long time, and he was the first in his family to start climbing the management ladder. General opinion was, those positions were kept for the Bonfils family and their cronies. But was that still true? Tate had fought for staff rights for so long, but against general inequality and discrimination, rather than for his own benefit. Mr. Charles and Mr. Henri were both pretty fair bosses, unlike some places Tate had heard about. If he could just pluck up a little more nerve and look into higher roles....

But. *But.* What upper-class, traditionally-run company would welcome an outspoken, working-class creature like him into the fold?

Alex tapped him on the shoulder.

"Sorry?" Tate asked. What had Alex asked?

"I reckon you know all about the Bonfils business, being on all these committees. Plus I believe you're in charge of security here in the warehouse? I just wondered..." Alex had half-turned his head away and Tate couldn't clearly see his expression. "...if there were problems in the company."

"Not at all."

"Oh. Sure. I'm just new to this place. I didn't mean to pry."

How did Alex do that? Apologise, yet *not?* "But you are prying, aren't you?" Tate felt an odd unease. He took a deliberate step away from Alex.

Alex held up his hands as if in surrender. "Sorry. I will curb my instinctive inquisitiveness forthwith."

"You what?" Tate couldn't hold back a short laugh.

Alex smiled in return, apparently encouraged all over again. "But at least there's no problem with us, is there?"

"I don't know what the hell you're talking about."

"We're both free tonight. You can come for a drink."

"I said no, didn't I? I have...." A genuine excuse? Another date? A trip to the moon? "I have to go grocery shopping." *Oh my God, how lame is that?*

Alex shrugged. "Good. I'll help you."

"Why on earth would you?" Rudeness was becoming Tate's default. But nothing seemed to upset Alex.

"I'd like to. As a friend."

"Don't you have anything better to go home to?" And that was just downright cruel. Even Alex's careless expression tightened at that. "I'm sorry," Tate said. "I shouldn't have said that."

Alex shrugged again, and his smile was warmer. "No, I asked for it."

But was that true? Alex's expression was momentarily blank, *too* blank. All he'd done was chat up Tate, amusing him, using language Tate hadn't heard since Gran had last back-to-backed her Agatha Christie box set. That wasn't a crime in anyone's books.

*And you want to share time with him, don't you?*

Tate's shamed fascination weakened his resolve. "Okay. I finish at six. Meet me by the side exit. I'm taking the bus, and that door's nearest the stop."

"I'll call a cab—"

"No, you won't," Tate said firmly. "I can manage by bus. And it's not a date."

Alex nodded, though he looked amused rather than chastened. "We'll do things your way, Tate."

"What makes me think that's a novelty for you, Alex?" Tate sighed, but felt an unusual hiccup in his breath in anticipation of unexpected company. "Do you always do just what you want? That's not going to go well for you, working here."

"It just has to go well enough," Alex said cryptically.

And Tate didn't know what to make of *that*.

# CHAPTER 6

So how on earth had he been talked into taking Alex Goodson grocery shopping?

Tate had no clear idea, but here they both were in Tate's local store. For some reason, Alex had seemed reluctant to go home—and Tate didn't fool himself that it was only because Alex was chasing a date. But Tate, God help him, seemed to be equally reluctant to resist more time with Alex. Looked like he needed to get out more, if he was so delighted to stand next to a clueless new intern in the vegetable aisle, right beside the packs of French beans, however handsome that intern might be. That was what Lou was always telling him, anyway. But Alex had pursued him, and befuddled Tate's traitorous libido with those particular, handsome looks, and basically worn Tate down with his daft chat-up lines.

Tate was honest enough to realise he'd actually enjoyed it.

Shopping turned out to be an adventure from the very start. Tate had managed to finish his work a few minutes early and left the warehouse in Percy's capable hands promptly at six o'clock. Alex was already waiting at the exit, happy smile on his face, hair brushed back—that hair, so glossy!—and wearing a rather new-looking dress shirt instead of the work polo shirt. A rather *expensive*-looking shirt, if Tate was any judge of how the other half dressed.

"I'm ready for whatever you have for me," Alex said.

Tate shook his head wearily. It wasn't his idea of fun, shopping after work, but the list of things they needed at home had grown alarmingly this week. Gran must have been raiding the larder at night again. "You'll find this deadly boring," he said. Was that one last try to shake off Alex? "It's just a normal domestic chore, you know how household shopping is."

Surprising Tate again, Alex looked almost shifty. "Whatever. I'm looking forward to it. Lead the way!"

Things went from the sublime to the ridiculous. The bus journey to the store was interesting, to say the least. After years of the same route to work, Tate knew how to push through to the back to find a spare seat, when to move toward the exit in time for his stop, and when to lean to one side as the bus took the sharp bend around the clock tower a little too fast.

But Alex? The whole thing seemed to be an alien experience for him, as if he really had taken cabs all his life. Who could afford to do that? Within seconds of climbing aboard, Alex infuriated the whole queue when he had no travel pass or debit card—Tate finally paid for him—and almost fell over a double buggy, parked awkwardly in the designated area. When the bus lurched, Alex lurched too, with such a look of shocked disgust and his glasses hanging loose from one ear that Tate laughed aloud. And when it came to jump off at the supermarket, Alex would still have been on the bus if Tate hadn't hauled him off by the sleeve. It was almost as if Alex were waiting for someone to call him personally to the exit. Probably expected them to hold it open for him too, because he only just managed to yank his ankle out of the way of the automatic doors.

In the supermarket, Alex continued to chat along, and Tate found he actually enjoyed the company. He shopped with the kids sometimes—and Gran, if he couldn't avoid it, because she could be more of a liability than a help, often wandering off to the cake aisle—but it wasn't the same as having another similar-aged adult around. And Alex was extremely entertaining, though maybe not intentionally so.

"Let me take half the list," he'd said to Tate as soon as they arrived. "Or give me a couple of items to find."

It was like he'd found a whole new game. Tate had genuinely never known anyone with such a cheerful attitude when faced with fighting for the last family-sized chicken pie in crushed cardboard packaging. Funny thing was, he found himself playing along as they trudged up and down the aisles. And smiling more than he could remember for ages.

It was soon obvious that Alex had no idea of how similar foods were displayed together, or that there was a wide choice of brands. He was also crap at steering a shopping cart—he kept forgetting it was there, darting off to look at something on a top shelf or chatting to one of the assistants, or forgetting it turned on four wheels and couldn't spin around on a fixed spot. Admittedly, his apparent clumsiness meant he nudged against Tate almost every few minutes. The touch was both startling and fun. Tate started to wonder if Alex were actually that crap at driving at all.

They paused a few times, chatting aimlessly about the job at Bonfils. Tate found it a great relief. Yes, a lover outside the company was good for broadening his horizons, offering other points of view and life experiences. But a guy who knew where Tate worked and had some idea what the working day looked like? Tate could appreciate that.

*A lover?* Jesus, where was his mind leading him? Or rather, his other head.

"What's amusing you now?" Alex's curious voice broke in over the piped music wafting through the freezer section.

Tate tried desperately not to blush. "Um. The price of frozen sausages." They were Amy's favorite.

"What do you mean, the price?" Alex peered at the display cabinet where Tate had paused. "Where's that?"

Tate stared at him. "Are you having problems with your sight?"

"What?" Alex looked confused, then reached for his glasses as if he'd forgotten they were there. "Oh. These are just for... um." He folded them and shoved them in his jeans pocket. "I don't really need them. You know."

*No, I don't.* But Tate pointed at the price tag on the shelf.

"Oh. Yes, I see. That seems ludicrously cheap. Are you sure they're safe to eat? You should check first with the butcher."

Where on earth had Alex been shopping before? He didn't seem to realise how odd his behavior was. What other grocery store showed prices in any other way?

"What's next on the list?" Alex asked blithely. "I found you the tea." He held out an embossed tin almost proudly.

Tate shook his head. "That's the most expensive brand, Alex. And what's it blended with?"

Alex looked at him blankly, then turned the tin over. "Ginseng. Lime leaves. I've had this before and it's gloriously aromatic."

"I'm sure it is. And three times the price of the plain supermarket version. Gran likes the generic breakfast tea bags."

No doubt about it—Alex paled. "*Bags?*"

Tate laughed. "Yeah. You look like I asked you to eat a baby's head. It's a perfectly good option. And safer for Gran, whose hands can't always grip a spoon very well."

"Oh." Alex frowned, as if he'd never had to think of that before. "Is she ill?"

Tate drew a deep breath. "Just arthritis. But bright as a button still." He didn't often talk about Gran to people. "Um. Don't tell her I said that about her hands. She doesn't like admitting it. Well, if you ever meet her, that is. Which is, you know. Unlikely, I expect."

"I don't know about that," Alex said.

"You—? What?"

"You'll need help with all this on the bus." Alex said the last word like it was a bizarre spaceship of some kind and piloted by a hostile nation to boot. He reached across Tate to pull a packet of sausages out of the cabinet, his forearm brushing against Tate's. His skin was warm, set against the chill from the open door. Tate felt the contrast all the way to his neck and throat, a trickle of goose bumps along his flesh.

"Oh," Alex said very softly. Had he felt something too?

Tate stilled for a long moment, unable to respond. He could only watch as Alex gave him a mock salute and abruptly wheeled away with the cart. He didn't look back at Tate, but Tate was vividly aware of every single goose bump as it gradually faded. Only then did he feel braced enough to set off after his loose-cannon companion.

Lou was right—he really did need to get out more.

The minute Tate opened the front door to his family home, his hectic household greeted him in its usual fashion. Someone was singing a Beyoncé hit at painfully top volume, crockery clattered in a clumsy spin on the distant kitchen table, and Freddie started barking from the front room, as if he only just realised he was meant to be guarding the house from intruders. Young footsteps thundered along the hallway toward Tate, as the children appeared from the kitchen.

"Tate! *Tate!*"

"Did you remember the sausages?"

"Sausages! I want sausages!"

"Hattie won't share the laptop. Make her, Tate!"

"Hugo's a liar, liar, pants on fire."

Tate felt Alex tense up beside him, shortly before Amy hurtled into view and, without any break in momentum, threw herself at Alex's legs.

Tate raised his voice to be heard over the ruckus. "Let me get in the house without you yelling, kids. Hattie, Hugo, help with the shopping bags. Amy, leave Alex alone."

"Alex, Alex," Amy chanted into Alex's denim-clad leg.

"Who's Alex?" Hattie said.

"Is he your boyfriend?" Hugo challenged.

"Can he be my boyfriend?" Amy whined.

Tate groaned inwardly. Alex had stood stock-still beside him while all this was going on—an explosion of kids, four-way conversations, and— *oh, God take me now*—here was Gran tottering down the hallway with a plastic spatula in her hand and sporting a bright yellow kid's apron, covered with red stains that Tate hoped weren't blood but would need to check to be sure.

"You missed dinner I'm afraid, Tate. I was trying out a new Moroccan recipe, too." Gran grinned rather mischievously. "But don't worry, I left some in the fridge for you for later."

Tate opened his mouth to reply, then shut it again when words failed him.

Beside him, Alex tentatively moved his legs, but Amy clung tight. "Good God," he said weakly. "Are you running a school?"

Tate winced. "This is my family. There's my gran. Hattie and Hugo are the twins—"

"I can see," Alex said drily. "They're wearing the same clothes." He peered at the H's. "Don't they have any sense of personal identity at that age?"

"I wanna wear a pink skirt," Hugo said loudly, with a triumphant glare at Tate. "But Tate won't let me."

Alex raised his eyebrows and turned to Tate. "I don't know for certain your personal situation, but surely you wouldn't prevent him expressing whatever he wants—"

"You misunderstand," Tate said grimly. "It's got nothing to do with gender stereotypes."

"It's 'cos of me," Hattie chimed in loudly and gleefully. "Pink makes me *sick*."

Tate sighed. "You just don't like it, Hattie. *You* make yourself sick. Deliberately."

"And you're not the one wearing it," Hugo snapped at her.

"Wear it and I'll vomit in your lap!" she snapped back.

Alex blinked hard.

"They like to bicker," Tate, frowning, explained to him. "That's the only explanation I have for them not murdering each other by now." He grasped an arm from each twin and marched them in front of him into the kitchen. "Punishment for disgraceful behavior and talk of vomiting? Unpack the shopping for me, and then wash up after Gran's cooking." Their aghast expressions were enough to make him smile again. Gran could be trusted to make a meal, albeit a bit wacky on the ingredients, but the mess she made of every saucepan and utensil was legendary.

Then he turned back to see Alex still frozen in the hallway. God, the embarrassment! Yet another reason why Tate rarely dated.

"Sorry," he said, quickly sidling in front of Gran who was now a foot away from Alex, peering up at his face with undisguised interest, and waving the bloody spoon—surely it *was* only tomato sauce?—a dripping inch from Alex's smart shirt. "Um. Thanks for the help with the shopping. You'll want to get off home now."

"I will?" Alex tilted his head. Just slightly, but in some unfair way he looked even sexier. His smile seemed genuine, though his expression was definitely puzzled.

"The kids," Tate said, and threw his arms wide as if that was surely enough excuse. "Evenings are a noisy, frantic time for us, what with meals, and the excitement of all being together again after the day at school and at work—"

"Where's home, Alex?" Gran suddenly seemed to remember the spoon in her hand and licked the end of it experimentally.

"Oh, just a local budget hotel. The Crown."

"Budget? Hardly." Gran raised her eyebrows. "I'd say it's very smart."

"Is it?" Alex looked pained, as if he'd messed up with something.

"Gran," Tate muttered. "Alex *only* helped me with the shopping. Can you leave me to have a quiet word with him?"

Gran's smile at Alex turned to a frown when she faced Tate, but she sighed theatrically, wiped the spoon on her already stained apron, and pottered away into the living room.

Tate sighed. He could feel Alex's intense gaze on him, and he had an overwhelming desire to smooth down his hair. "Well. I have lots to do, so this isn't really a good time to... you know."

That tilt of Alex's head again, and the smile grew.

"Chat, I mean," Tate added desperately. "Relax. Whatever. I need to make the meal plan for the week ahead, the H's will need to finish homework, and Amy needs a bath and a bedtime story—"

"Story! Story!" The limpet on Alex's leg that was Amy piped up happily. "I want Alex to read to me."

Freddie gave a muted bark in the background; Gran was probably tickling him. Tate wondered if his family actually had a Grand Plan for whenever they saw their brother/grandson with a potential date, involving a whole bunch of devious ways of making him feel the most uncomfortable. "Amy, don't be ridiculous."

"I'm not rickerless." She let go of Alex, and sat

back on her heels, gazing up at him with soulful eyes. "Do *you* have a dog?"

Alex blinked hard. "A dog? No, I don't. Not at the moment, anyway."

"They can host billi-virus, y'know. It will kill the whales."

"No, I didn't know," Alex said. Tate was secretly impressed with how calm he was under Amy's questioning. Her thirst for knowledge meant she was often super-precociously blunt. "Is billi—what you call it—common in the UK? I wonder how frequently a British pet dog may meet a whale to pass on the infection."

"It's morbillivirus," came Gran's voice from the living room. "She's investigating whale diseases now."

Amy's expression lit up at Alex. "We could 'vestigate them together!"

Tate broke in sternly. "Bedtime is not negotiable, Amy." He glanced at Alex's cute gray eyes. When he smiled, the skin crinkled more beside his right eye than his left, though both were equally attractive. "She loves searching the internet, some people would probably say she spends too long on there."

Alex nodded sagely, though Tate suspected he hadn't had much experience with small children. "I believe current studies do recommend that young people only spend a few hours a week—"

"Ten minutes is too much for Amy's skills and imagination," Tate said frankly. "By that time, she'll have researched everything from whale diseases to a life in the Mafia, and a family tree that links her with Lucrezia Borgia. Amy, go and get your towel and pajamas ready, I'll run your bath. I can unpack the shopping with the H's, and Gran will cover bedtime routine."

From the living room came a dog's yelp and a loud, cackling whoop. Gran was obviously enjoying some TV program or other. The cheer sounded strong enough for a much younger and lustier football supporter, though Tate suspected Gran's current attention was on one of her beloved cookery channels. She did get overly excited by some of the chefs.

Alex touched his arm. "Don't disturb her," he said. "I'll happily do the story reading. Or if you don't feel you can trust me...?"

From halfway up the stairs came a small "hooray" from Amy, on her way to the bathroom.

"Well. I hardly know you," Tate said. He wanted to trust everyone, he really did, but he'd make sure Amy's door stayed open so he could hear what was going on. "And that's not the only issue."

"I know it's not."

"What?"

Alex moved nearer, now that they were mostly alone in the hallway. His shoulder brushed against Tate's. "You don't let go, do you? You have control issues. I understand. But you'll exhaust yourself if you don't allow others to take on some of the burden."

"They're not a burden," Tate said hotly.

Alex just rolled his eyes. "I didn't mean it like that. I was talking about you and your need to relax and enjoy life."

"My—?" *Just give up, Tate. This strange man is beyond your understanding.*

"Please," Alex said more softly. "After you've done Amy's bath thing, sit with your gran, or with the twins—" He smiled and waved a hand vaguely in the direction of the kitchen where there were sounds of splashing and raucous laughter. He'd obviously forgotten their names. "Just one question. What do I read?"

Another call came from upstairs. "I've got my favorite book right here!"

When Alex looked at Tate, Tate could only give a rueful smile in reply. "I'm afraid I have no idea what it is tonight. She has library tickets of her own. It could be anything from Dickens to Spot the Dog."

"I'll be led by you," Alex said gravely, though the smile still lingered. "As long as it comes recommended by educational authorities—?"

"It's my *absolute* favorite," Amy's call interrupted, more firmly this time.

"That's that, then," Alex said. "I assume?"

Tate laughed. "You learn fast, newbie."

# CHAPTER 7

Tate scrabbled awake with a shock, realising he'd dropped off to sleep on the sofa. Beside him, Gran snored, her mouth wide open and her apron skewed around her waist. Freddie was slumped on her lap, also snoring. The last Tate remembered was finishing Amy's bath, then sending the twins to their rooms to revise for the next day's geography test at school. He vaguely recalled offering to watch *Supreme Sausage Suppers* with Gran, or something similar. The TV was now showing a gritty Scandinavian crime drama with a dismembered torso being dragged up out of a frozen river, so something had definitely slipped in the space time continuum.

My God, he must have needed the rest. But what about Alex? *Is he still here?*

Groaning a little, Tate eased gently off the sofa and padded upstairs in his socked feet, picking up a small handful of laundry that had been left at the foot of the stairs. On the top landing he paused, listening to the gentle bickering from Hugo's room where the H's were currently based. From the occasional word he caught clearly—like "volcano"—it sounded like they were successfully getting on with their homework.

"Tate?"

Alex was just coming out of Amy's room. He smiled as Tate approached; Tate felt rather oddly vulnerable in front of him. Had Alex seen him fall asleep?

"How did it go?" Tate said softly. He peeked into Amy's room to find her warmly wrapped up in her *Frozen* quilt and fast asleep. He closed the door as quietly as he could. "She can be a little madam, if you know what I mean. At heart she's just a little kid, but she's so very bright for her age, you need all your wits about you."

"Well, I couldn't read this to her, I'm afraid." Alex said in a similarly lowered voice, holding up the luridly covered book that Amy had presumably chosen. "The story didn't make any sense, and the language was bizarre. Plus none of the characters are anatomically correct. Don't they have curriculum-based reading matter nowadays?"

Tate chuckled. "I'm sure they do, but that doesn't always appeal to Amy. But she still fell asleep okay?"

"Of course. After I recited some Keats."

"You...?" Tate was startled. It was becoming his default response to Alex Goodson. "As in John Keats, the poet?"

Alex shrugged easily. "She seemed to like it. I find 'season of mists and mellow fruitfulness' has a cadence that lends itself to sleep. I certainly drowsed through most of my English lessons at school. That's one of the few poems where I can remember all the verses."

Tate really, *really* wanted to let loose a proper

laugh. "Dammit, Alex. You're...."

Alex seemed to lean in more closely. "I'm what? Handsome? Irresistible? Just the kind of man you've been looking for to take you out and show you some fun?"

Alex's scrutiny made Tate feel hot, which was very odd, standing on his own home landing on the rather worn carpet, hoping against hope that wasn't a boner he was springing. "Astonishing. That's all I'm prepared to say." He pressed the pile of clothes into Alex's arms and took a step away before he admitted something he regretted. "I must look in on the twins. If you're okay to help out some more, perhaps you can dump this laundry in the basket in the bathroom on your way back downstairs?"

Despite his success with Amy, Alex was no help to the twins with their homework—his geography knowledge seemed to have skipped all mountain ranges and major lakes, concentrating only on the location of certain international airports—so Tate left him downstairs with Gran while he helped the H's collect their books together for the morning and get ready for bed. Thank God his family home had enough space for them all, though there were times the house felt stuffed to the gills with humans and all their belongings. When he finally came back down to the living room, Freddie was back in his basket and Gran was awake. She was rather flushed, with a suspicious twinkle in her eyes. Tate saw she'd been watching an episode of *Game of Thrones* and he sighed inwardly. He usually kept her away from the whole series, though Alex wouldn't have known that. She just got too lively after it, and Tate had his hands full at the best of times. It wasn't so much the sex and violence—to say nothing of the dragons—but rather the bizarre meals some of the characters ate. He'd never forgotten the time Gran asked in the middle of Tesco's for dried horse jerky.

Alex looked up at him and gave that smile again. Not the polite one he used at work or in front of Tate's family, but the wide, hungry one, full of delight and temptation. But as his gaze flickered over Tate's face, his eyes narrowed and his expression grew more serious.

He stood slowly. "I'd better be going. It's getting late."

"Never too late," Gran said.

"Not for some things, Gran," Alex said easily. "But maybe for young men during the working week. I'll see you again soon, I hope."

"Don't forget that recipe for quails' eggs." Gran gave a peal of happy laughter.

Tate watched with an astonishment that was getting weary, as Alex bent over Gran's hand and kissed it goodbye. After a farewell scratch to Freddie's ears—when the dog shamelessly, cravenly whined for more—he accompanied Tate to the front door, where they paused.

Tate spoke in a lowered voice. "I doubt this was what you expected to happen tonight."

"How?" Alex asked.

"How, what?"

"How do you know what I expected?"

"Alex, you made it pretty clear you were after a date, not a… a… Gran-and-pet-sitting-cum-child-education session."

Alex laughed gently. "I wanted to spend some time with you. That's all."

"For God's sake."

"What's your problem, Tate Somerton?" For the very first time, Alex seemed annoyed. "Are you calling me a liar? People appear to have an issue with my voice, and maybe I haven't mastered the arcane rituals of warehouse life yet, and maybe I don't always think before I speak, and I'm too damned provocative—"

Tate nodded. *All of that.*

"But I can't be accused of not speaking the truth, however inconvenient. I mean every word I say."

Tate hesitated. "Don't tell me you weren't just thinking of a quick tumble."

"Would you believe me if I did? Of course I want to seduce you. I'm really attracted to you, you're hot, and…."

"What?"

"Astonishing," Alex said. A sly smile crept over his face as he turned Tate's earlier words back on him. "That's all I'm going to say."

Tate laughed, but this time he heard the rare relief and ease in his voice. "You're used to having things your way, aren't you?"

Alex nodded. "Yes, I am. But you'd want me to

be honest about that, wouldn't you?"

"Yes." Tate realised Alex was right—it was both refreshing and relaxing to find someone who apparently was exactly what he seemed. "Sorry. I might come across as a bit overcautious." He gave a slightly bitter laugh. "It's not been a good year for dating, for me."

Alex's touch on his arm was warm. "Can only get better, right?"

"I hope so," Tate said, almost a comment to himself. When Alex braced his free arm on the doorframe and leaned in toward Tate, Tate didn't veer away. Instead, he leaned in too.

"This is okay?" Alex whispered.

Tate nodded. Alex must know by now he was both gay and interested, and oh my God, he was so very eager, was that obvious to Alex too—?

The kiss was gentle but oh, so good. So good that Tate couldn't remember ever experiencing such a wave of delight and need. Alex's lips were full and warm, and the tip of his tongue teased at Tate's. It was enough to set all Tate's nerves a-jingle; he was very afraid he moaned aloud. Alex kissed with all of his mouth, not in a gross, sloppy way, but with a possessive desire that made Tate feel treasured. There was no tentativeness, that was obvious. No nervousness, no hesitation. But although Alex took with confidence, his touch was full of respect, so that Tate found himself very ready to give in return. As Alex had said, Tate felt he could set his own pace. He sighed softly and leaned into Alex, sliding his hand around Alex's waist. Alex lifted a single hand and cupped Tate's cheek as they deepened the kiss.

Tate felt himself molding to Alex, becoming part of a single unit. They were of a similar height and build, and it seemed both comfortable and natural to link his arm into Alex's and press his legs against Alex's thighs. They both had an evening bristle, but it brushed rather than scratched. Alex nuzzled at Tate's ear, as Tate tried to resist the urge to lap gently at Alex's throat. Desire grew slowly rather than as a lustful rush. His cock was stirring under his jeans, no doubt about it, but he was relaxed, savoring each second of delectable taste, of the smell of Alex's skin, his quickening breath. Oh, but Alex knew his attractiveness, he knew his skills....

Tate knew with sudden, blinding certainty and a fast-beating heart that Alex Goodson would know how to treat a man well.

Finally, Alex sighed and gently pulled away. "Definitely," he murmured. He sounded breathless.

"Definitely what?"

"Worth waiting for," Alex whispered in Tate's ear. "Thank you."

Tate could still feel the press of Alex's fingers, the warmth of his lips, the tease of his tongue. Who was thanking whom?

"No strings, okay?" Alex's lips ghosted over Tate's jaw. "I hear enough to understand that's what you want. I can do that, no problem."

"Yes," Tate said. "No strings is good." Exactly what he wanted. Maybe this wasn't so lunatic a step, after all. He smiled and cleared his throat.

"You're... um... okay with where the bus stop is? The 94 will take you back toward the Crown."

Alex was watching Tate's mouth. "That's fine. Thanks."

"Or the 113." All Tate could hear was his own gabbling.

Alex smiled, his gaze drifting up to meet Tate's. He looked slightly drunk. "You want to come with me and show me the way?"

*Yes.* "No. I'll see you at work tomorrow. Don't be late."

"Or Tate Somerton may put me over his knee and chastise me," Alex said blithely. "The big, bad manager."

*Ouch.* Tate felt himself flush. "Jesus, if you're just going to poke fun—"

"No!" Alex must have realised he'd overstepped, he looked horrified. "I'm sorry, that didn't come out quite right. It's not a joke at all."

"No. Not at all."

"However edgy my sense of humour may be—"

"Edgy doesn't do you justice, Alex."

And despite that hiccup, as they parted, they were still both smiling.

# CHAPTER 8

When Tate wandered back into the living room, he was disappointed to see the twins were up again and cuddled up to Gran on the sofa. "It's a school night, kids. You need to get to bed and asleep, smartish."

"Just one last cuddle for Gran," Hugo said, his eyes wide with pretended innocence.

"We were worried, Tate. We didn't know where you'd gone," Hattie added.

Tate rolled his eyes at them. They knew he wouldn't fall for all this. They must have crept downstairs while he and Alex were on the doorstep. Tate was glad he'd pulled the door closely behind him.

In his basket asleep, Freddie snuffled and twitched his back leg.

"Your young man is handsome," Gran said. "Knows a lot about those TV chefs, even says he's met a couple. Promised me recipes, too. Handsome is as handsome does."

"Gran, we say hot nowadays, not handsome. Hot, hot, hot!" Hugo hugged her, laughing.

"Ooooh, Tate and hot Alex, smooch-woochy!" Hattie squealed, and Hugo joined in with her giggles.

"He's not my young man." Tate tried to be

heard about the whoops of laughter. Just sometimes, they all drove him mad. Just sometimes, like now, when he wanted a few minutes of his own, to think about Alex and his mysteries and his dancing eyes and flirting talk, and oh my God, the taste of his mouth…. "What bloody chance do I have of dating *any* young man," he spat out, "when this chaos would chase them off at first base?"

The room fell unusually silent. Even the TV had slipped into a run of bland commercials. Hattie thumped Hugo surreptitiously on the arm, and he halfheartedly kicked her shin in return.

"Sorry, Tate," they chorused, looking suitably sorrowful.

Gran looked apologetic too. "We're your family, Tatty, that's all. We care about you."

It was the nickname that broke him, time and again. His mum had coined it; now Gran was the only one who used it. "I know. I didn't mean it, not like it sounded." He dropped into the armchair with a sigh. "And it's not as if I'm looking for someone. But if I did… oh, never mind. I'm just bloody tired."

"Tate said bloody," Hattie whispered to her twin, but loud enough for everyone to hear. "Twice."

"Another two pounds in the Christmas swear jar," Hugo mouthed back, equally obviously.

"Off back to bed, the two of you," Gran said gruffly. She hauled herself off the sofa, watched over the twins as they kissed Tate good night, then herded them upstairs to bed like an elderly sheepdog with her small flock. The H's were unusually subdued, but did Tate care? No. The quiet was a rare treat. And to be honest, it was just what he needed at the moment.

Gran shuffled back in after fifteen minutes or so. She plumped down on the sofa and patted the cushion for him to join her there. "Tired, you say. Trouble at work, Tatty?"

"Some bits and pieces, Gran." He couldn't give her details, even the ones he had. It was important competitors didn't learn about Bonfils's plans, especially with a new launch on the horizon. And unlikely and daft as it might seem, who knew who Gran was line dancing with or challenging at indoor bowls during the days' activities? She was a member of virtually every community club in the city. "There's just a bad feeling in the warehouse at the moment."

"Nothing to do with Prince Harry?"

"Oh, dear God. Did he tell you that's his nickname?"

Gran smirked. "Doesn't seem to bother him. Though he told me Harry isn't as good-looking as him in real life."

Tate raised his eyebrows. "Did he really say that?"

Gran nodded and started groping around on the sofa cushions for the remote control. "That's what it sounded like to me. My hearing's good enough, y'know? Funny thing, it was like he'd really met the royal family, and not just packaged on TV like the rest of us."

"Bloody show-off," Tate muttered. "Like we'd

believe that kind of crap." Gran must have been concentrating on her search, because she didn't reply to that. "Anyway, what *were* you talking about?"

The remote had been found, and triumphantly, Gran turned the TV to a foodie channel. "Oh. This 'n' that. Homework. Schools. Hairstyles. Morbillivirus."

Tate smiled. She was a dear old lady, and he loved her sense of humour. "Not the kids, Gran. I meant with Alex."

"Like I said." Gran had a sneaky grin she used for when she caught him out or bested him in something. "We were talking about homework, schools, hairstyles—"

Tate laughed in surrender. "All right, all right."

Gran snuggled back in the sofa, obviously settling in for the rest of the evening. "He may speak like a bloomin' royal, but he can chat about anything you like. Good to find that in a young sprog like him. They don't usually want to waste their time on the older generation. Though he talked about the kids like they'd come from another planet."

"I think they had, from Alex's point of view."

"Talked about you—"

"Me?" Why was his throat suddenly dry? *I mustn't ask, I won't ask—*

He didn't need to, Gran was going to tell him anyway. "—what you did at work, how long you'd been working at the warehouse, what your job included, if you ever talked about how the company was doing."

"Well. I suppose I do." Bonfils Bibendum was an important part of his life; had been for three generations of his family's working life. But he never shared anything confidential, even with his family.

Gran nudged him in the ribs. "Keep your hair on. I told him you were no kind of decent gossip."

"Oh yeah?" He nudged her back, though not as hard, and she chuckled.

"He left his specs behind too," she said, pointing to Alex's glasses on top of the TV. She shrugged. "Didn't seem to be bothered without them."

For a few moments, they were silent, Gran's gaze back on the TV and a bizarre omelette challenge. Then, "You know what?" she said. "He just talks as he wants, doesn't stop to think about what's right to say to an old bird."

"I know, he's an arrogant—"

"And thank God for that!" she broke in gleefully. "It really pisses me off when people stop swearing in front of me, or don't mention hospitals, or think I don't understand how bloody Instagram works."

"Gran, please." Tate had a shocked thought. "I don't do that, do I?"

"I wouldn't let you, Tatty." She leaned into him and kissed his cheek, a dry but loving brush of the lips. "No, I just liked the boy. Fairly up his own arse, but genuine."

"Sounds schizophrenic to me."

"You're a case in point, yourself. Coiled up tighter 'n a spring with all your control freakery, but a flood of easy pleasure when you let loose."

Control...? And a flood of *what*? He wasn't entirely sure what she meant—or whether he liked the implication. What had possessed Gran this evening? "Control's important," he said, a bit tightly. Why wasn't she engrossed as usual in the cooking? She loved all those mature Italian chefs.

"You think I don't know that, but I do," Gran said. "Just as I know I can afford to ignore it now I'm old and have got you lot to look after me. And I know you *can't*."

He relaxed and grinned. "But in compensation, my knees are better, right?"

"Too bloomin' right." She thumped him on the arm and they both laughed.

Things were quiet for another few minutes while Gran flicked between the omelette challenge and the Bake-Off semifinals. Tate was feeling drowsy again, but in a very different way than his usual weariness after work. Had it really been so long since he relaxed properly, enjoying a selfish, self-centered delight just for himself? This was a sensual kind of ease, seeping through his body, warming and relaxing him, like easing himself into a hot bath. That first contact of tired muscles with the soothing water was one of the best sensations in life, he reckoned. Well, apart from Alex Goodson's kiss....

"So, when are you going on another date?" asked Gran.

"Another? Gran, this wasn't a date. Dammit, if it had been, he'd be running for the hills after this family baptism of fire."

Gran's laugh was mischievous. "Didn't see any dust around his heels. In fact, you were an interesting time on the doorstep, saying good night to him."

Tate closed his eyes briefly. "'Nuff said, Gran. It's just a casual thing, it's not like it's going anywhere. We're completely different guys, after all. No strings, we've agreed." When she patted him on the hand, he opened his eyes.

"He wondered what your ambitions were," she said. "You know, I do too."

*Ambitions?* "Just to keep the roof over our heads, Gran. Food on the table, the kids' schooling uninterrupted. They need stability and lots of love. The warehouse job is full-on, but also gives me some flexibility."

"Not just the job, love."

*Oh gawd, was this dating advice?*

"Give Alex a chance, Tatty, love. He's unusual. That's what you need."

Tate couldn't have articulated the shiver of sensuality that ran through him if his life had depended on it. "You mean weird?"

"If I did, I would have said it, boy. I said unusual. He stands out from the crowd."

"Okay, I get the point."

"No, you don't," she said, more sharply. To Tate's alarm, she clicked off the TV altogether and turned abruptly to face him. Her expression was fierce. "Do you think your parents would want you to be alone? Yet I've seen the mess you've made with the boys who occasionally pin you down to a date. You're running away from it."

"Gran, that's not—"

"It's totes true, as the H's would say. They want you to be happy too, Tate. We all do. You're run ragged with everything else in life. Louise sees it too. We think it's about time you took a break and had something for yourself. Something or someone that doesn't need your protection or campaigning—something just for fun!"

Tate shifted uncomfortably on the sofa. They were ganging up against him. "Don't play that card with me, Gran. I don't have any choice. It's only four years since the accident, remember?" That was clumsy, of course Gran remembered. He gentled his voice. "The kids need me."

"Not *all* of you, Tatty. We can cope with much more than you think. And that unusual boy—"

"Don't say any more," Tate said, too sharply, he knew. "Isn't there a Gordon Ramsay retrospective series on tonight?"

Gran grumbled, but was distracted, and the TV came back on. Tate was left with melancholy thoughts of his deceased parents, his adorable but needy family, and his ridiculous—yet undeniable—attraction to Alex Goodson. Could he really think about dating Alex for real?

Tate was used to handling decisions on his own, even when surrounded by people. Things had been that way ever since he was orphaned. Oh, he didn't look for sympathy, because there were plenty of folk worse off. It had been a terrible, gut-wrenching time when his parents were first killed, but he'd just dug in and determined to carry on. The family had already brought Gran into their house to live, but Tate was only in his early twenties, working hard at his own job, and ill-prepared to take on primary care for all his siblings. However, he couldn't bear the thought they might be fostered out to other homes—however well-meaning—or split up as a family. Luckily, he had good support from social services, was given sufficient compassionate time off from work to sort things out in those first few grief-stricken months, and his colleagues and friends had stepped in to help when they could. Louise, of course, was the best of them all.

Tate had dated before the accident—he now envisioned his life split that way, before and after—but there'd never been anyone special. And he still tried, now and then, not *just* because Gran and Louise nagged him. A guy needed comfort, right? He had fun, he had occasional sex, and he had such a lot going on in the rest of his life, he didn't usually notice how few and far between his nights out were.

Gran might have been annoying, but Tate's innate honesty made him face the fact she might also have been *right*. Had he messed up his private life by being so fierce about protecting his family? Was he out of the habit of dating or, worse still, giving out hostile vibes in the first place? If Gran was so right, where was *he* going so wrong?

The rest of the night didn't lie easy for him.

After waving goodbye to Tate on his doorstep

and waiting for the front door to close behind him, Alex sneaked around the corner of Tate's street and jogged for another couple of blocks before hailing a cab to take him back to the hotel. He slid quickly into the back seat and allowed himself to slump down and relax.

What had just happened? The evening had been astonishing and, as Tate himself had said, not at all what Alex had expected when he inveigled his way into Tate's personal space. He'd met a whole adventure park full of kids and a rather slutty but cute dog, run the gamut of an old woman who was too perceptive for her own good, and kissed the most exciting man he'd met for a long, long time.

*That kiss....*

Alex imagined he could still taste Tate, even though he must have licked off all traces by now. What's more, he could still smell Tate's shampoo from where Tate's head had rested against the crook of his neck and shoulder, still feel the press of Tate's muscled thigh. Plus his heart was still racing, and he was hard and uncomfortable. And ecstatic!

Tate wasn't like anyone he'd dated for years. Maybe ever. He was cross and tousled, and suspicious of Alex. He was gorgeous—the fire in those eyes!—and overworked, and so tightly wound he could explode any day. Yet he didn't; he coped with the warehouse, with Percy and the other staff, with the senior Bonfils, with feeding and caring for a family that both adored and clung to him. Jesus, he coped with *public transport*!

If Alex had been back in his normal life, he would never have left without Tate's mobile number and an arrangement to wine and dine him as soon as possible. Instead, he'd left with a tease of a kiss, Tate's scowly smile, an unrelieved erection, and a purple plastic ring in his pocket that Amy had insisted he wear as reward for reading to her, at least while he was in the house.

What the hell was up with him? He couldn't stop thinking of Tate....

*No!* he told himself sternly. *No distraction. No strings, remember?* He'd had plenty of practice with that kind of relationship, it was his default mode after all. Sexy fun with a gorgeous man, just in passing.

Yes, tomorrow he had to get back on track. He had to start his investigation in earnest.

# CHAPTER 9

It had been a weird week for Tate. It took several days to get the confiscated shipment released and, back in the warehouse, the damaged labels on existing stock had to be replaced. This was far more than just printing something off themselves—they had to reapply to the French producer who determined the appellation on the wine.

Tate's concern about these random, yet potentially damaging, interferences grew by the day. He found himself watching his staff with suspicion rather than supervision, yet no one seemed to act oddly. Well, more oddly than usual. Jamie still trotted everywhere with Stuart like a puppy, Percy seemed even more growly, Penny in Packaging added a new piercing to her lip, and the married couple who organised the warehouse refreshments had been persuaded by someone to offer homemade cakes at the afternoon break. Tate had a pretty good idea that persuasive person was Alex Goodson.

Yes, indeed. *Alex.* Tate had conflicting reactions to that.

The main reason was because Tate had been seeing Alex. Socially, that was. Well, he wasn't sure he'd call it actual dating—just a few times they'd gone somewhere after work. That was all, right? *Grow a pair, Somerton*, he imagined in a voice that sounded remarkably like Louise's. Okay, they'd definitely been dates, he couldn't deny it. He wasn't entirely sure why he kept trying to, except from some kind of self-preservation instinct.

Yet it had been such a lot of fun.

After that astonishing shopping evening, they fell into the habit of having coffee after work at the small café on the edge of the industrial estate. Tate wasn't keen on being seen, and then mercilessly teased, by other staff members, but at the end of the working day, most of them had already gone home. If Tate was in charge of locking up, or preparing for the night shift, Alex would wait around until he was free, then meet Tate at a small table at the back of the cozy café.

Despite having been in the same warehouse every day, they always seemed to find more than enough to talk about. What on earth *did* they talk about? Movies and books; the latest dramas in Tate's child-ridden household; cars; wine. Tate had been intrigued by Alex's knowledge of matching wines to food, and in return, he knew he'd surprised Alex more than once with his own knowledge. He might only work in the warehouse, but his interest in the job extended to knowing about the product as well. In fact, he'd already rashly applied for the sommelier internship, but no one needed to know about that yet, did they? At least, not until they got back to him with yes or—more likely—no. In the meantime, he'd discovered that Alex was startlingly easy to talk to: he made Tate laugh. Such a silly thing, but Tate realised how little he did of it recently.

Alex's latest story had been how he dropped his pass under the forklift tracks that morning. Now it was mangled so badly—

"—I look like the Hunchback of Notre Dame's younger brother," he announced plaintively. "If there were a prime suspects lineup—"

"Your own mother wouldn't recognise you?" Tate realised he'd miscalculated the joke, as Alex's expression went suddenly blank. He hurried on, trying to recover the moment. "So do you think this job is really for you?"

"What do you mean? Are you here to fire me?"

"No. You think I'd do that on my own time?" Tate laughed. "But you must realise you're not the usual type of intern we get. At least, not of the ones who stay. You've obviously been very well educated, you're not lacking in assertiveness, and I for one can't reconcile you working on the shop floor."

"That's what an internship is, right? It's important I see all aspects of the business."

"Yeah. But I'd expect you to have been fast-tracked to one of the specialist training programs. Sommelier, marketing. That kind of thing."

Alex didn't laugh back, but looked serious.

"You're intelligent, too, Tate. Nor are you lacking in confidence. You could go for the fast track, too. Why is it different for me?"

Tate didn't know what to say. He struggled for a convincing shutdown on the topic. "Oh, I'm not the same kind of guy. I mean, maybe I've never had the urge to go further. I like my job as warehouse manager, and I love this part of the country." He loved Bristol, had always lived here, and had no desire to work in London, for example. The West Country was buzzing with activity if you wanted it, but also close to the most wonderful countryside. And the people were friendly and neighborly.

Alex didn't look convinced. "There isn't more you want to do with your life?"

*Let it go!* "I have a lot to juggle, you know that. This job fits with my life, which I appreciate. When would I have time or resources to do further training?"

"That's not an actual answer," Alex said gently.

*No way.* Tate wasn't going to confess his secret plans, his hopes of rising through the ranks, not if they never came to anything, despite his late-night studying and his regular, surreptitious analysis of other jobs available at Bonfils.

"It's enough for me." He nodded firmly. *End of.*

Alex sipped his coffee, quiet for a moment. "But there are things you'd change if you were in charge?"

"Hell, yeah. Better conditions for the staff," Tate said promptly. He so rarely talked about himself, it was a heady feeling to let loose. "Our facilities are always the last to be renovated. More flexible shifts, better pay. We're loyal, but that shouldn't be assumed, and people should never be seen as a cheap resource. Most of us have families to support. More input to the management agenda—"

"Hear, hear," Alex murmured.

"And the chance to suggest improvements. We're the ones who work with the system—we're the ones who often know what could make it run more smoothly. We're all invested in the Bonfils reputation, as much as Mr. Charles and his team."

Alex's gaze was locked on his coffee cup for once. "I guess there are a lot of opinions in the warehouse."

"That's unusually diplomatic of you," Tate said with a grin. When had that extra slice of cake appeared in front of him? He hadn't seen Alex gesture to the counter, but now they both had a fresh, generous slice of chocolate fudge cake. Apparently, talking made them both hungry. "Yeah. Many of us aren't backward in coming forward when we see—"

"Things going wrong?"

Tate was a little startled. "Sorry? I mean, yes, but... that wasn't what I was talking about."

"Ignore me," Alex said quickly. "I just heard some gossip, that's all. That there have been problems at the warehouse. I thought it would be best to get the real story from you."

Tate wondered why Alex was so interested. Alex was cheeky, definitely, but he'd never seemed particularly malicious or a gossipmonger. Yet this wasn't the first time he'd asked Tate about recent events. Apparently, according to Percy, Alex had been talking to some of the other staff too. "Yes, I admit there have been some issues. But you have to expect ups and downs at such a busy enterprise."

"Do you know why?"

"Why these things happen? Too much activity, too tight deadlines, too few resources. Probably all the usual reasons. Plus we're all human, and make mistakes."

"Even Tate Somerton?" Alex asked slyly, his smile taking the sting out of the tease.

"Yeah. Even me." Tate sighed. "And I don't know everything that's going on. Bonfils is a successful company, much envied for its quality wines. And it's no secret we're planning to launch a new one at the UK Heritage Wines Awards. The pressure's on us all to do well with it. Mr. Charles has been working for several years to develop something very exclusive."

"Very British." It sounded more of a statement than a question. Maybe Alex had done more research on his new job than Percy had accused him of.

"Yes." Tate was proud of the homegrown products they already had, but Angel's Breath would be a market leader if it launched well.

"Very expensive?"

Tate laughed. "Inevitably. Out of the range of our pockets, anyway." Alex seemed to be concentrating again on his coffee, so Tate was also quiet for a moment, using a mouthful of cake as a valid excuse. When he'd finished, he leaned back in his seat, happily filled with sponge and sugar. Lucky that Gran was cooking for the kids tonight. Tate reckoned he'd eaten enough now not to worry about an evening meal.

He snuck a glance at Alex, who was playing idly with the froth left in his coffee cup. He really was gorgeous: what they called sculpted features, and a body that wasn't pumped up or anything, but skin that seemed to glow with the health that only came with good care and attention. Tate knew he often looked dog-tired, plus he didn't have time to go to the gym anymore or play football with his mates after work. Maybe when the H's were older, he could get involved with the school sports matches. There was always a shortage of adult assistants with any after-school activity. He treated himself to another self-indulgent ogle of Alex. It wasn't just his looks, though Tate really liked the full lips, the breadth of Alex's shoulders, the way his skinny jeans clung around his thighs. His eyes were almost always alert, always searching; he'd never asked for his glasses back since the day he left them at Tate's. No, it wasn't just his looks, but the way he carried himself. So confident, so certain of himself.... Then Alex looked up and caught his eye.

"Tate," he said softly, his eyes gray pools of fascination. "*Oh.* That look on your face."

"What about it?"

Alex's eyes narrowed. "Don't jump down my throat like that, you'll spill the cappuccino. Hasn't anyone ever told you how good you look? Can't a man compliment you?"

*Not often. Not at all.* It made Tate itch with embarrassment. "You just surprised me, that's all. I thought you were going to say I had frosting on my lip, or something." Bad choice of phrase— Alex's gaze dropped immediately to Tate's lips. Tate's jeans tightened noticeably across his crotch. "Anyway, this started with my question, not yours. Why you applied for the intern job in the first place."

"Applied...? Oh. I see." Alex had that sly smile again; he had a whole portfolio of them. Tate found himself enjoying trying to guess which would come next. "Let's call it fate. It's a good company, I think I'm demonstrating that I can do the work, and I needed a job."

"You?" Tate couldn't help the exclamation.

Alex flushed. "Yes, difficult though that seems for you to believe. I lost my last... position and decided to seek a useful role elsewhere."

"Jeez, Alex. You would have done better to look at Head Office in London—"

"No!"

Tate was startled at Alex's cry. "Shit. I'm sorry. Though I'm not exactly sure why."

Alex grabbed his hand across the tabletop. "No, I'm the one who's sorry. You touched a nerve, but there's no way you could have known that. And no," he continued as Tate opened his mouth to protest, "I don't want to talk about that tonight."

"Okay." Tate had shied away from showing vulnerability, only moments ago. He could show Alex the same latitude. "Enough warehouse talk, okay? I have plenty of it during the day."

Alex chuckled, and the tension eased. "So let's talk about the product. Do you drink a lot of wine? What's your favorite vintage?"

Tate wasn't going to get into that, either. He knew his place. "Red."

Alex blinked hard. "Sorry?"

"I don't drink much," Tate hedged. "House red is usually good enough."

Alex actually blanched. "There's so much to enjoy! Surely you must be tempted, working at Bonfils? How can you bear transporting the stuff to clients all over the world and not tasting it yourself?"

Tate felt a prickle of shame at the nape of his neck, and his reply was instinctively cool. "Bonfils's wine isn't the kind of thing I can afford on a weekly basis."

For the first time, Alex looked discomfited. "Well. I mean, I'd rather have a single glass of a good quality wine than a bottle of the inferior."

"And I agree with you. But, to be honest, I don't drink that much of it anyway." That was also true. Tate's knowledge of good wine was growing by the day, but his natural caution kept him from boasting about it, and his bank balance kept him from indulging it. "I'm impressed with the English vintages, though."

"They're enchanting!" Alex's enthusiasm was so attractive. "You should visit the vineyards, too, see the grapes in situ. When they get close to harvest, they're heavy and plump on the vine. There's nothing like the southern English soil for producing grapes that lush. It's to do with the right pH balance, then a mix of loam and sand, plus added charcoal. It's glorious to see in spring, when the berries start to swell, though that's when they need to be thinned. And they're always hungry plants, so they need to be fed regularly with a liquid feed, like seaweed."

There was such a sparkling look in Alex's eyes that Tate was momentarily silent. He wondered where Alex had learned so much about wine growing. When he got the chance, he was definitely going to dig a little deeper into Alex's rather sparse resume. "Maybe next time—"

"—we go out?" Alex interrupted, returning to his raised eyebrows and eager grin.

"Next time I have a glass of wine," Tate finished firmly. "I'll take longer over the wine list." Not that he ate very often at places with a wine list. His preferred family takeaways tended to ask if he wanted salt and vinegar with his fish and chips, rather than which vintage he'd drink it with. "Maybe I should ask Mr. Henri for a recommendation when he next comes around," he added teasingly.

Alex started and pushed his chair back. "Where?"

Tate held up a hand to soothe him. "No, not here, you idjit! Calm down. He comes around the warehouse once a month or so, is that a problem?"

"Once a month?" Eyes wide, Alex was definitely shocked.

"Yeah. The staff really appreciates the way he shows interest in the day-to-day running of things, even if it's only in passing. I mean, he's grown up in the business, knows all the wines and their clients—" He didn't know why Alex had such a strangled expression, but never mind. "Though it's not just altruism. It's a check on how well we're performing. The whole organisation has to run like one well-oiled machine."

"What about Mr. Charles? I mean, what do they call him, the big boss." Alex had settled back at the table, but when he moved his coffee mug, it rattled. Were his hands shaking?

"Yeah, he's been known to visit too, though less often. He's already been around this month, you just missed him."

"I hadn't thought," Alex said ruefully. He seemed to have relaxed. "I never considered it."

"Considered what?"

"Nothing." And Alex wouldn't be drawn any further on the topic.

Eventually, the café owner insisted he had to lock up if they all wanted his breakfasts to be served on time the next morning. Tate glanced at his watch, amazed it was already ten o'clock. Thank God Gran was on hand at home to look after the kids.

"Do you have any more time tonight?" Alex asked. "There's a late-night showing of an art house sci-fi movie at the Everyman."

"No, I have to get back," Tate said, and realised his reluctance was genuine. "After all, this is what Gran calls a school night—you and I both have work tomorrow. Plus Gran's had a busy day and I don't want to overtire her. She's just joined a new ladies' barbershop quartet and they had a rehearsal this afternoon. It means she'll be knackered tonight and will probably fall asleep on the sofa. Last time Louise and I went out for a drink, we came home to find Hattie had put a Post-it Note on the TV screen to say they'd taken themselves to bed, and they hoped Gran would keep the snoring down!"

It was good to see Alex laugh again, and even better to know that he, Tate, had caused it.

"Maybe see some music next week?" Alex said gently. He drew Tate under the small awning outside the café. The shutters rolled down behind them with a final clatter. The air was sharp with chill but not uncomfortable. There weren't many people about this time of night on the industrial estate. "There's an excellent jazz band at a place called the Old Duke that the music press has been raving about."

"I know the pub, and I like gigs. That'd be great," Tate said, and meant it. Something about being with Alex eased his usual caution, lifted his mood, offered opportunities he'd passed over before. "Hopefully Louise will babysit for me. But if you like live music, what about seeing a rock band later this week? I go to the Fleece now and then, and I confess I don't know a bloody thing about jazz."

Alex chuckled. "Excellent. We'll teach each other new things. That's just as I like it" He hugged Tate closer as if trying to keep him warm, because Alex always seemed to have internal heat. Now, as his face pressed against Tate's, their noses rubbing together as they tilted and slotted together, his lips descending onto Tate's, Tate felt warm in a way that had nothing to do with degrees centigrade.

He          really          liked          the          feeling.

# CHAPTER 10

"So how are things going with you?" Louise asked as they drove into work two mornings later. "This is the second morning in a row you've called for a lift—though you know I never mind offering, in fact I like the company—but I reckon it means you're, *you know*."

Only Louise could articulate ironic speech marks with just her voice. "No, I don't know," Tate said, slumping back in the car seat. And yawning.

"A-ha! Proof indeed, members of the jury." Louise snorted. "I mean *dating*. And you are, aren't you? In the sense of being out late unusually often, drinking beer, finding a reluctance to leave said boyfriend, therefore missing sleep, subsequently oversleeping on a work day and needing the speedy vehicle of your dearest friend and trusty confidante Lou—"

"Lou, please. It's too early for jokes." Tate yawned again. "It's not really dating."

"Damned well is!" Louise said gleefully. "Every day after work? Looks it, sounds it, and definitely *quacks* like it, my BFF."

"Jesus, are you stalking me?"

"Don't need to." Louise looked horribly smug. "I have my spies. And I've also offered to babysit the brood—that's including Gran—while you go

109

out with him again on Friday, to that Tyme and Tyde gig at the Fleece."

"Him?"

"Don't be coy, Tate. I know you're seeing Alex. Why d'you have to be so secretive?"

"Because it's... personal. Anyway, it's not anything special. You'd think it was your love life we were discussing, you're so damned excited."

Louise wriggled in her seat and nearly swung the car onto the pavement. "Oh, it's far more exciting than mine. I haven't met a girl I've liked for longer than two hours since last year, though there is Penny, and she's warming to me, I reckon...."

For one brief, wonderful, relief-filled moment, Tate thought he'd dodged the bullet of talking about his dates.

"And while we're on that subject, Tate—"

He hadn't, obviously. "We're not."

Lou ignored his protest. "Tell all! Have you done the deed? He's such a cutie, and he's so obviously hot for you. Inquiring minds want to know all the gory details."

"Twisted, perverted minds, more like. And no, I'm not telling you anything about that." He thought he'd shut her up pretty successfully until he saw her mouth hanging open and her eyes wide. "What's that look for?"

"You've always told me in the past, Tatty." It was serious when she used his family nickname. "All the updates on anyone you've been dating. I mean, maybe not *all* the gory details, but definitely how things are progressing in general in the, you know, bedroom department. Or couch, or car, or shower, or anywhere else." Lou's expression was mischievous, but was that the glisten of almost-tears in her eyes? "This must be serious, my dear BFF."

"Oh, for God's sake."

But, *was* it serious? Tate felt uncomfortably shaken. Lou had only been teasing, but Tate hadn't. For some reason, he wanted to hug the details of him and Alex to himself; to keep the chatting discreet, to savor the touches and kisses. Everything seemed very different from the usual hookups he'd had before—all the *other* hookups where "no strings" had been the implicit name of the game.

Not that there was much sexy detail to report to Lou. They hadn't progressed much beyond kissing and cuddling. Tate wasn't the sort of guy to rush at the best of times, but frustration was starting to bite. He reckoned it was the same for Alex too. Their make-out sessions were increasingly heated. It was only casual making out, of course... *oh, please, who are you kidding?* It was proper make-out, with proper sexual chemistry. Alex was obviously highly experienced—the places he found to lick and probe inside Tate's mouth were a testament to how well he knew how to excite his partner—but Tate had therefore assumed he'd get tired and move on to a new boyfriend soon enough. He'd been wary of going too far with Alex and making a fool of himself.

It hadn't happened yet. And he was getting eager to make a wonderful, sexually satisfying fool of himself, indeed.

One of the problems was that Tate had nowhere to go. He was limited in the time he had the house to himself. When Gran's joints were free of pain, she'd take the kids out for the day, being a firm believer in the restorative powers of open, green spaces, and Lou often took them to the cinema for the evening if there was something suitable on show. The kids had occasional sleepovers, but what were the chances of coordinating three of those so he could have a night of passion with a boyfriend? With previous guys, he usually went to their place. But Alex hadn't suggested going back to his hotel room, and Tate was *not* going to mention it. He didn't want to look uncontrollably horny with the need to see more of Alex—as in skin, not hours of the day—and wanting to jump him at the earliest opportunity.

Which, unfortunately, he was.

Alex was deeply concerned—with himself. He'd seen Tate Somerton for over a week, every day at work and most evenings on a date, and he was eager for more. Or rather, s*till* eager for more.

He couldn't remember the last guy he'd dated where he was quite so keen to keep things rolling. He loved men's company, some of his exes had been really hot—and dammit, he liked sex as much as, and usually more than, the next man— but he really could take or leave the relationship side of things. Tina had been right when she accused him of avoiding monogamy. But now? Now, unexpectedly, he'd discovered a man who fired up all of Alex's hot buttons, even when they'd barely started on the physical side of things, and Alex just got more and more fascinated. It was as if he'd taken on a whole new persona, not just a new name, when he'd launched himself as Alex Goodson. Maybe it was because he couldn't move on to something new that kept him in Tate's zone—or maybe he didn't want to.

God, it was a trial. He hadn't expected this kind of soul-searching when he went undercover. As far as the TV programs went, the boss was usually in and out within the week, with a camera crew to stop him straying into inappropriate territory. Pity the program had never mentioned the critical logistical issues, like the mystery of income tax, timekeeping, and rabid coffee vending machines. What with trying to keep his identity secret, and training as fast as he could in the actual job so he didn't get thrown out, Alex also hadn't found it as easy as he'd thought to discover details about the potential sabotage.

And he definitely hadn't intended to fall for one of the staff.

Tate was good-looking—the unruly hair, the sharp, dark, eyes, the wiry strength in his body— but it was so much more than that. Tate didn't know who Alex was, so he couldn't be suspected of playing up to the rich heir. He obviously fancied Alex, but wasn't giving in submissively, like Alex's previous lovers almost always had. Tate had a lot going on in his life, and Alex was gradually finding out how he, Alex, was only one, single part of that—and not necessarily the most important one.

Alex wasn't insulted by that; he wasn't in a petulant sulk. He was just trying to get used to it, and decide what he could do to change it. He was a naïve, unpracticed stranger in the strange land of relationships, he guessed. *How ironic.* It would give Tina a good belly laugh, if only he could tell her.

In the meantime, he had to grit his teeth, get on with his prescribed job, and fulfill his secret mission. Then he would return to the Bonfils boardroom, beaming with success and proof of his worth. As soon as possible. Really. And if that meant leaving Bristol—and Tate—behind?

He wasn't going to think about that just yet.

The rock gig that Tate suggested for Thursday night after work turned out to be dire. Both of them thought so, not just the gig-virginal Alex, who might have dated rock stars but had rarely put himself out to go to their events. In fact, he'd really enjoyed the evening with Tate, despite drinking warm beer and being jostled by sweaty, overexcited people who stumbled across the venue floor in groups like confused lemmings. It had been good to see Tate's eyes shining, to try to make out his shouted words over the noise, to soak up the undeniable enthusiasm of the band's musicians.

But they both agreed that Tyme and Tyde were a crap group. The singer was out of tune, the drummer wasn't strong enough to control the beat, and it was really only the tight trousers that made the young female fans squeal every time the lead guitarist struck a chord. Alex and Tate weaved to the back of the room during one of the lulls in music and left the building.

"Bloody dreadful." Tate sighed. "If that lead guy ran his hand through his hair one more time, I'd have leapt up on stage and cut it off."

"The hair, or—?"

"Both, the gurt vain spanner he was."

"Love that Bristol talk," Alex said with a smile. "That means idiot, right?"

Tate laughed and took Alex's arm quite naturally. "What did you think of the support group? The couple with the guitar and keyboard."

"They were very good," Alex said truthfully. He was keeping his arm as still as he could, so Tate wouldn't be tempted to let go. "I thought the lyrics were very original."

"And that from a man who prefers instrumental playing with a sax." Tate grinned. The good mood from the gig still shone in his eyes. "The man is local, you know. One of Lou's distant cousins, actually."

"So you mix with the famous," Alex joked. When he slid his arm around Tate's waist, Tate leaned into him. "I'm honored to know you."

"Stupid arse," Tate said, almost fondly. He was a little tipsy from the beer, though neither of them had felt brave enough to battle to the bar inside the small venue more than twice. "I'm starving."

Alex checked his watch. "What's still open?" It wasn't terribly late, as they'd left the gig early, but many places would already be filled until closing time.

"All the fast food venues," Tate said helpfully, then laughed at Alex's instinctive grimace.

Alex had accepted Tate's education in fast food menus, but the going was tough. Alex had quite enjoyed fried chicken, and had now developed a guilty hankering for a decent kebab, but his allegiance still lay with "proper" restaurant food. Yet he knew Tate couldn't afford to eat out very often.

"There's a French place." He pointed to it, tucked down a narrow turning off the main road. "Let me treat you."

"We share the bill," Tate said firmly, though Alex was happy enough to have fooled him into agreeing to go there in the first place.

It was a small restaurant, with only six tables, decorated in the usual bright white tablecloths and wine bottles ranged on a high shelf around the room. Four of the other tables were occupied, so they were shown to one of the two remaining at the back of the room. A basket of fresh, warm-smelling bread arrived promptly, along with a bowl of plump olives and a dip of fragrant oil and vinegar. The aromas coming from the kitchen were marvellous, full of garlic and tomato. Alex had a really good feeling about this place, despite its size. When he opened the menu, he found a modest but imaginative menu of traditional dishes.

He glanced over to see Tate had just picked up the wine menu. Alex quickly swapped with him before Tate even had a chance to open it. "House red?" he asked with a smile.

"Are you mocking me?" Tate smiled too, not taking offense. The light from the candle inside a glass on their table flickered in his pupils.

"No. But I'd like to order for us, if you don't mind." Alex was excited to see that the wine list was as imaginative as the menu. He was torn between a bottle of Bordeaux and the featured special for this week, a Cabernet Sauvignon. Of course, it depended what Tate ordered for food.

"Alex...." Tate looked wary.

He was too late to complain, because Alex had already lifted a hand to order. The waiter darted across and nodded enthusiastically at Alex's choice of the Cabernet. Tate sat in silence while the bottle was fetched uncorked and left to breathe on their table.

Alex decided to address the elephant in the room before Tate had a chance to. "I know you worry about the money, Tate. Just let me have my head this time. I... came into a small win today."

"You gamble?" Tate frowned.

Damn, Alex had chosen a wrong cover story. "No. I mean, it was like... like a Premium Bond win. I want to spend it on our evening. Let me get the wine. Here, try a taste. It's full-bodied, you may even find a blackcurrant note. The grapes originated in France, though they're grown all over the world nowadays." He poured into their glasses quickly, before Tate could refuse. Would he? Alex still found it tricky to gauge the effect of Tate's pride.

Tate sighed with resignation, then took an aimless sip. Then another. He looked up at Alex, his pupils dilating slightly. "A good choice. Yes, the blackcurrant is there, but also notes of black olive and cherry. Rich, but not heavy."

There was a sudden, pregnant silence.

"I see," Alex said slowly. "You've been fooling me all along, haven't you? You know plenty about wine."

Tate had the grace to look ashamed. "I'm sorry... I couldn't resist. Usually, I don't give away so much about myself."

Alex was startled by the sudden twist of anguish inside him, but he spoke quickly over it. "You don't have to apologise to me, Tate, for anything, and certainly not for protecting yourself." If anyone knew about living with the pressures and restrictions of family and social expectations, it was Alex himself. "But I'm not sure what from. I'm not going to laugh at you or argue with you for that matter. It's a treat to find someone who can talk about a subject I love." He took his own sip, letting the wine settle gently on his tongue before swallowing. It would be perfect with their meal. It was a lesser quality than many of the Bonfils wines, he admitted, but delicious regardless. What a find! "Tell me more about how it tastes."

"I just did, didn't I? You obviously know it, you chose it—"

"No, not like that. I want to hear what you think of the effect, not just the taste."

"Is this a joke?"

Alex rolled his eyes. The man was infuriating! "Tate, can't you take a rest from defense for once? I'm not out to fool or humiliate you. I mean it genuinely."

Tate still looked bemused. "Why do you want to know? It's obvious you know just as much, if not more, than I do."

"Well, yes. I suppose you could say... wine is my hobby."

"A damned sight more than that, I reckon. But okay, I'll play along." Tate was slightly flushed. God, but he was even more gorgeous when he smiled. Alex watched carefully as Tate took another slow sip.

"It's smooth. The alcohol is there, I get the buzz. But it seeps in slowly, seductively. No pulp, no fiber, no sugar. Just the flavor, the essence. Blackcurrant, like we said, but also a hint of sweet pepper. It fills my mouth, it's rich in my throat. I smell it as well as taste it. Weird, but delicious. It's like summer—the heat, the flowerbeds, the cut grass." He laughed self-consciously. "I can't express it properly."

Alex realised he'd stopped breathing while Tate spoke. Tate's tone had been softer than usual, more thoughtful. Their rustic fish soup had arrived but neither of them had reacted. Tate's eyes were slightly dreamy as he concentrated; Alex had such a strong desire to put out a hand and caress Tate's cheek. To kiss the words as they drifted out of his mouth.

"You just have," he said softly, awed. "Perfectly. You have an excellent palate. You should apply for the sommelier track at Bonfils."

Tate flushed even deeper. "Shut up."

Alex rolled his eyes and laughed along with Tate, but he hadn't been lying. Tate obviously did have a talent for both tasting and assessing wine. God, he wanted to share many more wines with Tate Somerton. He'd love to introduce him to a fine St. Emilion, even a Chateauneuf-du-Pape. And they could share many bottle of Angel's Breath, until the bubbles ran through their blood, the light, sparkling taste of British summer suffusing them and their kisses. He would woo Tate with sweetness and sensuality, with richness, and delightful, enchanting, irresistible sensations.

But would he get that chance? Something inside him twisted again; the doubt made him nauseous. Was this what caring for someone felt like?

Tate was staring back. He'd broken some bread for the soup but was still holding it between his fingers, as if suddenly distracted. "Am I... what you said earlier. About me not taking a rest. Is that how you see me?"

"Defensive? Overcautious? Downright off-putting to a date?"

"To hell with you, too." But Tate's mouth twitched at the corners. The wine must have mellowed him.

Alex determined to speak the truth, as usual. "You're a hard man to get to know."

Tate's face fell. "Well, if that's more than you can cope with, you can just—"

"Stop!" Alex grabbed Tate's hand so hard, Tate dropped the bread into his soup with a *plop*. "But I want to. So I'm sticking with it. Your principles do you credit."

Tate's smile was like a candle in itself, suddenly lit, casting brightness over the whole table. "No one has understood before. There's such a lot of unfairness out there. Injustice. People taking advantage. I want things to be right, not just for me, for everyone."

Alex nodded. Maybe it wasn't something he'd ever spent much time thinking about, but in Tate's voice, with Tate's bright eyes and earnest expression... it was perfectly understandable. "So that's why you do so much work?"

"Huh?"

"I know how many committees you're on. Community associations. School trips when you can get time off."

"How the hell?" Tate frowned and sighed. "Gran told you."

Alex smirked. He'd only met Gran that one evening, plus a brief chat when he and Tate arrived home late one night, but he really enjoyed talking to her. And that was in spite of—or as well as—her championing of her grandson.

"I just help out. I want things to be... fair."

Tate must think his life had been desperately unfair, to feel this so deeply. Alex wondered what had happened to his parents. "Don't get defensive. Again," he half joked. "That's a good thing."

They started on their main courses. Alex had pheasant, and Tate the steak poivre. The food was hot and fresh and very tasty. For a while, they just enjoyed the meal and wine, occasionally praising it to each other, or just smiling over the table.

After the main course, Tate sat back and took a deep breath. He seemed to be bracing himself to say something. "There's been more trouble at the warehouse. Some pallets of Sauternes have been moved."

Alex was startled that Tate would now discuss it with him, but this was what he needed to know. "Is that bad?"

"I suppose you wouldn't know. We have the stock in specific areas, rotated according to orders and shipments, so there's never any mistake made with a client's order. These were designated for a select presentation at the Savoy, yet when we came to load up, it was another wine, not as superior. It's just luck I happened to be there at the time and noticed the wrong packaging. We finally found the right one stacked haphazardly with a group of unrelated wholesale wine."

"Was anything else moved?"

Tate looked shocked. "Hell. You mean, there may be more mistakes on the shelves? I'll have to take a closer look. Jesus, Alex. It could be disastrous to our shipping schedule."

"Do you have CCTV?" They could look at that, see who'd been creeping around the warehouse on their nefarious business.

"It covers the main entrance and dispatch exits only, not the central storage area. It's there to catch intruders or thieves."

Alex nodded slowly. "Not to deter mischief from within."

Tate stared back at him, stark realisation in his eyes. "I know that pallet had been moved because I personally booked it originally into the right place."

"So you understand what I'm saying. It wasn't a mistake. It's an inside job," Alex said. "Someone with knowledge of the stock, and access to the forklifts."

The waiter called at their table right then to clear the plates, so they fell silent. As soon as he left, Alex rushed to speak again.

"Tomorrow," he said. "We'll look seriously into this. I'm assuming you will let me help you?"

Tate's expression was a little dazed. "Looks like I'm assuming it too."

"But for tonight." Alex said, lifting his wineglass and gesturing for Tate to do the same. "We'll just decide on what dessert!"

# CHAPTER 11

The kiss as they prepared to part that night was deeper than usual. Alex drew Tate back against the wall of the bus shelter, his hand around the back of Tate's neck, his lips searching, needy. He could taste a delicious mix of salt and lemon on Tate's tongue from the meal.

"Who the hell are you, Alex Goodson?" Tate whispered into Alex's neck as they huddled together in the chill.

*What did he mean?* Alex tensed.

"Why are you here?" Tate continued. "Why are you so worried about the warehouse? How do you have the knowledge and the money to make wine your hobby? It's all a bit of a mystery to me."

Was it time to tell Tate who he really was? What he was doing here? Surely it was still better that no one knew. He would never suspect Tate of the sabotage, but it was still important to keep under the radar. "There's nothing sinister, Tate, and I will tell you everything you want to know. One day. Just not right now. Can you trust me just for a while longer?"

Tate hesitated for only a moment, which Alex was going to take as a small victory. "I guess so. After all, you take me to all the best places. The restaurant was great—"

"So was the gig, in some ways," Alex protested.

"And this is a perfect end to our evening, making out at the bus stop." Tate chuckled, gesturing at the shelter with its cracked roof, LED letters missing from the revolving schedule, a stooped, half-asleep old man leaning on the frame at the far corner, and a pile of fast food wrappers under the seat.

Alex only had eyes for Tate, but now he took in their surroundings. Yes, it was pretty seedy. "Tate, I wish there was somewhere else."

"No, it's okay." Tate ran his tongue daringly, teasingly along Alex's jaw. "That was tacky of me. I don't want to rush you into anything."

"*You* don't—? But I'm the one watching my step."

"You are?" Tate stared at him, brow furrowed.

Alex gave a shaky laugh. "It's early days. I've only just captured your attention for a few dates. You've made it clear you think I'm a smooth-talking playboy. So I assumed you wouldn't want to get further embroiled with me." Tate's mouth was twisted. Was he angry? Or was it the start of a grin?

"Embroiled?" Tate said innocently. "Is that even a word?"

"Yes, it is. Its roots are in seventeenth century France, I believe," Alex said pompously.

"Right. Well. I still think you're a smooth-talking playboy, but luckily you have a sense of humour to balance that."

Alex was trying to keep up with this new

development. "I do?"

"You know damned well you do. And... I like that. And so I think you should take me back to your place. If you want to, of course."

"*Fuck.* I mean. Sorry."

"Don't apologise." Tate was smirking now. "Here's hoping you'll walk the talk, though. Or have I misjudged this whole thing?"

"Jesus. No!" Alex's head was spinning, and he didn't think it was to do with the wine. "It's just... my hotel room is very basic."

"Well, shit. That's that, then." Tate pulled back, his expression glum. "No way I'm having sex with someone who hasn't furnished through IKEA, at the very least."

Oh God. *Oh God!* Alex opened his mouth to defend himself, then caught the twinkle in Tate's eyes. "You bastard! Now who's got the sense of humour?"

Tate laughed with him and nuzzled into Alex again.

Oh, joy! Had Alex ever had such weird and wonderful foreplay? "So," he said tentatively. *Me, tentative?* "You... um... will be?"

"I will be what?"

Alex gave an exaggerated sigh. "Having sex with me?" Out of the corner of his eye he thought he saw the old man jerk awake and shuffle a few steps away. Ah well, it'd give the guy's imagination something to conjure with on his journey home.

Tate pointed out a bus just turning the corner toward them. "I'm not gonna talk about it all night, Alex. Let's just get to your place and do it before the rain shrinks my baws to the size of marbles."

"I love your vocabulary."

"You could see your way to expanding yours, y' know."

"I'll work on it. But maybe not tonight." And with that, Alex—now ridiculously pleased he'd learned the bus routes on the ludicrously tortuous system called public transport—hauled Tate onto the bus back to the hotel.

Alex had never worried about his rooms before. In fact, he'd rarely worried where he had sex, as long as it was relatively comfortable and borderline private. But when he and Tate stumbled through the hotel room door, breathless from running up the stairs, clumsy with the key card, and laughing with desire and some nervousness—well, the room struck him yet again with its bleak aspect.

"I've just gotta go for a leak," Tate said. "And I'll send a quick text to Gran so she knows I'm not coming home."

When Tate went to the bathroom, Alex quickly turned off the main light and clicked on the bedside lamp, in the hope of creating some better ambience. What else could he do?

"Jesus, Alex," came Tate's voice from the bathroom. "Are all these posh bottles yours? I've never seen this shampoo in any supermarket. And is this hairbrush *silver*?"

"No! I mean... they're samples. Giveaways.

Came with the room. Someone else must have left them behind." Alex was scrambling for excuses. Suddenly he realised his naivety in thinking he was *slumming it* here. Luxury was relative—Tate would judge from the point of view of someone who rarely stayed away in hotels, let alone spent nights in the Park Lane Hilton, or enjoyed the hospitality of foreign diplomats and minor royalty. Alex had misjudged things—again—and badly. How arrogant of him! He quickly opened the drawer of the bedside cabinet and swept every piece of junk off the top into it, *junk* that included his Rolex, his exclusive gold credit card, the personal bits and bobs from his washbag—

"Alex?" Tate stuck his head around the doorframe.

In the middle of kicking his handmade shoes under the bed, Alex was panicking in case Tate noticed the monogram on his socks. "I'm afraid I don't have any drinks here, and there's no provision for music apart from on the TV—" He never finished; in fact, he never even had time to settle his tousled hair. Tate's mouth was on his before he could grab another breath. *Oh*, but it was fine! Tate's tongue plunged into his mouth with possessive need, far more aggressively than ever before, with the taste of wine, the chill night air, and the heat of passion. Tate physically pushed him too, his hands gripping Alex's biceps. Alex took steps backward under Tate's force, kissing back as best he could, until his back hit the wall beside the bathroom door. The artistically ghastly sea scene hanging beside his head rattled on its hook but stayed put.

Tate paused, his lips still resting on Alex's, his breath harsh and hot on Alex's cheeks. "Fuck. I've wanted to do that since we left the gig."

"We should have chosen fast food," Alex joked. Was that his voice? He sounded years younger, almost as nervous as his first time.

"No. The meal was... it was lovely." Tate chuckled shyly, his hands still tight on Alex's arms. "And Jesus, you taste so good as well."

Alex felt the laugh ripple through his own skin, Tate's chest hard against his. He could feel Tate's heart beat, his pulse race. Alex's cock hardened, frighteningly quickly. "Better than the wine?"

"Yes. Much better. And there's way more than a glassful or two of you."

"Are you saying I'm full-bodied?"

Tate was laughing freely now, his shoulders shaking, his hair tangled over his forehead, those eyes—those eyes!—expressing pure, simple, perfect joy, full of amusement and anticipation. "No. Human. Sexy human. Very sexy human—"

"Enough. Yes. Enough of my stupid questions." Alex gasped and pulled Tate back in for another kiss. Oh, the joy of laughter in among lust! Alex had never appreciated it so much before.

Tate wouldn't let go of him, not that Alex was trying to escape, and they stumbled back across the room toward the bed. Alex stubbed his toe on the cabinet, and as they staggered against it, the lamp fell over. The room went dark as the light now illuminated their feet rather than the walls. Alex's reading book fell onto the floor with a thud.

"Shit." Tate tried to twist around to see what they'd swept off the unit, but Alex held him too tightly. "Was that important?"

*Wine Legends of Bordeaux?* Alex wasn't admitting to that expensive tome, especially not a first edition signed by the author. "A minor novel. Secondhand. Maybe third. Anyway, it's nothing. N-not like you." He could barely make sentences. Enough talking! Tate was warm and hard in his arms, and nothing was going to distract him. He felt clumsy, stupidly overeager, as unlike his usual self as he'd ever been. His heart was beating so fast and his throat was so tight, words lodged in his throat like pebbles. Tate's skin was salty on his lips, Tate's throat taut and shiny with sweat as he swallowed hard.

"I'm still sweaty from the gig." Tate gasped. "We could shower—?"

"No! Later. Not now." Alex could hear the panic in his voice. Tate was smiling at him, laughing at him, but there was a fond, almost tender look in his eyes. "Tate, I can't wait—"

"Shhh," Tate said, whispering the sound into his ear. "Let me."

It was a time of ongoing discovery, Alex thought, as Tate tumbled him onto the bed. He wasn't used to being on the receiving end, he was so often the initiator. Tate straddled Alex's hips, his deceptively strong arms locking his upper body in place as he leaned down to Alex's mouth and kissed him, then kissed him again and again, until Alex's head began to spin from an overload of sensation. The bed creaked underneath them, and the bathroom fan was whirring noisily since Tate had turned the light on and off again. There was a chemically floral smell lingering in the room from the products used by the hotel's daily cleaning staff, and Alex knew that on the hour, the boiler behind the hotel kitchen would groan and knock as it reset itself.

But nothing bothered him tonight. *Nothing.*

Yeah, Alex's hotel room was plain, but Tate barely noticed. Why the hell would he, when he had such a delicious specimen as Alex Goodson to attend to? Besides, they were warm and comfy here, the door didn't stick like it did at home, and there wasn't any risk of being heard by Gran over the late-night TV or being interrupted with Amy's occasional nightmares.

Maybe it had been the wine: maybe it had been the pleasure of a more intimate evening with Alex. Whatever the reason, Tate realised he'd suddenly begun to relax. The kids were all okay tonight—though, my God, he'd owe Gran and Lou a million favors after being out so much these last days!—and Alex had proved himself great company, and understanding of Tate's situation. There hadn't been many men who met those requirements over the last year. And more important? His desire for Alex hadn't eased off in the daily workplace. It had grown, until he couldn't bear to wait to touch him properly.

Alex was spread beneath him, arms now

outstretched, legs pliant and graceful, his dark hair fanned out on the pillow. Tate nudged Alex's shirt up his torso, revealing the soft skin and defined muscles, running his finger through Alex's paler treasure trail until Alex sucked in his stomach and moaned aloud.

"You are fabulous," Tate breathed. "You're so pale."

"Last year's tan has worn off, I don't hold colour for very long—"

"It's fabulous," Tate repeated. "Gorgeous. I'm not complaining. Against your dark hair, too."

Alex tensed. "You too," he whispered quickly. "Gorgeous. Can't chat anymore. Strip. Strip us both."

Tate laughed and obeyed happily. Alex lifted his upper body so his shirt could be removed, then raised his hips for Tate to pull off his jeans. Tate took Alex's underwear with the jeans and might have accidentally-on-purpose run the heels of his hands over Alex's swollen cock as he did. Alex gave a small, sudden gasp as Tate moved down his body to remove his socks.

Then Tate slipped off the bed and quickly pulled off his own clothes. It was only as he bent to unlace his shoes that he glanced back up at Alex. A sliver of light through the hotel room curtains caught Alex's eyes, making them gleam like fireflies in the room. His gaze was concentrated on Tate's bare back and down to his arse. His mouth was slightly open. Tate grinned to himself. That look was so damned *hot*.

He straightened and turned to face the bed

again. His vision was getting used to the minimal light by now. His cock was already plumped, and a few slow, teasing strokes brought it back to full hardness. Alex's gaze followed every single movement. "We can just mess around," Tate said. "Don't have to do anything you don't like."

"May I provide a list of those likes?" Alex said, his voice cracked with lust and amusement. "It'll be a very long one."

"I see. Good. Best to know where we are from the start. I have no problems with anything, unless you get really kinky—"

"Not tonight," Alex growled, so low and fierce that goose bumps ran down Tate's spine. "Tonight, I just want you the hell back here, and that gorgeous cock in my mouth."

Tate didn't exactly run to the bed, but he moved damned fast. They lay side by side, naked, exploring each other. Alex's hands were sure but respectful; Tate had been right to assume he knew how to treat a man in bed. Alex knew when to stroke and when to grip, especially when Tate let him know he liked a firm hand. When Alex folded his fingers around Tate's cock, Tate groaned. "You said something about your mouth and my dick?"

Alex grinned, his perfect white teeth bright in the dim light. He kneeled up on the mattress and bent over Tate's groin. The first touch of his lips on the tip of Tate's cock had Tate gasping. Slowly, Alex slid down the shaft, his tongue slicking the skin, teasing the vein, his mouth moving down, down, right down to the pubes.

Tate yelped. "Fuck!" He hadn't ever been deep-throated; hadn't been sure he'd even like it. *Jesus*, but it seemed he did, and how.

Alex murmured, a chuckle barely possible with his throat occupied on Tate's dick. Tate thrust gently, carefully, feeling Alex's lips tighten around him, his throat convulse around the head. He thrust some more, Alex allowing it, encouraging it with rumbles of pleasure from deep inside his chest. Tate had never felt so sensitive, so worshipped, so savored. Alex's right hand rested on Tate's hip, keeping both of them anchored. His other hand was in his lap, stroking his own cock.

"I'm... fuck... soon." Tate gasped, hoarse with the excitement. His back arched, his fists clenched. *God.* The image of coming down Alex's possessive throat was so strong, he had no idea how he'd kept an orgasm at bay this far. To his almost-despair, Alex slowly withdrew and sat back. Tate's skin felt cold and damp with loss, his breath rasped in the still air, his cock ached with unrelieved need.

Alex felt around his jaw, as if loosening it up again, his eyes preternaturally bright with passion. "Ride me," he said, his voice rough.

Tate's whole body flushed. "Can I?"

Alex's eyes darkened so much, Tate could barely see the whites any longer. "I don't know. Can you?" he breathed.

Tate laughed softly. "I mean, may I? You don't catch me out with your proper English rules, man."

Alex laughed too, but his was ragged. He rolled Tate gently aside, then lay back down and brought his legs together, allowing Tate to straddle him. "I want to see you," Alex said. "I want to see you take all of me."

"Lube?" Tate could barely cough out the word. He reached between his legs, under his tightening balls. The skin was hot and smooth as he slid his finger back, reaching for his hole. He knew Alex couldn't see that far back, but he'd know what Tate was doing.

"Bedside drawer," Alex said. "Unless it's on the bloody floor by now."

Tate leaned sideways, acting all casual and easy, his obliques stretching, his skin tightening—Alex's eyes widened and his breath shortened at the sight—and fumbled in the drawer. He impatiently pushed aside a watch, plastic card, a pad and pen, something like the usual hotel bible, until he found a couple of condom packets and a small bottle of lube. He popped open the top and poured some on his fingers.

"We should share that," Alex said, slyly, and held his hand out for a squirt.

Tate gently eased fingers into himself, watching as Alex slid on the condom and slicked up his cock. Tate was finding it hard to breathe, and his heartbeat felt so close to the surface of his chest it may as well have been on the outside. He shifted a little nearer Alex's waist, getting the best angle, letting his bum settle into the dip of Alex's lap. He caught Alex's heated gaze.

"Yes please," Alex said with a strained but greedy smile. His hands tightened on Tate's hips.

Carefully, Tate pulled himself up, took his weight on his knees, and guided Alex's cock to his arse. One initial press against the pucker, then he was in. Tate sighed happily, full and tight and deliciously conscious of every nerve in his body flashing alive.

"*Oh*," Alex whispered. "Oh, yes."

They moved together, slowly at first, just rocking, getting used to each other's body. No words, just sighs and smiles. Tate felt his impending orgasm bite again, more insistent now for its completion. His body shuddered and he folded a hand around his cock, began stroking. Alex moved his grip to Tate's arms, helping to support him. Their movements became fiercer, harder, both of them grunting with effort. Tate's thigh muscles worked hard, holding him as he rose and fell, feeling Alex slide slowly out, then thrust back in. Alex's head pressed hard into the pillow and his eyes half closed. His mouth opened wide, any words articulated only as moans.

Tate gazed at him, stupidly happy, affectionate, thrilled... then Alex's eyes opened very wide and his whole body tensed as he came. His hips thumped up against Tate, forcing his cock deeper, tighter. His grip loosened on Tate as he started to keen. Tate held as still as he could, loving the ecstasy on Alex's face, the pleasure of bringing *him* pleasure. Then his own climax crawled its demanding fingers from his groin all the way to the back of his neck and back down again, making his skin tingle and his blood race. He came with a cry, spilling onto his hand and Alex's belly, writhing on Alex's lap. He had just enough time to slam his sticky hand back on Alex's chest to keep himself upright, to stop his shuddering body from tumbling off balance. The ecstasy ran through him, shivering, crawling, bringing a few tears to his eyes as he began to calm again.

The room was quiet apart from their heavy breathing. Panting, Tate stared down at Alex. "Bloody hell," he said, realising immediately what a very inadequate description that was. His hand slipped an inch on the sweat all over Alex's chest.

"Yes," Alex replied, still breathless. "But bloody good, right?"

And they both laughed until Tate lost his grip completely and collapsed down beside Alex, their limbs tangling and their bodies already starting to cool.

In the middle of the night, Tate stumbled to the bathroom in the dark, his legs still seeking the return of their strength. His hands were shaky as he reached for the taps, and he knocked over a tube of toothpaste and a capped bottle of some kind of cologne. Behind that was a packet of something that looked surprisingly like hair dye. He only knew the brand because Mum had once touched up her roots in defiance of her first few gray hairs. Odd thing to find in Alex's bathroom, but men were just as entitled to a refresher on their highlights. He'd always admired Alex's hair. Now his fingers itched to touch it, to run through it, to tug it back *hard* to bare Alex's throat to him—

His cock jerked on his thigh. *Ever hopeful!* Tate turned sleepily and reached for the bathroom doorway to guide himself back to bed.

"Tate? Are you okay?"

Alex sat up in bed, eyes heavily lidded, his body half-shadowed by the crumpled sheets. He yawned, swiftly lifting a hand to cover his mouth.

*Adorable.* Alex's quaint manners were becoming endearing. When Alex patted the mattress beside him, Tate slid back into bed. "I'm fine." He smiled at Alex, though the room was dark and maybe Alex didn't see it. "I just... something made me think of Mum."

There was a small silence. Alex slid an arm around Tate's shoulders and guided him back onto the pillows. They smelled of Alex's skin.

"Tell me?"

It wasn't a demand. Alex's voice was like the gentlest caress and Tate discovered that at last he wanted to talk about his parents.

"Both Mum and Dad died in a train crash four years ago. Gran had moved in with us, I'd just been promoted at work, and so they took the opportunity to have a weekend away for their anniversary. They'd been married twenty-six years."

"Oh, Tate...."

"Gran's arthritis wasn't as bad then, plus Louise was—is—always on hand to help out. We wanted Mum and Dad to enjoy their time out. So as things were running smoothly at home, we didn't call them over the weekend." His throat tightened, but that was compensated by the gentle wash of relief, in getting things off his chest to another listener. "The crash was on the news that night, but only Gran knew the details of where they were staying. It was an Intercity route between Wales and London. On their way home. The points on the track failed and the train derailed. Over seventy people were injured, and six... died."

Alex hugged him closer. His breath was shallow, and his cheek felt damp against Tate's. Why on earth would Alex cry at Tate's story? "Don't say any more."

"No," Tate said. "This feels right. The police and social services came to the house on the Sunday night. That was the first we knew. I took over the family duties from then on."

And then he cried, too. Just quietly, and lightly, but he shut his eyes and let the tears come, trickling onto Alex's shoulder. He didn't feel as humiliated as he'd imagined. There was something about Alex that reassured him, that made him trust the man to be compassionate. To respect Tate despite his weakness.

"I miss them," Tate whispered.

"I know how that is," Alex replied, His voice sounded odd. "I miss Mama every day."

"Your mother?" Tate opened his eyes and caught Alex's gaze. His eyes were glistening in the dark.

"She died of cancer when I was thirteen. My brother was sixteen. Papa was devastated."

"You too." Tate was startled by the seriousness of Alex's expression. "I'm sorry, Alex, I... didn't know anything about your family."

"Don't apologise. I knew nothing of yours."

"A fine pair we are." Tate rubbed a hand over his face, until Alex caught him by the wrist.

"And don't deny it, either," Alex said. "Your grief and your love are genuine and true."

"Doesn't help with the grind of daily life."

"Hush." Alex's breath was hot against Tate's neck. "It's all right. Let me."

"Let you… what?"

"Show you what a pair we can really be." Alex's voice softened to a whisper and then he slid under the covers, his fingers trailing down Tate's chest. Tate's nipples hardened, fast, with an ache that reached deep into his gut. Alex's tongue lapped at his navel, and the muscles of his belly tightened as Alex nipped at the flesh there. He rutted against Alex's body, seeking friction. His cock bobbed and nudged Alex on the nose. They both chuckled.

"Come back up here," Tate murmured. He tugged Alex back up the bed so they were chest to chest. Then he slid a hand behind Alex's arse, his fingers reaching between the cheeks. Alex arched against him, gasping. "Hold on," Tate whispered.

Alex's slipped his hand down between them and he fisted around both cocks. Tate groaned, and wriggled his middle finger into Alex. Their sweat gave them lubrication, but even so, they had no desire to go further. They rocked tightly against each other, Alex rubbing them gently but firmly toward climax, Tate fingering him boldly, their mouths mashing onto each other whenever they didn't need to draw in more breath.

Tate's head swam when he came, his throat

tight and his heart hammering. *So* good!
They made a damned good pair, indeed.

# CHAPTER 12

The next morning in the warehouse found Tate in a rather delicate condition. He'd probably drunk too much wine, plus the full, unusually late evening meal hadn't settled well in his stomach. And every time he swung himself off the forklift seat too quickly, his arse stung.

That made him smile, though.

He was on his way to the office when Percy intercepted him.

"Tate, boy?" Percy's expression was unusually difficult to decipher. "Somethin' y' need to look at."

"A problem?"

"It's Prince Harry."

Tate's gut tightened, and not from indigestion. "Has he done something wrong?"

"Nope. Not exactly." One of Percy's bizarre skills was saying no while radiating yes with every muscle and fiber of his being. "You seen his handwritin'?"

"His...? Alex's, you mean? Well, yeah. He printed up some notices for me yesterday." Alex had used a lovely italic script, like something out of an illustrated bible. Tate had admired it, but then had to ask him to rework it in sensible block capitals because biblical script was never going to be suitable for NO ENTRY TO THIS STORAGE AREA WITHOUT AUTHORISATION.

Percy grunted. He carefully placed a sheet of paper in Tate's hand, then turned and walked back across the warehouse.

Tate glanced down. It was a reference for Alex Goodson, something the company always requested. Alex had provided several character references, but only one from previous employment. It had been emailed from Ibiza, of all places, on a hotel's headed paper, and announced that Alex had been "a model of diligence and attention to detail." The stilted language might have caught Tate's eye as incongruous, but now he also noted the lovely italic script for the signature and printed name at the close of the letter. The suspiciously *familiar* script.

*Bloody hell.* Had Alex forged his reference?

Tate wasn't a fool: he knew it happened. He and Percy had coped with it a few times to their knowledge. Whatever the reason, any evidence like this led to the employee's dismissal, and immediate removal from the premises.

And what exactly was he going to do about it?

Over at bay six, Alex was daydreaming about Tate while he labelled shelves.

Tate had left the hotel bed in the small hours after dawn, explaining in a sleepy whisper that he had to get the kids ready for school, Gran couldn't cope with it all. Alex had insisted he'd pay for a taxi. He'd watched, only half-awake himself, as Tate scrabbled for his clothes and went to wash up quickly in the bathroom. The fan started up again: a car's headlights outside the hotel arced across the curtains. Somewhere along the corridor, someone else was leaving early. Alex could hear the trundle of a small suitcase as it passed the door.

Suddenly, fiercely, he'd known he didn't want Tate to leave. He wanted more. He wanted the whole package: to go to sleep with Tate, wake with him, have gasping morning sex, eat breakfast, maybe travel into work together. And not just for this one day.

Dear God. What was happening to him?

Tate had poked his head out of the bathroom. His hair was spiked up on one side, flat on the other. Catching Alex's raised eyebrows, he tried to balance it out with his fingertips through the tangles, but finally gave up. "I'll sort myself out at home. No one expects me to look perfect first thing in the morning, anyway. And I'm not due on shift until noon, so I'll have time to iron a shirt and stuff." He was gabbling, Alex knew. He was nervous, maybe unsure about what they'd done, now facing the ominous morning after—

Then Tate had smiled, and Alex knew everything was all right. Tate wasn't the kind of guy who regretted things—he took his time deciding to do them in the first place, so he was sure of himself. It was so unlike Alex's usual mad dash to experience anything and everything while the slightest passing opportunity was there, then face any regrets after the event. No, Tate wasn't like Alex at all. He knew and trusted himself.

What was that like, on a daily basis? Alex had wondered, with more than a touch of jealousy.

"Goodson? Hey!"

Alex snapped back to real life in the warehouse. Percy was calling.

"No daydreamin', boy! Give us a hand here."

He was trying to move one of the crates off a low pallet. Tate's conversation last night sprang back into Alex's mind. Had there been more disruption in the storage? "Where's it got to go?" he asked, jogging over to help.

"It's the good stuff." Percy huffed as he set the crate down on the floor. "Shouldn't be put here at all. It belongs in bay four. Don't know what the hell's goin' on with the storage this week. Stuart? Bring that forklift over."

Alex took hold of one side of the crate and between him, Percy, and Stuart, they shifted it onto the bed of the forklift.

"Why is this in the wrong place? What do you think happened?" Alex said, trying for a casual tone.

"No idea. And be careful with this lot." Percy scowled at Alex. "Worth about eighty quid a bottle."

"Wow," Alex said, as he assumed he was meant to. The last bottle he'd opened at his London apartment had retailed at two hundred and fifty.

"Yeah. Right. Not the sorta thing to drink with y' cockles on a Friday night."

145

"Of course not," Alex said quickly, wincing as he heard his clipped vowels against Percy's easier, countryside chat. Funny how he'd only recently begun to notice the contrast. "I mean, I haven't tried cockles before, at least only in a Mediterranean seafood medley—"

"Seafood medley?" Percy interrupted with a snort. He made it sound like Alex dined as far away from Bristol as Saturn. "That's in a plastic rather than a polystyrene tray, right?"

"Lay off," Alex grumbled.

"You gotta learn to take a joke, boy."

"I will, when I hear one," Alex snapped, too late to bite it back.

But Percy's raised eyebrow implied that, this time, he appreciated Alex standing up for himself. For an odd moment, his gaze rested on Alex, as if unsure what to make of him. Then they were both interrupted.

"Don't think Harry is into cockles, Percy. More like caviar and canapés for him." It was Stuart, chipping in with his pathetic jokes again. Plus he scandalously mispronounced canapés. Alex sighed to himself, wondering how much longer he could last without punching Stuart in the mouth. *Dammit.* He couldn't get fired yet.

At last he had Tate on his side, and they were going to sort this out together. Alex had taken every opportunity he could to investigate on his own, but while the warehouse guys were eager to gossip about the recent hiccups in the distribution process, none of them had offered much in the way of what or who was at fault. Nor did any of them look particularly guilty.

The one unassailable fact was that the worst mishaps had happened with the high net worth wines. It made sense, Alex supposed, that if someone were looking to sabotage Bonfils's business, they'd target the profitable lines. The stock held up at customs had been one of the more expensive wines; the labels that had been defaced were on a pallet of the best Bordeaux. And the latest confusing movements in the warehouse were also affecting the premier stock.

The most treasured product should have been the safest. There was a separate secure storage area for it in the warehouse, with a specifically designated unloading bay. Alex had been keeping an eye on the store whenever he could, but it didn't look as if anyone had tampered with it. The room was controlled with a key card lock and, as far as he could see, access was restricted to only a few people: Percy, Tate, and Stuart were among them. Jamie and a couple of other employees sometimes worked with Stuart on unloading and loading, and Percy accompanied an extra cleaner into the store on one occasion. But no one, including the cleaner, was ever left alone at any time. That was where they stored the early bottles of Angel's Breath, which were still going through final quality control. Imagine something going amiss with them!

Alex continued to be both astonished and depressed at how little he'd known about the working of Bonfils business before he started here. How the hell could anyone evade the authorised staff to get inside the warehouse and do any damage? Unless the mischief-maker *was* authorised staff. That was his conclusion, and Tate seemed to agree with him now.

A hand landed on his shoulder, a warm breath at his ear. Alex nearly bit through his tongue with shock.

"Sorry if you didn't hear me coming. Are you okay?" Tate sounded just as startled.

"Oh. Yes. I mean, of course. You just caught me—"

"Woolgatherin' again," Percy grunted, appearing behind Tate. "Keep y' mind on the bloody job, boy. Tate, are y' here to help or get in the way?"

Tate rolled his eyes. "No, I have a new transport company representative to meet in five minutes' time. I'll be away from the warehouse for an hour or so. Just wanted to let Alex know I need a word with him later."

Alex didn't take much notice of the brief look Tate and Percy shared. He'd been plunged back into his daydreams. Tate had a tantalising scent that was less cologne than caramel. It made Alex's mouth water at the same time as his cock stirred. Alex knew it wasn't likely—as they'd both showered since last night—but he imagined he could still smell Tate on his skin, see the glimmer of Tate's sweat, feel the strong palms, the limber legs thrown astride Alex's hips, Tate's sticky seed on Alex's belly....

"See you later?" Tate murmured to Alex. For a moment, he looked as if he had something more to say, but it passed. Taking his hand off Alex's shoulder, he turned to leave.

"Bloody well hope so," Alex replied quickly. When Tate's mouth twisted into a wry smile, Alex's heart stuttered and damned near sang.

There was one more box left in bay six to move back to its correct place. Alex had offered to do it on his own, but it was heavier than he'd expected. He and Henri had occasionally helped Papa and his managers move stock in the London stores when they were young teenagers, and he'd managed perfectly well. Had Papa been humouring his sons with lightweight stock, or had modern packaging increased in weight? Despite his firm grip, the box shifted against his chest, and he staggered a step backward.

"Easy, lad," Percy growled from somewhere behind him.

Alex twisted to avoid Percy—or the place where he thought Percy was standing—and the box shifted in the opposite direction. He stumbled again, his body now off-balance, his hip jolting hard against the edge of the shelving. "Ouch!"

To his shock, the shelving shuddered on its foundation, and dust blew up from the stacked pallets to tickle his nose. He sneezed loudly, confused. Surely he wasn't heavy enough to have moved the unit just by knocking into it?

"Stuart, get over here, you bloody idjit boy!" The shout came from behind the shelving, in

Percy's voice. Alex was concentrating mainly on keeping his balance while a whole stack of packaged wine loomed above him. The shelf shivered, as if the boxes were moving of their own volition, shifting the pallets toward the edge.

"What the fuck?" came Stuart's growl. "You said move the stock in bay seven—"

"I need you in six, you fool! *Now!*" Percy again.

The pallets creaked, a suddenly ominous sound. The highest ones were empty of boxes, lighter than the rest of the stack, and therefore quicker to slip their moorings. The top one reached the edge of the pile, and slowly but inexorably started to tip over. All Alex had time to notice was a dark mass out of the corner of his eye, then a wooden corner caught him a glancing blow to the head. With a gasp of pain, he buckled at the knees.

"Boy!"

Alex couldn't speak, even if that "boy" had been intended for him. A heavy weight caught him in the lower back, spinning him around by 90 degrees, hurling him down toward the floor. He instinctively threw out his hands to catch his fall, and the box in his arms crashed down ahead of him.

*Shit!*

The pungent smell of wine rose from the floor, filling his nostrils. It was the good stuff, he remembered suddenly with a sinking feeling. *I've smashed thousands of pounds' worth of product!* His hands had thudded against the cold floor, the palms felt bruised. The vibration of running feet juddered through him, shouts echoing in his hearing.

He tried to rise, to call for someone. Pain sliced through his head.

*What the hell is happening—*

Another creak. A wheeze of loose packaging.

Even as he straightened up, still on his knees, the second pallet fell. There was a whistle of air, the earthy smell of untreated wood, and a blow squarely on his shoulders that knocked all air from his lungs. He was squashed flat onto his face. *Hard.*

He didn't register anything else after that except darkness.

# CHAPTER 13

Something was really wrong with the world, Alex thought.

Not in a metaphysical sense, but a very real, physical sense. For a start, things were very dark. And not just dark, but thick and sticky and oddly painful. He wondered if he was trying to open his eyes in a dimly lit room. Or maybe he already had opened them, and the room was totally dark. The circuitous thought processes hurt his head. *Try it out, idiot.* He opened his eyes and stared up into a more familiar brightness, wondering idly why all he could see were ceiling tiles and fluorescent light fittings. Why his back was up against something cold and hard. And why his head hurt like the blazes.

"Harry? Can't he hear us?"

"Christ, that was a hell of a hit."

Gabbling voices and the sweaty smell of bodies crowding around him.

"Don't move him 'til we know how badly he's hurt, y' know?"

"He's awake!"

"What?"

"His Highness—he opened his eyes!"

Gruff. Excited. Worried voices. The bodies clustered nearer.

Several faces swam into view. A handful of young men, in matching polo shirts; one older one, his fierce face creased with concern. They were all vaguely familiar, but damned if he could remember any names.

"Can you sit up?" the older man asked him.

*Sit up?* Oh, right. Alex realised he was lying on the floor, which accounted for the bizarre view. He had no idea why he was resting here, rather than in his own bed. Wherever that may be. "Of course I can," he said, a little shocked at the sound of his own voice. He wasn't sure what he'd expected to hear, but... everything seemed startling at the moment. The old man dropped to an awkward crouch beside him to help and, slowly, he pulled himself to a sitting position.

The older man breathed a sigh of relief. "Okay, the rest of y' can get back to work. Give the boy room to breathe, okay?" As the other workers shuffled a few feet backward, reluctant to leave just yet, the old man peered more closely. His expression was seriously anxious. "Sit here for a moment, boy. Gather y'r wits. That was a hell of a thump y' took. Luckily y' weren't out for more than a second or two."

*A thump? Out?* Something floated in Alex's memory, becoming clearer. He was in the warehouse... a pallet had shifted, then another, he hadn't been able to move out of its way fast enough—

"The wine!" he gasped. "Dammit, I dropped it!"

"No problem." The older man shook his head impatiently. "That's only wine, it can be replaced.

But y're one of my boys."

"Percy?" Two remaining employees hovered behind the older man—Percy, of course that was his name, why had that been so hard to remember?—and the one speaking was skinny and apparently nervous of approaching any nearer. "If Harry's okay, d'you want me to mop up the spillage?"

Percy looked briefly irritated, then nodded. "Put it in the breakages ledger, too, Jamie. It was the good stuff, and we have to keep separate record of it. Y'll have to access the secure store for the book, but don't take anyone else in with y'. I don't want every damned Tom, Dick, 'n Harry with access."

"I'll take Stuart wiv me," Jamie said quietly. He looked so shocked, he might be ready to throw up. "Just us. Then I'll fetch the first aid kit. You can rely on me, Percy."

"Good boy." Percy spoke absentmindedly, obviously still concentrated on his injured employee, because he didn't bother to watch Jamie scurrying away.

"Wait! You mustn't—" Alex barely recognised his own cry.

Percy's eyes narrowed on him. "What's up, boy?"

Behind Percy, Jamie paused, staring back with wide eyes.

"I don't expect y' to clean up, son," Percy said quietly. "Y' need to get checked out."

"No, don't clear up at all!" This was so irritating. Alex's head ached and he couldn't think clearly enough. But he had something important to tell Percy, to tell someone else he couldn't remember at the moment.... It was about the pallets. Yes, that was it! "You need to check the pallets. They weren't fastened properly."

Percy's hand was a solid presence on his arm. "It's all right, boy. Y' had a nasty shock."

"Don't patronise me!" he snapped back. It made Percy frown, and Jamie sucked in a startled breath.

Another man jogged over to stand by Jamie. "What the hell's he on about?" He glared down suspiciously. "What does Harry know about anything, the clumsy sod?"

"Back off, Stuart," Percy said gruffly.

*Harry?*

"My name isn't Harry." Alex was still snapping but, in justification, the pain was really fierce. "It's Alex. I thank you to remember that. The joke's run its course, don't you think?"

Percy raised his eyebrows and seemed to let out a breath of relief. Stuart started to laugh, then when Jamie jabbed him in the ribs, bit it off.

"Get back to your damned truck, Stuart," Percy growled. "Or I'll dock y'r pay for rubberneckin'."

Jamie scuttled off after the grumbling Stuart, and the other workers also drifted away. Percy was left to help Alex to his feet.

"Good to hear y're as feisty as usual," he said. "Looks like there'll be no lastin' damage. But come sit down by the cooler, I'll get y' some water. Do y' remember what happened?"

"Why wouldn't I?" Though everything hurt,

trying to get things straight. Harry—Alex. Wine—water. Or maybe it was the physical pain racketing around in his head. Good God, as a child, he'd dismissed Mama's migraines as headaches, time and again. He'd never do that now. *Mama?* The vision of a tall, slim, woman with a ready smile and the same dark blonde hair as his, flashed before him. His memories were all out of kilter: he hadn't thought about Mama with such anguish for some time. When he moved to follow Percy over to the chairs, a sudden stab of agony down his left side made him wince.

"Go slow, boy." Percy's voice was astonishingly gentle.

"It's important. You have to check it out," Alex muttered.

"Believe me, I will," Percy said sharply, then he gentled his voice again. "But y'll rest first." Percy helped him into a chair and started to draw a cup of water from the cooler.

"Has he broke anyfing?" Jamie was back again, pale face, wide eyes, clutching a green box with First Aid stamped on the front of it, and staring at Alex like he'd never seen anything like him on the planet before.

"Don't think so, but I'm no *Holby City* consultant," Percy growled. He pushed past Jamie to give Alex his water. A few staff from Packaging had sidled over to see what was going on, as well, but Percy pointedly ignored them. "Where's Tate? Is he back from that meetin' yet? Go get him, Jamie boy."

Tate? *Tate!* Alex felt a wash of relief and need.

That was whom he was waiting for—whom he had to tell! He tried to jump up from the chair but his legs felt suddenly like limp spaghetti. His head throbbed even harder—was that possible, for God's sake?—but he knew he had to reach Tate. He *needed* to.

Luckily, the decision was made for him. Tate strode toward them across the warehouse floor, his expression a mixture of alarm, anger, and confusion. "What the hell's happened? I was told there's been an accident." As Percy moved aside, he caught sight of Alex for the first time and his face paled. "Alex? My God, are you—"

Alex didn't let Tate finish. "Thank heavens you're here. Someone will listen to me now."

"Listen to you? What about?" Tate's gaze ranged over Alex, his eyes wide and worried, his hands half lifting from his sides as if he wanted to run them all over Alex to check he was still in one piece. "Where are you hurt? Are you thinking straight?"

*Explain. Find the words!* "The pallets were loose. Bay six. You see, I helped Stuart strap them together when we were moving some of the wine back to its proper place." Despite Percy staring at him with total amazement, he struggled on, now desperate to be heeded. "It was loosened."

"It got loose—?"

"It. Was. Loosened." Alex was firm.

Percy glanced at Tate with a frown. "What's he mean? And how come he knows about the boxes put in the wrong place?" He peered at Alex, brow furrowed. "You sure, boy? The bays all look the same to some. Y've only been here a coupla weeks."

"Tate." Alex leaned in, his face inches from Tate's, startling himself with the urgency in his voice. "I know."

"You'll check it out," Tate said slowly to Percy, who nodded.

"Thank God." Alex grasped Tate's arm. "Thank *you*."

"That's okay. Trust me, we've got it." Tate glanced around at the spectators. "But let's not talk anymore about it, with an audience, you know?" He placed his hand over Alex's, then patted it tentatively.

"I'm not an invalid." Alex sighed, but he didn't pull away because it felt really good. He wondered if he could slide a hand around Tate's waist and pull him in closer? Maybe not in the workplace. *Shame.*

"He still looks confused," Percy offered helpfully. Or not, Alex thought, depending on whose viewpoint it was from. "Somethin's not connectin' in his head."

"I'm fine," Alex said earnestly. And *so* much better now Tate was here. "You want proof? Let me tell you. I've been working in the warehouse for two weeks, your refreshments are appalling, and Tate is my boyfriend."

A bubble of shocked silence enveloped everyone within hearing. Then one of the Packaging girls giggled.

Tate briefly closed his eyes. A flush coloured his cheeks.

Percy snorted.

"Tate?" Alex was suddenly worried. "Isn't that right?"

"Sort of." Tate looked very uncomfortable. "I mean. You know?"

Alex didn't know, actually, but he didn't mistake the warmth of Tate's hand on his, or the smell of his skin. That was vividly familiar.

"You lot?" Percy gestured fiercely at the packaging crowd plus Jamie. "Y' can all get back t' work now, everythin's in hand. And I'll thank y' to be discreet about this. I'll have no bloody gossip in my warehouse about who does what with who in their private time. Y' hear me?"

A chastened "Yes, Mr. Grove," "Sorry, Percy, of course, Percy" came from the workers as they turned and scurried away. A couple of the girls still hung around, giggling.

"Oh, dear God, I'm so sorry." Alex turned to Tate, suddenly realising what he'd done. "Doesn't anyone know you're gay?"

Percy gave another snort.

Tate took a long, deep breath. "Yes, they do. I mean, I don't talk about my private life with everyone, but I've never hidden being gay. Maybe there was a problem with a few people when I first started here—"

"We soon sorted them out, boy," Percy growled protectively.

Tate smiled. "Yes, Percy did, though you both know I can fight my own battles. And now everyone just knows me as Tate, which is how it should be. But...."

"I should never have announced it like that. I effectively outed you!"

Percy muttered something into his hand that might have been "Bloody drama queen," but Alex couldn't be sure.

"It's no problem," Tate said gently. "The important thing is for you to be okay."

"He needs to go t' hospital," Percy broke in, bluntly.

"No!" Alex knew he didn't want that. No trips where he'd have to explain who he really was. He had to stay under the radar for the time being. "I feel fine, just a bit weary. My back hurts like hell." He straightened, determined to look as fine as he said he was. "But I'm sure it's just heavy bruising."

Percy was still doubtful as he spoke to Tate. "If he takes ill after the fall, it'll be on us, boy."

"I know." Tate looked torn between worry for Alex and respect for his wishes. "Well, I'll take him home for the time being and see how he feels later. Good thing it's Friday, and he's not on shift for the weekend. He can take time to rest. He doesn't seem to have any problems with motor skills or his memory—"

"I remember everything!" Alex said brightly. "I'm at Bonfils Bibendum. You're Percy and Tate, and the other guys were Stuart and Jamie. Jamie appears to have a bit of a puppy fixation on Stuart and eats two packets of licorice toffees a day. Stuart wants to be a racing car driver and once took a girl he wanted to impress on the forklift to the local café. And one of those girls from Packaging is called Penny, she's training for the

London Marathon, and I seem to remember Tate saying his friend Louise has a crush on her."

"She does?" came a startled female voice in the background.

"Christ on a crutch, get him and his loose chatter away from here," Percy groaned, "Before he outs every damned person on the shop floor, and tells everyone I borrowed a fiver from petty cash last week."

"It was a tenner," Alex said smartly. "But I believe you left an IOU and repaid within the day." Weren't they impressed at his ability to watch, learn, and clearly recall all the peccadilloes happening in the warehouse? "I repeat, I'm fine. I could get back to work if you like." He mocked a salute, though touching his temple made him wince.

"No way!" Tate snapped this time. "Home immediately for you."

"Um. My hotel?" Alex tried not to sound too pathetic, but the thought of that bare room wasn't appetising.

Tate grimaced. "Yeah, that's a problem. You need to have someone keep an eye on you. You could... well. Rest at my house? If you don't mind. We'll go and check you out of the hotel, then ferry your stuff over to mine." He looked a bit flushed. "Gran can watch out for you. And we'll see how it goes."

"Thanks," Alex said. He wasn't sure what "it" was going to be, but did that matter? He was keen to go home with Tate, for whatever reason.

# CHAPTER 14

Tate drove Alex home in the warehouse van. It was a very slow journey, because Tate was determined to follow every single traffic restriction to the letter, even though he was pretty sure Alex hadn't broken any bones when he fell. Hell, what a way for the day to end! He'd made a quick report to the Health and Safety committee before they left—the new guy in HR, Liam, had initially been horrified to hear what had happened to the new intern, but then settled briskly into assuring Tate he could leave it all in his hands. In fact, he'd insisted Tate didn't worry about it *at all*, Liam would deal with all the paperwork. Tate was secretly relieved, because he knew there was a pile of forms to fill in to cover the company's liability. He could ill afford the time, what with the Awards coming up.

He also had his own concerns. Why on earth *had* the pallets shifted and fallen like that? The shelf units were sturdy, and—Alex was right—the pallets should have been fastened securely, even if they were empty. Alex could have been far more seriously hurt if he'd fallen awkwardly, if the pallet had been packed with full boxes, if he'd been standing a little nearer the pile.... Tate barely held back a shudder at the thought.

As it was, Alex had been really shocked. Was he right in his suspicions—which Tate couldn't have failed to understand—that it had been deliberate? Maybe done the same time the stocks had been mixed up, or before or after. *Who knows?* Well, Tate needed to find out. This had been a far more serious type of sabotage, threatening the staff. Threatening *Alex.* Were the troubles escalating?

Tate snuck a sideways glance at his passenger. Alex was pale but seemed otherwise okay. Tate really thought he should see a doctor, but Alex had refused time and again. Obviously, if he'd only just moved into the area, he wouldn't have a local doctor of his own, but he was very firm about not contacting anyone about the accident. He was hiding something, though when Tate pressed him, he wouldn't give any reasons why.

"Just because I can't," Alex had insisted. "Please take my word for it."

And that was that. Tate didn't want to harass the guy any further. Tate was shocked, too, though he'd keep that hidden for the time being. When Jamie came running with news of the accident; when Tate had seen who was slumped in a chair, white as a sheet of paper, favoring his left side and barely clutching a cup of water...? Tate's whole stomach had roiled with nausea.

He was worried about running the gauntlet of his family's interrogation, bringing Alex to the house, but luckily Gran had taken the younger kids to the Friday afternoon movies after school. Freddie rushed from his basket in the living room to greet them, but Tate was able to calm him quickly, then he guided Alex up the stairs toward his bedroom.

Alex paused in the doorway. For a long moment, they just stood there, Alex resting against Tate, his gaze on his feet. His breath was warm on Tate's throat, and Tate's hands nestled with familiarity in the small of Alex's back. Tate looked around Alex's shoulder into his room, wondering if he'd cleared away his dirty clothes, taken that coffee cup back downstairs, put away the romance suspense thriller he'd been reading....

"Tate? Are you sure?" Alex's voice was very quiet.

"About what?"

"Me. In your bed?"

Tate flushed. What did Alex mean? "Last night you didn't worry about it."

Alex's smile was a little slow but had a flash of his usual mischief. "Last night we were in a hotel. Last night was...."

*Oh God, what?* Tate found he was holding his breath.

"Special," Alex murmured. He leaned closer and brushed his lips against Tate's cheek. "Very special. But you live here with Gran and the children."

"Oh. Shit. Yes, I see what you mean. How it might look to them. I mean, I'm just helping you out—"

"As a friend, yes—"

"And it's just to rest, isn't it—?"

"Of course, nothing more provocative than that—!"

They both stopped talking over each other and laughed gently.

"You're *very* provocative," Alex murmured. "At least, you are to me."

Tate didn't know how to answer that, when his emotions agreed wholeheartedly, but his head told him to be wary. "Okay. Come along to Hugo's room," he said. "Just for an hour or so. You can sleep there. When the kids get back, we'll sort something out."

Alex barely made any comment on the posters, or the scattered Xbox games on the floor of Hugo's bedroom, before he tumbled onto the bed and fell asleep within the minute. Tate sat with him for a while, until he established Alex was breathing regularly. He'd fetched a pair of his sleep shorts in case Alex wanted to borrow them, but there'd been no time to suggest it. Tate satisfied himself with pulling off Alex's boots and socks, then peeling his jeans down. Alex barely stirred, the accident finally catching up with him. Tate left him in his underwear and the Bonfils work shirt, sure he'd be comfortable enough to sleep in them, and just pulled the quilt over him. After pausing for a few more moments, that was.

Damn, but Alex had lovely long, strong legs. Was it only last night they'd been pressed against Tate's inner thighs, Alex's hands gripping him, begging to go deeper, exhorting Tate to move faster, rougher—? He fancied he could still hear Alex's strangled groan, his bitten off laugh of happiness as his climax shuddered through his body. He could smell the sudden spurt of warm seed as he came all over Alex's belly, the slight tang of sweat as Alex wrapped an arm around him as they lay together, panting, on the mattress.

Tate had a wild desire to wipe his brow at the mere memories. This was a rare, quiet time, without the others in the house. Time for Tate to sit on the end of Hugo's narrow single bed and watch Alex sleeping. To wallow in sexy memories—but also to worry. Tate worried about anyone who had an accident like that, especially if it was one of his workers. But if something dreadful had happened to Alex...? It was time to examine why he was both upset and fascinated by how much that distressed him. Alex was able to talk about the attraction openly, Tate's caution was another matter.

They'd only known each other a short time. They'd said no strings, right? But.... *Crap. Face the truth, Somerton!* Tate had enjoyed every minute of Alex's company and found he was looking forward to each day at work, just to see him. *I've got it bad, haven't I?* Alex lightened his day and made him laugh, even if it was at Alex's often ridiculous behavior. Their shared laughter was all the more precious because of it. Alex was attentive to Tate, and he didn't hide the fact he was keen on him, and oh God, but it was good to have attention again! Alex was a breath of fresh air in Tate's life. He made Tate feel that dating and companionship were attainable, even in Tate's full life. And that was, oh, such a dangerous route to take.

*Yeah.* Dangerous, because it wouldn't last. Tate

carried the pain and stigma of those he loved leaving him. When his parents were killed, he'd been the one to comfort Gran, and somehow explain it all to the kids. How could such a tragedy be explained at all? Not with his life experience, at least. All he could do was his best, knowing that was so often lacking. He'd had to grow up pretty quickly after that day. Any plans for further education had been shelved in favor of keeping the family afloat and together. His parents had sensibly arranged some life insurance, but that had to be kept safe for what the kids might need in the future. Everything—and Tate meant *everything*—had to be secondary to his family's welfare.

Tate smoothed the duvet around Alex's chest, remembering the times he'd sat with the kids when they were younger. The time when they all came down with chicken pox had been the worst: three invalids at the same time. Alex snuffled, shifting under the bedclothes, his broad shoulders snuggling into the pillows, those long legs stretching out under the covers.

*No kid, that.* Tate smiled to himself. Despite the inappropriate setting, his cock hardened. And despite it being his younger brother's bedroom, he wanted nothing more than to slip under the covers beside Alex, just for a cuddle. How long, he wondered, before the kids came back—?

Downstairs, the front door slammed behind a hubbub of voices.

"Tate? Tate!"

"We've brought fish and chips for supper!"

"Gran fell asleep in the movie! Twice!"

Tate smiled ruefully to himself. He'd just have to hold that thought.

Friday evening was traditionally a hectic but fun time for the Somerton family. Even if Tate was working over the weekend, they all relaxed with takeaway food and tales of their week at school or work—or, in Gran's case, at her many social clubs—and stayed up later than usual. Tate even avoided dates on Fridays, albeit that hadn't been difficult in his recent dry love life. Tonight, they all clustered together in the living room, the H's reenacting every frame of the movie, Gran hogging the ketchup for her chips, and Freddie hopping up and down in anguish in his basket because he knew he shouldn't beg for food but was *itching* to. Amy sat on the sofa next to Tate, hugging him close in between eating her food, as if they'd been apart for weeks rather than just a normal day. Did she pick up on his somber mood after the day he'd had at the warehouse?

Gran caught Tate's gaze once, over the heads of Hattie and Hugo who were practicing a weird kind of salsa dance on the rug in front of the TV. She tilted her head up to the ceiling—Hugo's room was directly above them—and waggled her eyebrows quizzically.

*Blimey.* Did she guess there was someone there? Tate couldn't hear a single sound from upstairs, and he hadn't told anyone yet that Alex was in the house, he was waiting for the right moment. But Gran had her own mystical ways, he should know by now there was no fooling her. He nodded briefly back to let her know everything was fine. The disadvantage of having the kids around them right now was that he couldn't talk openly about adult things. He'd give it another half hour, until the kids' bedtimes were due, and he had to shift Alex somewhere else.

Then the *right moment* chose itself. The twins were playing cards on the rug, Amy was snuggled up to Gran on the sofa, playing rock, paper, scissors—and winning as always—and Tate was crouched by the TV, scratching behind Freddie's ears and driving the dog to ecstatic delight, when Alex appeared in the doorway to the living room, yawning.

"Alex!" Amy whooped. Every head whipped around to look at him. The H's jaws dropped in unison; Gran froze in position, both her hands in "scissors" position.

"Hello, everyone," Alex said slowly.

He was dressed in his jeans and socks, plus a clean T-shirt Tate had left on the bedside table; it was one of Tate's better ones, now stretched across Alex's broader chest. Tate found it embarrassingly difficult to take his eyes off the effect: the raised shadow of Alex's nipples was particularly distracting. Alex smiled at him as if he knew exactly what Tate was thinking and ran a hand through his hair. It was plastered awkwardly against the left side of his head, and Tate caught sight of a few oddly light strands in among the rich chestnut brown. He stood abruptly. Freddie rolled onto his back and sniffed in disappointment at being abandoned.

"Um. Tate?" Alex said.

"Oh. Yeah." Tate hurriedly spoke to his family. "Alex had a bit of an accident at work today so I brought him back here to sleep it off." At Gran's raised eyebrows, he added, "We used your bed, Hugo. I mean *he*, Alex, used your bed, I hope that's okay with you."

Hugo all but plumped up with pride. "Happy to help," he crowed, and jabbed Hattie in the ribs with a "he needed *my* bed!" gleam in his eyes.

"How are you feeling?" Tate asked Alex.

"Fine—" But Alex didn't have a chance to say more as the Somerton clan rushed into action.

"Sit down at once, Alex." Hattie was in bossy nurse mode, determined to regain ground with her twin. She all but pulled him into the room and onto the sofa beside Gran and Amy.

"What happened, Alex?" Hugo gave him a fierce look up and down. "Did you break something? Was there blood?"

"Are you hungry? There are some chips left," Amy offered, though there were only a few scraps left in her polystyrene tray. She poked around at them, as if looking for the best specimens for Alex.

Only Gran greeted him calmly. "Alex."

"Gran," he replied, just as equably.

Tate wondered when Alex had started calling her Gran. "So. Just to update you all. Alex had a fall in the warehouse today. He's bruised but okay."

"Ouch," Hugo said gleefully.

"Aww," Hattie sympathised.

"Where's the bruise?" Amy asked. "Can you show me?"

"Hush, Amy, Alex isn't a project," Gran said. "He's walking wounded. And it's your house, Tatty. You can invite whoever you like." She peered at Alex like the most thorough Harley Street doctor. "You're white as a sheet, boy. Plenty of sleep and hot baths is my prescription, that'll get your mojo back in a couple of days. We don't have any spare rooms, but I'll make up the couch for you. Easy enough to set up and break down every day."

"Gran, it's just for tonight—" Tate started to protest.

"Until he's better," she said firmly. "He can't go back to a *hotel*, Tatty." She made it sound like the black hole of Calcutta, and Tate was a slave master. "And of course," she continued blithely. "It's good for you, too."

*What is?* Tate thought, alarmed, but didn't dare ask.

"Just one thing worries me...."

Tate sucked in a breath. *Here it comes.*

"We're gonna need another loaf of bread if you eat toast for breakfast. We're down to the crusts again." She grinned and gestured to the children. "Come on now, time for bed for you lot."

There was a chorus of disappointed groans, as if they were missing prime entertainment. Tate glanced quickly at Alex, who was smiling gently— and a little bemusedly—from his seat. Maybe this

171

*was* prime entertainment. Hattie and Hugo were all but shoving each other out of the way to look after Alex's needs, Gran had slipped an arm into his, and Amy had fetched her toy stethoscope to listen to his pulse. But no one had complained or argued with Tate about letting a virtual stranger into the house. *Wow.* His heart felt warm, his emotions shaky. His family was wonderful. Welcoming, tolerant, even though bizarre at times.

Alex met his gaze, smiled more strongly, and Tate's warmth increased fortyfold.

# CHAPTER 15

The weekend morphed into Monday, then Tuesday. Alex kept suggesting he should go back into work, but while his bruises passed through the gloriously vivid purple and yellow phases, Tate and Gran insisted he continue resting. The Somerton sofa was old but ridiculously comfortable to sleep on; Alex found he was sleeping more deeply than usual at night, wrapped in soft blankets and mismatched but vividly bright linens.

However, there wasn't much rest in the Somerton household by day. Alex couldn't ever remember being in such a busy scenario. Tate was up early to see to the kids, worked a long, busy day at the warehouse—and sometimes evening shifts—and then came home to another virtually full-time job as parent. For the first day, Alex found himself retreating into the role of fascinated observer, then he relaxed, finding himself alternately astonished and delighted by the family members.

Gran was a warm, enchanting soul, but when her arthritis was bad, she couldn't do much apart from passive babysitting. But she told a wicked joke and knew everything that was happening in *Love Island* or *Eastenders* on TV, and she cooked a mean shepherd's pie, Alex could attest to that. It was fast becoming his favorite meal. He'd even asked for her recipe.

"You can cook it tonight," she announced gleefully, in trade. And although he'd meant to pass it on to the family housekeeper, he let himself be chivvied into the kitchen and he'd... good God, he'd cooked a family meal! He found he actually enjoyed the physicality of chopping vegetables and mashing potatoes, and Gran encouraged him to use his imagination with the herbs. He instinctively caught himself wondering what wine to serve with it, but discovered he was just as happy with a glass of what the family called fruit squash. And when the kids liked his food? How weird that he was so delighted!

But there was so much more to this family business. Alex remained astonished at how long it took to organise. The schedule started at godawful-o'clock when Amy and the twins had to be roused from sleep, dressed—and in the right clothes, not just any old pair of jeans, and Tate always insisted the socks matched—and fed breakfast. Then Gran had to be helped with her breakfast, Tate would sort out the selection of tablets she took, remind her if she had to collect the kids after school from the same neighbor, or if he could do it on his way home, then check Gran's dog was let out into the garden to relieve itself, then fed and watered. Alex had never had a pet before. From the look on everyone's faces, it was an irritating yet strangely rewarding commitment. Bizarrely conflicting, in his opinion.

Tate would then hustle the kids out to the bus stop across the road, where he'd wait with them until they caught the bus, or into a helpful neighbor's care, if they were also going to the school. One morning, Tate's friend Louise stopped by to take them in her car. Tate didn't let her into the house, which was odd, and according to everyone's chorus of disapproval, not the usual way of things. Alex had seen her grinning broadly and peering at him out of the car window when he went to see Tate off at the door. He made sure to send her a cheerful wave.

During the day, Alex slept, exercised carefully, and was co-opted into helping Gran with the laundry and other household chores, to the extent he might find himself at the kitchen table with her, snipping discount coupons out of the local newspaper. *Coupons!* And after work, it was the same routine but backward. The kids arrived at the house as a small hurricane of noise and activity. Coats and backpacks were discarded anywhere, until Gran reminded them to pick them up and change out of their uniforms in their separate rooms. Funnily enough, she seemed to have to say this every time: did children never learn, or were they deliberately challenging? Hattie and Hugo were learning to cook supper but Tate liked to be there to supervise, and mostly did it all himself until they rousted him out of the kitchen. They all needed lots of attention with their homework—the twins because they got distracted too easily, and Amy because she was shockingly bright and often needed adult input—

yet none of them appeared to welcome it. The TV went on, as per the kids, as soon as Tate's back was turned, then off again—per Tate, accompanied by dire threats of sending the equipment back to the store—several times. The persistence and single-mindedness of children was a revelation.

It was a unique situation for Alex, finding himself a spectator of other people's lives. No one ignored him *per se*, but his was by no means the loudest voice. He began to realise how selfish his life had been before now, run purely to his own schedule. Now, at the Somerton house, he was learning to help out where he could, answer questions if directed at him, and in all other cases, try to keep out of the way. It was, at times, exhausting.

And yet....

He'd also noticed how suddenly the chaos and mayhem could ease. Everyone would dart in and out of the living room all evening, but for one moment they'd all be together. The whole atmosphere in the room would change, as abruptly to Alex as if a switch had been flipped, yet he had no idea where, how, or by whom. The discordant voices would settle into the same pitch, even some of the same words. Someone would laugh, and everyone would join in.

Then Hattie and Hugo would hug Tate, two similar blobs of affection clasped to his chest. Tate would laugh, too, his face cleared of the stress of looking suddenly younger, freer, more Amy would snuggle up to Gran and oth sing along to adverts on the TV or tickle Freddie with their toes as he lay on the carpet at Gran's feet.

They acted as if they were one being, one emotion, one love. Alex would watch it happen, unable to explain or analyse, hoping that no one took offense at the look of bemusement he was sure was on his face. Hoping that they would continue to tolerate him with them there, in their lives. That tolerance and welcome suddenly seemed very critical to him.

Was this the real meaning of *family*? It was odd. He felt inexplicably breathless.

And, he confessed to himself, lonely.

On Wednesday morning, they all congregated at the kitchen table as usual. Gran had a cold and was wrapped up in her duvet on the living room sofa. Tate didn't think she needed to see the doctor—or an expert on tropical viruses, as Amy suggested blithely—but he was reluctant to leave her without help all day.

Hattie said, "She's not alone. There's—"

"—Alex in the house," Hugo finished.

"And I will not take offense," Alex said rather primly, "that you don't think I can look after her."

Tate privately worried that Alex had never shown any aptitude for or experience of looking after anyone but himself—and maybe Tate—but he wasn't going to argue. Just because a man had never changed a nappy, cleared up dog poo, or mashed up a tin of beans when his grandmother misplaced her teeth, didn't mean he shouldn't be given a chance.

"We need more bread, milk, and eggs. I don't know where it all goes, but we're constantly out of them."

"Gran eats eggy fried bread for lunch every day when you're at work." Alex said bluntly. "It usually takes her a few attempts to get the consistency right."

Tate blinked hard. He'd never known that. No wonder his frying pan was always so messy.

Alex continued, "And I can jog down to that bijou little store you have on the corner of your street and get more supplies. I've done that a few times already, although I'm appalled at how much extra they charge per item just for the convenience. I'll wait until she drowses off in front of *Ramsay's Kitchen Nightmares USA*."

"Um. It's also her day to pick up the kids from school, because I have a union meeting early evening, and Louise is busy at her mum's after work—"

"I can do that too. It's only a short walk away. However, I believe you need to let the school know it'll be me accompanying them? One can't be too careful with young people's safety nowadays."

"No," Tate said, biting back a grin. "No, you can't be."

"Can we have the art lessons next weekend?" Hattie leaned toward Alex across the kitchen table, her best adoring-puppy smile in place.

"Art lessons?" Tate asked, puzzled.

"Well, I did a semester at the Slade in Paris, until they asked me to leave for disrupting the class," Alex said blithely. "I promised the twins help in developing some basic sketching techniques, though maybe just in pencils to start with. I have recently learned that certain paints are virtually impossible to wash out of man-made fibers."

"Back up a bit. You were disrupting...?"

"Personally, I believe an artist should be allowed to draw whatever he wishes, with full creative license."

*What the hell did he draw?* No, Tate wasn't going to ask; he didn't dare.

"I also want to go through online grocery shopping with Gran when she's better," Alex continued. "I'm getting a good idea of what's where in the store, Gran's guided me toward the discount shelves, and they also offer a surprisingly wide selection of family meal recipe cards. Also, I'm researching the best deal for a new washing machine, yours is apparently—according to Amy's vernacular—on its last legs. I will be negotiating the delivery charges downward, I can tell you."

"I. Right. Okay." Tate was stunned into almost silence by this new side to Alex.

"And then I'll come back to work with you," Alex finished firmly. "Will we do the bus journey again? I've been studying the local timetables. Though Louise called the house yesterday to offer her informal chauffeur services anytime, so I could call her back to see when her shifts coincide with ours. And neither of us knows why you're embarrassed for her to see me here."

*Good God.* Tate didn't know whether to laugh or cry. The accident seemed to have opened the floodgates on Alex's careless frankness. "You've had a serious work injury. The company medical officer will need to know you're over that completely, but I don't see why you shouldn't return next Monday. And the embarrassment thing? I've been trying to protect both our reputations."

Alex made a snort that sounded suspiciously like one of Percy's.

The kids scrambled from the table and left the room, laughing, jostling, seeking the items they needed in their backpack for school. Tate was left momentarily alone with Alex. "Be honest," he said. "How *do* you feel?"

"You mean, about how to continue our investigation—?"

"No," Tate said firmly. "I mean, about your health."

Alex sighed. "Still bruised, but I must go back to work."

"Look, the investigation doesn't need to concern you—"

"Tate, I can move, speak, and follow instructions. And of course it concerns me!"

Tate had a lightbulb moment: he could have kicked himself for being so insensitive. "Oh my God, what an idjit I am. You need the money." Alex was at the end of the sickness period he could self-certify, and if he still wouldn't see a doctor, his wages would stop.

Alex blinked hard. "Oh. Dammit. If that's what you... yes. That." His expression softened. "Thank you for caring."

"Alex is much better now," Amy said, suddenly appearing at Tate's elbow, making both men start. "I love him here. He reads stories like he lives in them. But he should do some work too."

Tate smiled and tried not to roll his eyes where she could see it. Amy was a bold but sensible soul. "I guess that's okay then," he said drily. "I mean, God forbid I, the warehouse manager, should try to run the place without consulting my seven-year-old sister."

"Glad to hear it," she said, missing the irony completely, but happily satisfied her point had been made. She rejoined the twins in the hallway, meeting Louise at the front door. Over the heads of the welcoming children, Louise winked at Tate and waved hello to Alex.

Tate nodded cheerfully at Lou. "You're now fully introduced, I see."

Alex smiled at him. It was a slow, gentle smile, nothing like his cheeky, arrogant smile that had been so evident when he joined the warehouse. Tate liked this smile much more. He'd seen a lot of it this week, at breakfast, in front of the TV, over the kitchen hob, laughing together while they made up the sofa for Alex's sleep each night. And snatching kisses and touches that teased the libido to a way too painful level. Tate's memory lingered again and again on that night in Alex's hotel room, on the too-soft mattress, savoring cool, clean sheets he hadn't had to iron himself....

Oh God, Tate thought, as he so often did nowadays. It wasn't just thwarted lust that made him dread Alex going back to work. He was used to having Alex around. He'd still have Alex's company at work, but obviously Alex would move out of Tate's house. Get his own flat or check back into another hotel. A deep, ugly ache started in Tate's chest at the thought of that. And the next step? Alex would move on completely. Tate knew that now. He'd lose another person he'd come to care for.

Don't mince words, his internal voice told him. You mean, to love.

*I am so screwed.*

But all he said to Alex, the man whose eyes lit up when he saw him, whose determination Tate could only admire, whose body Tate remembered as clearly as if they'd slept together last night and not a frustrating week ago, was, "That's fine. I'll get Percy to put you back on next week's shift schedule.

# CHAPTER 16

That night, Alex woke suddenly with a shocked gasp. The living room was dark, and a quick glance at the TV showed it was around 2:00 a.m. His right arm had flopped off the sofa, banging his elbow on the low coffee table, and he was sliding off the edge of the seat. Swallowing hard, he grabbed the back of the sofa with his left hand and pulled himself to sitting. The cushion he'd been using as a pillow had already tumbled off, and the duvet was tangled up around him. His heart was racing and the back of his neck was sweaty. He slept in his T-shirt because of the kids, but now he peeled it off, grateful for the cooler air on his skin.

*Hell of a dream!* People dreamed about their whole life when they died—or so the books said, though Alex personally couldn't imagine ever recalling *everything* he'd done and dammit, he hadn't really been *that* assaulted—but the scenes in his mind had been extraordinarily vivid. There had been people around him all the time.... Papa, so stern, so businesslike, with Henri similarly dressed in a sober suit beside him. Then a blur of older, happier scenes, with Mama in the group. He'd heard music, felt the sway of plane travel, smelled the soft leather of limo seats. There'd been snatches of school days, where Alex sat at the back of a room full of desks, young men lounging in their seats, chatting and teasing. A sports field... a party with champagne. Snow... a beach. Fast cars. It was presumably a potted history of him—and his family.

But the last, most explicit visions before he woke had been of Tate Somerton. Laughing, frowning, scooping Amy up in his arms, running beside Freddie on the pavement outside the house on the way to the local shops, eating popcorn in front of a late TV movie, washing up after dinner, earnestly explaining the rights of his staff, the need for better school equipment for his siblings and others, the plight of local senior residents, how to treasure and maintain local parks....

"Alex?" Tate stood in the doorway, half in silhouette, dressed only in sleep shorts and yawning, rubbing a hand through his messy hair. "Are you okay?"

"Yes. Just a dream, I think."

"Sounded like a nightmare." Tate came into the room, quietly closing the door behind him. Light from a small lamp in the hallway shone underneath it, giving a shadowy illumination to the living room furniture. Tate sat down gently on the sofa at Alex's feet. "You were calling out."

"My God, was I?" He'd never been aware of sleep-talking before. "What did I say?"

Tate's face was guarded, at least as much as Alex could make out in the dim light. "Nothing sensible. I... to your mother maybe. You said... *Mama.* Several times."

*Dammit.* Alex ran his hand back through his

hair.

"You miss her?" Tate was watching him closely. "Well, of course you do. You haven't told me much about her—and there's no need to, I know—but I'm here if you want to talk about anything."

"I don't want to." Alex felt inexplicably tearful. How bloody embarrassing. A burst of rash honesty ambushed him. "I mean, I do. Maybe. And if it were to anyone, it'd be you."

Tate's flush was a darker gray on his cheeks. "Well, hopefully you can get back to sleep. There's a school trip tomorrow, so they don't have to be in as early as usual. I'll try and keep the kids out of the room so you can sleep later."

"No," Alex said absentmindedly. He'd almost added he was used to kids in the house by now, but how weird was that? The important thing was Tate; being with Tate; trying to make sense of this overwhelming *need* for Tate. "It's fine. Sorry I woke you."

"That's what I'm here for," Tate said easily, quickly, though he flushed again as soon as the words left his mouth. "As a friend, I mean. If you've recovered from the nightmare, I'll leave you be—"

*As a friend?* Alex reached out and grasped Tate's hand on top of the duvet. "Stay. Please."

Silence for a moment. Tate's shoulders tightened but he didn't move away.

Alex rushed on, "This thing about friends... I'm also sorry for what I said in the warehouse, after the accident. About us being boyfriends." He knew Tate remembered: he turned his face farther into the shadows. Had Alex used the wrong term? Had he got the whole bloody situation wrong? Why was he angsting about all this, more than ever before?

"It's not a problem, Alex. I just don't think everyone needs to know my—our—business. And we've only just met. I'm not sure *what* we are, at the moment. You're just... you've had a disturbed night. You may not be thinking straight." He cleared his throat. "Didn't we say, no strings?"

*Ouch.* "I know we did. But I could see my way to reviewing that. What do you say?" When Tate stilled, Alex tugged urgently at his arm. He was startled by the edge of desperation in his voice. "Tell me the truth, please. Don't tease, don't brush me off. And most of all... don't say what you think you *should.*"

"Is that what I do?" Tate frowned.

Alex took his time answering. "You don't lie, no. But we joke a lot. And you're cautious, I understand that. It's just... tonight...." A stray bead of sweat ran down between his shoulder blades. "I need to ask. I need the truth."

A small smile teased the corner of Tate's mouth. "I reckon yes, then. I'd like that. But like I say, it's the middle of the night, you've had a weird dream—"

"Fuck all that," Alex said, probably too enthusiastically. But who wouldn't be enthusiastic to find the man he wanted might just want him in the same way? "God knows, after this week, the one real thing I feel most strongly is that you and I are meant to be together."

"Jesus, Alex." Tate looked a little stunned.

Had Alex gone too far? He'd never known what it was to be refused; with a shock that made his whole gut plummet, he realised this was the first time it would matter to him. He leaned over the duvet to grasp Tate's arm. "Don't back away, Tate. We felt something, didn't we, that night in my hotel room?"

That memory was stronger now than his unsettling dream, suddenly slotting into a full scene like a jigsaw in his mind, with all of his senses engaged. *Oh, joy!* The light of Tate's eyes in the dim room, the grip of his strong thighs as he reared above Alex, riding him with every muscle and nerve he had. Forehead sweaty, hair tumbled everywhere, a bead of moisture trailing down between his nipples. His body taking Alex inside, deep, hot, hard, hungry. His delight so blatant in every stretch of his limbs, every time he threw his head back. And the kissing... the *kissing*!

He realised he couldn't hear Tate breathing. He *had* gone too far, oh God, he'd messed everything up. "Tate?"

Tate slowly rose from his seat, but stood close to the sofa, close enough for Alex to see his shining eyes, the flush on his cheeks. "You mean all that?"

"Hell, yes. It was magnificent." A flush of pleasure shivered through Alex's body at the mere memory. "But not just the sex. I felt... it was something for us to build on." Were they the right words? That expensive, though erratic, education was letting him down again. What *were* the right words—when you really meant them?

Tate sat back on the sofa, but much closer to Alex this time. His gaze ran over Alex's bare torso and the pulse at his throat was fast. "Look. The trouble is... It's me, not you."

"Don't give me that tired old line." *How ironic.* Alex felt very sure he'd used it himself plenty of times, with men he didn't care about. "It *was* magnificent. The best time I ever had." He swallowed hard, suddenly disgusted with his own history. "I know I'm not as decent as you. But this is the closest to a guy I've ever been—ever wanted to be. To *you*, Tate."

Tate's eyes flared with something fiery, but his voice was cool. "In your own words, please don't tease or lie to me, and not about that."

"I'm not." *Dammit!*

But Tate still looked so pained. "Thank you for that, but it *is* me. I'm not very experienced in dating, Alex. In... talking about it, either. And it looks to me like you *are*. Experienced, that is. I mean, I won't pretend it wasn't pretty fabulous for me too. But please let's just take it slow."

No, that wasn't the whole story, Alex could tell. Tate was withdrawing from him. Panic fluttered like a trapped bird in Alex's chest. "And you don't trust me."

"I didn't say that!"

"But you did. Not in words, as such. In your wariness."

Tate's words were unusually hesitant. "I'm sorry if you're insulted. But you are a bit of a mystery, Mr. Goodson."

Alex slid his arm around Tate and pulled him closer. Tate's nude torso was cool against Alex's warmer one in the night air. "I'm the one who's sorry. I want nothing more than your trust. But I understand I have to earn it. Yes, I've dated a lot—" God, a *lot*, but such a lot of *nonsense* it now proved to have been, "—but this is different. You are different. You're special to me, and that means I want to give you special treatment."

"I'll admit, you're not the same man who started at the warehouse. The one I first met." Tate looked strangely sad. "But it's impossible to know more than that, after just a few weeks."

"Not at all." Alex was suddenly, totally sure. "Don't you ever just act?"

Tate obviously didn't have to think about that for long. "Rarely."

Poor, neglected Tate, Alex thought with a pang of sympathy and the overwhelming need to change that forever. "Spontaneity is fun."

"It's not an option."

"Just give me a chance," Alex urged. He was also suddenly, totally sure that he'd regret it for the rest of his life if he let Tate Somerton slip through his fingers. The last couple of weeks had been a revelation on so many levels, now unencumbered by his Bonfils persona. "Let me give *you* that chance."

"I want to." Tate looked as if that admission startled him. His breath was shortening, his hands clenched at his sides.

"Come here." Alex lay back on the sofa, tugging Tate down to lie beside him. It was a tight squeeze, but that was all the better for keeping Tate close. When Alex reached for Tate's mouth, Tate responded slowly but not unwillingly. Alex anchored him with a hand behind his neck, his fingers brushing Tate's fabulous curls, his mouth seeking Tate's like finding an oasis after all these days in a desert. Alex slipped his tongue into Tate's mouth, relearning the taste of him. Tate clung to Alex's shoulders, thrusting back into his mouth. There was no mistaking Tate's arousal, pressing insistently against Alex's thigh.

"Why won't you trust this?" Alex murmured. "Why won't you let go and enjoy it more?"

Tate's voice was tight, even as his lips ghosted over Alex's, desperate for the touch. "I'm not used to this, Alex."

"To feeling happy?"

Tate tensed in his arms. "It's different. It *was* different, in the hotel. That one night. But now... that's not my number one priority."

The issue became much clearer for Alex. "The family is?"

"Yes. I can't let anyone upset them."

"But I won't. Not intentionally. You can't protect against anything more than that."

"Yes, I know that," Tate muttered more angrily. "But I can't risk it. They could get to love you... someone... get to rely on them in their life, then they'd leave. Why invite the pain of that?"

Alex was stunned at Tate's harsh tone. "Your parents. It's about that, isn't it? Because they left you." Tate tried to wrench himself away, but Alex's grip was too secure. "Don't fight me, Tate, because I *know*. My mother left us too, remember?"

There was a long, pregnant silence.

"I remember," Tate whispered. "I didn't mean to upset you."

"It's okay." Alex held Tate even closer, like some kind of security, like his own personal buoy in a tumultuous sea. "You said the kids could get to love me?"

"Someone," Tate said quickly, "They could get to love someone."

"You mean, a lover. Does this mean you've never had anyone really special?"

Tate's sigh brushed across Alex's chest, making his nipples pebble. "The kids need me. I can't be distracted from that."

"What about what *you* need?"

"I'm happy. I have work, my family, good friends."

Alex was silent for a long moment. "I haven't either. Had anyone special, that is. No one I've spent time with regularly, had a real connection to." He was all too aware of his previous, brutally selfish behavior, but now it was as if it had belonged to someone else. Date, have fun, move on. Never more than a couple of days, or else boredom would set in. So many more fish in the sea, so much more novelty than comfort. God, who *was* that guy?

Tate lowered his face, hiding his eyes, his breath warming Alex's chin. "Maybe this is something new for us both. Maybe there's a chance. Or there would be...."

"But?" It hovered like the sword of Damocles over their future.

"But I still don't know enough about you, Alex Goodson."

What was he going to do? What could he do to clear up this mess? "Tate. Things are weird at the moment."

"I know. I can see there are things you don't want to share. But that's the same as me, isn't it? Neither of us wants to leap in with both feet without some kind of secure basis."

Alex would have done, in his past life, when he was *that guy* who didn't give a toss for the consequences of anything he did. "I will promise you, Tate."

"Hmm?"

Tate was both soft and hard against his chest, snuggling, burrowing against him. Alex could feel the man relaxing, as if the talking had somehow eased him, even if they hadn't made any decisions. Alex wanted this so much. The feeling was exhilarating, yet at the same time, very scary. He wanted to make Tate feel good, but not just physically. Tate deserved so much more. Brave, protective, wary, sexy Tate.

"I promise I'll tell you all my truths. Soon. I promise." What was he committing himself to? "In the meantime, though, *you* must tell *me*."

"Oh, really?" Tate sounded amused. "Tell you what?"

Alex's heartbeat sped up, and his groin tingled with a very familiar desire. He slid a hand down Tate's outer side, down the muscular groove to his groin, and up under the seam of his sleep shorts. "Tell me what you want right now."

"Jesus." Tate jerked and gasped, a short, sharp sound, as if he'd clamped his mouth shut to hide it. "What you do to me!"

"Say it," Alex growled.

"I want you to kiss me. Then I *really* want you to suck me."

Alex chuckled. "That's lucky. It's what I want too. But even if it wasn't, when you take that tone...."

"Wh-what tone?"

"That management tone. Does something to me, Mr. Somerton, sir. I'm happy to follow orders."

"You stupid arse." There was laughter in Tate's voice now, his eyes glimmering with excitement in the quiet, dark room. "But we have to be quiet. Gran wakes several times a night, and I won't have the kids disturbed. No shouts, no swearing, no loud groans—"

Alex kissed Tate's neck, lingering his tongue over the pulse. "Oh, that's good. Keep talking dirty."

Tate's stifled laugh came out as a gargled breath. "You're mad. A complete idiot."

"For you, yes. And you like that, don't you?"

It was a while before Tate answered. Alex wriggled down Tate's body, pushing the shorts down Tate's thighs to his knees. Tate's belly was warm and smelled of the clean cotton fabric. Tate's cock bobbed on his lower belly, and Alex took hold, licking hungrily around its glistening tip. The shaft was thick and heavy in his palm, and he kept his fingers circled loosely around its base as he slid his mouth down.

"Oh!" Tate seemed to have been suffering desert starvation too, judging by his immediate response to every twist of Alex's tongue. He arched beneath Alex's touch, obviously trying not to thrust too hard into Alex's mouth, but failing.

Alex paused for long enough to let Tate's cock slide off his tongue, then to lick a stripe of wet heat from Tate's balls to his entrance, and back again. He fondled the soft, crinkled sac in his palm, loving the feel of it shifting and tightening with anticipation. Tate was already close.

Tate's fingers tightened painfully in Alex's hair, and from the soft, strangled grunts he made, he was trying not to express his pleasure too loudly. With mischief and pure delight, Alex took him back down his throat and tightened his lips. One final suck should do it—

"Yes, I like it!" Tate hissed, bucking as his climax crested. "God, yes!"

Alex clutched Tate tightly as he writhed on the sofa. He happily swallowed Tate's essence, loving the smell of Tate in his nostrils, the muscles clenching under his hands, the muffled moans Tate was trying so hard to keep quiet.

This was the real madness.

# CHAPTER 17

In some strange way, Alex felt he was on borrowed time. This weekend was the last of his recovery, the final days of staying at Tate's. On Saturday, while Tate took the H's out for new uniforms—amazing how children grew so quickly, and so relentlessly—and Amy was at her adored maths club, Alex sat with Gran in the kitchen. He was trying to master pastry—how difficult could it be to mash some ingredients together, then roll them out again, without them crumbling or turning gray in the process?—and Gran was sitting with Freddie at her feet, browsing through the Bonfils company newsletter Tate had brought home that week. Alex glanced over at it: there were photos of the recent presentation at the Savoy, with Bonfils representatives announcing their great hopes for the UK retail wine trade, and the forthcoming Wine Awards.

Alex hadn't attended the presentation, but his stomach tensed suddenly. He let his spoon drop clumsily into his mixing bowl and white puffs of flour flew up his nose.

"That Mr. Charles looks very smart," Gran said, running her finger along the text of the middle page spread. "Though his father was a better-looking man."

"You knew my—Mr. Theo?" Alex asked, stunned, yet trying not to show it. He'd barely known his grandfather, who'd died when he was a toddler.

Gran shrugged. "Bonfils is a big name in Bristol. We all know the family."

How well, exactly? Alex wanted to ask but didn't dare. He'd never thought he looked particularly like Papa, but he had an overwhelming urge to hide his face behind even more flour. He should have kept up with the glasses as well as the hair colour, but the bloody things irritated his nose.

*Help!* His position was becoming untenable.

The other night, he'd promised to tell Tate the truth. But when, and how? Yes, he was meant to be undercover, but that all seemed like a rather immature game now. After the last two weeks, he knew the warehouse, he understood much better the way the business was run, and the trials and obstructions its staff had to work with. Most important of all, he'd met Tate, a man who demanded and deserved honesty.

*Deserves a better man than me?* Alex had never questioned himself before now. He'd always considered himself a charming, rewarding catch for any man. But Tate had challenged him head-on from the start, with no knowledge of Alex's background or assumed privileges. Tate saw and judged what was there—just the man, not the trappings. Alex was suddenly scared that he'd be found wanting. Not only could he lose Tate, he would lose Tate's family as well.

He was still amazed at his kindly assimilation into Chez Somerton. The family was weird and wonderful, full of action and conflict, noise and emotion. It was an alien world, compared to his experience as a Bonfils. Gran had a never-ending list of chores that needed doing around the house, even though Alex had proved he was no damned good with DIY, since he'd blown every fuse in the house trying to fix the toaster, and his attempts to bleed the radiators had soaked most of the hall carpet. So he was now in charge of organising dentist and doctor's appointments for the kids— was it some kind of family rule that one of the children must always be ill, or the sky would fall?—sorting the laundry, helping Gran cook, and assisting with homework as and when his knowledge base fit.

When he'd asked Gran about the children's blazers and caps, she'd looked at him askance. "Where on earth did you go to school, boy?" she asked. "It's polo shirts and sweatshirts for them nowadays."

When he discovered Hugo had no clean socks without holes in the toes, she just shrugged. "Darn 'em," she said.

Was that her version of a curse? Alex had assumed so, until she shoved a sewing kit into his hand and suggested he patch them up. Never— *never*—had he mended a piece of clothing in his life. It took the whole afternoon, while Gran snoozed in front of Nigella's latest TV cookery show, for him to thread a needle competently, then make a neat enough job of the hole.

Yet... this was the family life he was living. Comparisons were no longer relevant, he reckoned. He was growing used to the routine, ferrying the H's back and forth on the bus to their after-school clubs, reading to Amy, chatting with Gran about anything and everything, watching a disgracefully huge amount of cookery shows that he was developing a guilty pleasure for, even taking the animal—Freddie, that was his name— for a walk. He barely noticed the clamor around him now. In fact, he *liked* it. If his London friends had turned up on the doorstep with free VIP tickets for him to accompany them to the latest London nightclub opening... well, he'd have had to refuse, citing exhaustion as an excuse and preferring an early night. And he wouldn't have felt he was missing out, either.

But he did need to go back to work, for several reasons. He hadn't been brave enough to confess to Tate that money would never be one of them, but he knew now what money meant to the Somertons. They'd been feeding and supporting him for a full week, and he realised just how much it cost to maintain a family of hungry, school-aged kids. Also, his hair dye was growing out. He didn't dare ask Tate to add dye to the shopping list, when the money was better spent on the kids, and he had no idea how he'd explain why he needed it. So he'd used a cheap touch-up kit he found at the corner store, but he was struggling to find private time in the shared bathroom to make anything like a decent job of it.

Primarily he needed to sort out the problems at

the warehouse: the Awards were due in a few months' time. The last thing he wanted was for his family's business to be humiliated or ruined at a prestigious event.

The other, but much stronger, reason of all was that he missed Tate when he went to work. *How odd.* No, not odd, just unfamiliar. Alex wanted to be with Tate. All the time. Yet he realised that when he went back to work, Tate would expect him to leave the house and get his own place.

It was a bizarre and depressing conflict.

Later, after the kids were all settled in bed, Alex found Tate sitting in the kitchen, bent over the table. He looked so very tired, Alex didn't speak, just stood behind him and started to massage his shoulders. He'd dated a masseur once and was grateful now he'd picked up some techniques that were useful outside the bedroom. Tate's muscles were a mass of knots. Tate didn't speak either but sighed with relief and lifted a hand to grasp Alex's wrist in thanks.

Gran poked her face around the kitchen door. "I'm off to bed. You boys going too?"

Tate tensed underneath Alex's palms.

Alex paused in his massage. If there was a single flicker of doubt or distaste in Tate's expression because he was afraid of his family discovering he was spending most of his nights with Alex on the sofa, then Alex would move out straightaway and find another hotel, loneliness be damned—

But Tate smiled easily, with an adorable shyness. "Soon, Gran. We just... um... need to talk about Alex going back to work on Monday."

Alex made a feeble excuse and sneaked out into the hall to fetch some chocolate he'd bought for Tate—and hidden from the other family chocoholics, Amy and Gran—to find Gran still at the foot of the stairs. Freddie had already scampered up ahead of her, to his basket in her room.

"Good night, Gran," he said.

"I like you, Alex," she replied bluntly.

"Um. Thanks?"

"But don't play with my Tatty's heart, you hear?"

He was touched by Gran's fierce protectiveness. "I have no intention of playing with Tate's heart, as you put it. I care for him a lot. I had hoped you'd realise that."

"Oh, I do, boy. But you can still hurt him. I'm pretty sure you have a lot of resources in your life, but Tatty has few. And if you use them up, what will he have left?"

Alex was momentarily speechless. By the time his throat had cleared, she was halfway up the stairs. "Gran? It's not like that." But she didn't turn back, just shuffled along the landing and into her own bedroom.

*That* was unexpected.

"It's not like that" he'd said to Gran. But if not, what *was* it like? A temporary stayover to help him out after the accident was turning into something more—at least it was for Alex.

Gran's recognition of the Bonfils family had shaken him up. He had to clear the air before Tate found out from elsewhere who Alex really was and misunderstood the whole undercover mission thing. No, Alex would explain it all, but he wanted the time and the right setting to do it.

Things were heading for a crisis.

And Gran was wrong in one crucial point, as Alex also now admitted to himself. The days when he, Alexandre Bonfils, could have exactly what he pleased, whenever he wanted, and with no noticeable effect on his pampered life—they were gone. Tate Somerton was embedded in his heart by now and could hurt him too.

So badly.

# CHAPTER 18

The time had come, Tate reckoned, to have a showdown with Alex Goodson.

Tate didn't often feel tense—he had his life planned as best he could, most of the time—but this weekend felt like a tipping point. The warmth of their nights on the sofa flushed right through Tate. He was looking forward to repeating it tonight. And the night after.

More things than his sex life had changed over the last week, though. Having Alex around had been unsettling. There'd been a few times when Tate had instinctively acknowledged Alex in the house as if he'd always been a member of the family. *Very* unsettling, and yet... great, too. Tate didn't know whether to be annoyed or delighted at the emotional skirmish inside him. He'd never shared his daily life before with anyone but family or Louise.

The odd, disturbing feelings hadn't dispersed by the time Alex returned to the kitchen with a large bar of Tate's favorite chocolate. "Let's talk a while," Tate said. "Just us, in private. In the living room."

"Excellent idea." Alex waggled his eyebrows in a ridiculous way he'd recently picked up from Gran. What was amazing—whether for good or bad—was that it made Tate chuckle, every time.

"No," he said with a mock frown. "I mean, that's good, too. But I want to talk first."

He couldn't resist the excitement, though, at the thought of snuggling up with Alex on the sofa. It wasn't just the sex—which was bloody fabulous, no doubt about it—but the intimacy. To have another man to cuddle and hold was something new and scary in his life, but also the brightest part of his day. He loved it.

It was a word he usually avoided outside the kids. *Love.* It made him shiver with both delight and fear. It muddled his thoughts, shook his self-control. Was that why he was fighting it so hard? He would argue he didn't allow himself the opportunity, because of the kids, and Gran, and his carefully constructed routine to keep them all safe and happy. He owed that to his parents, didn't he? But what about his own need?

*This* was gradually becoming something out of control. *This* was the way his heart bounced when he saw Alex at the end of his working day, the way Alex made him laugh, the way Alex lay on the floor with Amy when they were working together on her history project, the way Alex's nose crinkled every time Gran lobbed a used tea bag into the sink, the hysterically funny, stunned look on Alex's face when Hattie and Hugo trapped him on the sofa to watch *Made in Chelsea* with them....

*God.* He'd never thought this would happen. At least, not when he had no time to manage it properly. After all, he and Alex had both insisted it was a no-strings arrangement from the start. It was obvious he and Alex came from very different worlds—even if he didn't know much about Alex's background at all.

Which brought him back to his intended confrontation.

They settled on the sofa, the room still warm although the heating would turn off soon. Alex broke off a piece of chocolate for them both, and chuckled. "Chocolate and a hot man on a comfy couch. I couldn't ask for more. I don't mind telling you, I'll miss the company when I start looking for my own place."

"You don't have to," Tate said, needing to clear his throat a couple of times. "There's no rush. At least until you're back on track financially." He gave a shaky laugh. "Gran would kill me if we didn't continue to look after you."

Alex's eyes looked very bright. "Are you sure?" He broke off some more chocolate and nudged a piece at Tate's mouth until he opened up and bit on it. His lips were only a fraction away from Tate's. Tate felt Alex's breath on his cheek; his mouth ached for the taste of him. His fingers unfurled, wanting to reach for him.

"Tate." Alex just breathed the word onto Tate's skin.

"Talking about your financial status…," Tate said, haltingly.

"Which I wasn't, but you are." Alex sighed. He pulled away a few, significant inches and leaned back on the sofa cushion. "There's a but, isn't there?"

Tate still ached; he hated to spoil this moment

and all it promised. But he had to do this. Only that morning, Percy had moved Alex's forged reference from the bottom of Tate's in-tray and laid it silently but deliberately on top. "You've been lying to me, I reckon. And I think I've guessed what about."

Alex went very still.

Tate looked away, suddenly afraid of seeing something awful on Alex's face. "You know far more about the business than any newbie intern would. You're used to money—I see it in your clothes, hear it in your voice, in the way you move and act."

Alex shifted, very slightly.

*Here goes.* "I think you're an auditor they've sent from Head Office to investigate the problems we've been having. I never received any briefing about it, but in the light of what we suspect, maybe Head Office didn't want to warn anyone in advance. That's the only explanation I can find for the timing of your arrival and the...." He laughed softly. "The overall weirdness of you."

"Me?" Alex sounded wary but also a bit offended.

"Admit it! You don't know how ordinary life is lived, you've been living in a hotel, you can't cook—"

"Hey! What about my smoky bacon beans on toast, for a start?"

"Well, okay, but you couldn't before you came to stay here. There's all that, yet you're fit and bright and have obviously had a superb education. I've heard you talking to Gran and the kids about a miraculously wide range of subjects." He sighed and finally met Alex's gaze. "Am I right?"

Alex was quiet for a long moment. He nodded, then shook his head. Then grimaced. "No. Well. Yes. But not exactly."

"What the fuck does that mean?" Tate didn't know if he was relieved or disappointed in Alex's admission. What was going on?

"I am with the company. Sort of. And I am looking into the sabotage. I decided to come in undercover."

Tate couldn't help himself, he smirked. "Like that *Undercover Boss* TV program?"

Alex bristled. "Possibly. Slightly."

"Why you didn't think to share all this with me?"

"Tate, please. I'm sorry. I've been thinking of how to tell you, when would be the right time. Well, at first, no one was meant to know because I thought it'd give me a chance to see what was really going on. If everyone thought I was just another worker—"

Tate tried to resist rolling his eyes, but... really?

Alex scowled. "Well, that was my theory, right? Obviously, I wasn't the world's best. But... there's more."

"More to your role?"

"More to *me*." Alex snaked his hand into Tate's lap and grasped his hand. "I'm not just with the company. I mean—I *am* the company, sort of. I'm Alex Bonfils."

"You're...?" Tate heard the words, but his mind didn't compute. He started to laugh.

"It's not a joke," Alex said, rather snappily.

"You mean.... Mr. Charles's other son? The one who never comes to any business meetings? Who only appears in the gossip magazines going the rounds in Packaging?"

"Have you read them?" Alex looked stricken.

"No way. I save the company newsletter for Gran and leave the tabloids for kebab shop reading. Which I don't read, anyway. I get all my work news from management and union meetings." He stared at Alex, aghast. "Is this really the truth? You can't be him. Last I heard, he was up to something with a circus performer—"

"Oh, for God's sake!" Alex snapped. "I *told* everyone that was just a joke. I'm just Alex, really, not anything special."

Tate doubted Alex had ever said such a thing before in his life. Realisation was seeping in, slowly and painfully. "Jesus, how stupid am I? I helped you out when I thought you had nowhere to go, you needed nursing—"

"That was true, for God's sake," Alex said hotly. "I didn't fake the shock, the fact that every movement hurt. And you've never been stupid."

"Tell me right now," Tate said in a very low voice. "Everything. Or you leave this house right away, whatever the hour."

When Tate hardened his expression, Alex stood and started nervously pacing. "I wanted to be part of the business, Tate, I really did. Papa and I could never agree on a role for me." But after he took another look at Tate's face... "No, that's not strictly true. I never put my heart into it before

207

now. Papa grew tired of me partying the family profits away and fired me."

Tate was momentarily shocked. "He fired you? His own son?"

"He's never been particularly sentimental," Alex said wryly.

"I can't believe I never recognised you." Tate glanced at Alex's hair. "Mr. Henri is blond."

"So am I. I dyed my hair. Not very well." He gave a rueful smile, but Tate didn't return it. "Is it really that different from me being from Head Office? I mean, I am from London, and I *am* looking into the warehouse problems. So the only extra thing is—"

"That you're the son of the boss, that you're an heir to the company I work for, that you have a personal fortune of what must be bloody millions, when I scratch a life out of a nonnegotiable salary each month? Oh no, stupid of me, that's such a *tiny* extra thing, we can just ignore it!" Tate snapped back.

Alex's own anger ignited. "Is that what's really annoying you? The money? Why does that make any difference?"

"You can't really be that naïve. Can you? It makes *all* the bloody difference!"

"Because I was born with it and you weren't? That's all it is, an accident of birth."

"You would say that. You've always had it." This was the first time Tate had argued with anyone for years. The words came easily, the anger more slowly. And the distress even more deeply.

"Give me a break!" Alex fired back. He looked

genuinely distraught. "All my bloody life people have judged me by my name, by those *bloody millions* you talk of. I thought we were more equal."

Tate felt as if he'd been punched. "*Equal?* You've stayed here—you've seen how we live. It must be as different from your life as a caravan is to Buckingham Palace." Another thought struck him, and his gut twisted in horror. "Oh God, you've shopped with me, with my housekeeping money as your budget. You've darned Hugo's socks. You've watered down the orange juice to make it last another day. You've sorted through the bargain bins at the supermarket—"

"Damned fine bargains too; that stir fry you made was delicious."

"Stop it. Stop it! This is so humiliating!"

"Tate!" Alex cried, such a pure expression of bitter misery and shame that Tate froze, startled. "Tate, *please.* You have nothing to be ashamed of. I have never thought less of you, or your family, or your lifestyle. I have loved every minute I've spent with you, and I've learned so much. If anything, *I'm* the one who's humiliated. When I remember the stupid things I've said and done, just because I arrogantly never took the time to find out how other people lived their lives... I'm surprised you've stuck with me, even before my pathetic confession. This is a family life I never thought to experience." Alex's voice was now ragged. "You've shared yourself with me."

They stared at each other for a long, painful moment.

Tate finally broke the silence. "It's the lying, Alex. I thought you were one person, only to find you're not. What's more, I knew something wasn't right. Percy and I knew you'd forged your references. I should have followed it up before, but I... I think I was in denial." He grimaced. "And it obviously wasn't my business to know why."

Alex sank back on the sofa beside him. "It wasn't anything personal against you, or Percy, or anyone I've met. It was all part of my desire to hide from my family, to be something apart from them. And my bizarre plan—as you said—to be some kind of undercover boss."

Another silence. Tate felt he'd gone a couple of rounds in a boxing match, but the bruises were all inside. "So what do I call you?"

"Alex. Just Alex." Alex ran his hand through his hair. "Are you really angry with me? It won't change anything, will it? I mean, with us."

"Us?" Something worse was nagging at Tate, churning his stomach. He threw himself back against the cushion with a groan. "Of course. All those questions you asked. Guess I was a good source."

"What?"

"Well, seduce the manager and you can find out all kind of things."

Alex jumped as if he'd been poked in the ribs. "It wasn't like that! You don't believe it was, do you? I never planned on meeting you—well, not that you'd be, you know. *You.* That I'd find you so attractive."

Oh, but flattery would be in Alex's weapons

cache, wouldn't it? Tate was in turmoil. The stomach-churning raised bile in the back of his throat. Alex had lied about so much already.

"Tate, it wasn't! Tate, look at me, you owe me that." Alex gripped him fiercely and pulled Tate to face him. "I liked you from the very start, on my own account, nothing to do with who or what you were in the company. Damn, I never intended to fall—!" He bit off the sentence.

Tate stared. "What?"

"Forget it. But believe me, we're on the same side."

Tate shook his head slowly, trying to bed down the whirl of thoughts. It was like a movie script. Alex the son of the Bonfils owner. Nothing like the Alex Goodson Tate had grown so close to. Or… was he?

"We can still work together on the sabotage, can't we? Tate, I swear to you that's the whole truth. Don't pull away now, not when we're close to finding out what's really going on!"

"Are we?"

Alex's eyes gleamed with what looked suspiciously like the light of battle. "Let's take a look around the warehouse tonight. You have twenty-four-hour access, don't you?"

"Yeah, but—"

"Neither you nor Percy saw anyone moving pallets when they shouldn't have been during the day. Let's take a look at nighttime, when the place is clear."

"Look for what?"

"Clues!" Alex all but crowed. Then another

thought struck him, and his eyes widened. "Maybe that was when the shelf unit was loosened—I mean, overnight."

Tate felt the blood drain from his face. "You think that was deliberate?"

"Perhaps. We'll consider it later." Alex seemed to brush away that topic. "I know you'll say you can't just come and go when you like. I understand as well as you do that the kids have to be looked after, that they're priority. But Gran's here. They'll be safe for a few hours."

Tate just stared at him. Why wasn't he more devastated, betrayed? All he could see was the excitement in Alex's expression, all he could feel was the thrill of being with him. *What a bloody fool I am!*

"It's time we went looking for proper answers," Alex said grimly. "Are you in?"

Tate just nodded, he wasn't sure what else he could say. He picked up the bar of chocolate and snapped off a huge chunk of what was left.

After this lunatic evening, he needed comfort of the simplest kind.

# CHAPTER 19

They let themselves back into the warehouse at around eleven o'clock. The security guard didn't even need to see them, as Tate's pass let him in via the senior staff entrance. He followed Alex, who strode ahead into the main warehouse.

"I feel like a bloody criminal.," Tate muttered.

"Well, you're not. We're on the trail of one," Alex muttered back. "We'll search your office, see if anyone's coming in overnight and messing with the records. Check the inventory, deliveries, and dispatches etcetera. Then take a look around the warehouse bays, see if there's any more trouble planned."

Tate shook his head wearily. "You're enjoying this, aren't you? All part of your undercover game."

Alex's expression hardened. "It's not a game anymore, Tate, though I know my record's not good. We need to start taking positive action. Whether you believe me or not, all I want is to catch this saboteur, once and for all."

Tate watched Alex as he peered off into the warehouse bays. "Whether you believe me or not"... was that the issue? *Did* Tate believe Alex? It had been a night of shocking revelations. And while Tate appreciated Alex telling the truth—

well, how did he know he was? Or whether it was the whole truth. Tate's head hurt, worrying about it, what it meant for anything he and Alex had going on between them. Tate prided himself on judging everyone on their dealings with him, rather than any knowledge of their background or privilege. And yet... Alex was the son of the ultimate boss. Alex was a Bonfils, rich, powerful, from a different world. And who was Tate Somerton, in comparison to that?

He glanced into his office, dark and silent. All the filing cabinets were locked and didn't seem to have been tampered with. "Nothing looks out of place here."

Alex frowned. "Maybe this all started as a way to disrupt business and cause delay at this crucial time."

"Perhaps a competitor's behind it, you mean?"

Alex shrugged. "It's not unheard of, industrial sabotage. I've seen plenty of vintners smiling sycophantically at Papa at industry dinners but letting the mask slip long enough for me to see they're eaten up with jealousy."

"Wow." Tate knew there was heathy competition in the market but as he never went to events like that, he supposed he was sheltered from the commercial cut and thrust.

"I think the distraction is being stepped up, with the illicit movement of the pallets and—no easy way to say this, Tate—I think the next step could be theft of the new stock."

"Shit. Not the Angel's Breath? It's not even ready for sale yet."

"All the more reason. Can you imagine what it'd be worth to keep Angel's Breath from its carefully timed launch? How humiliating for Bonfils to lose control of the product! To say nothing of competitors having access to the wine itself."

Tate looked instinctively toward the secure store at the far end of the warehouse. "But whoever it is, they'd need access firstly to the warehouse, and secondly to the store. Only Percy and I have access to the key safe. You saw the cabinet. It needs a combination that's changed regularly."

"Hm. Maybe they're planning something done under cover of the deliveries. They come and go around the secure store, several times a week. If stuff's been moved around in the main warehouse, that could cause enough confusion to swap out Angel's Breath for another line. Who sets the delivery schedule?"

"It's organised and monitored separately by Percy and Stuart. And me, too—" Tate's heart stuttered suddenly; a lump of hot anger formed in his throat. "You don't suspect *me*, do you?"

"Of course not!" Alex looked horrified. "No one has ever mentioned any specific suspicions. I was just told that things had been going wrong. But I pay enough attention to know that if the aim is to destroy the Bonfils name and reputation, this would be the most devastating way. And for that to happen? It's *definitely* an insider. We're looking for someone already working in this warehouse."

It was a contradiction Tate couldn't get his

head around. He trusted his workforce—but one of them obviously *couldn't* be trusted. He glanced back into the deserted office. He knew it almost as well as his own home. The familiar, subtle smell of paper and printer ink; the tang of past cups of tea. A pen had rolled to the edge of the desk and hung there, equally likely to roll back or fall off.

"Why are you smiling?" Alex said.

Tate hadn't been aware he was, but he definitely knew why. The semidarkness made him bold enough—insane enough—to speak it. "The first day I saw you in that office, on that chair, facing Percy's interview with such arrogance I thought he'd see you off within ten minutes? I wanted you."

Alex flushed. "You did?"

"There was something about you made my spine tingle. My palms itch."

"In what way?" Alex said very, very softly.

The devil was in Tate tonight. His heartbeat quickened. "With hindsight, I think I wanted to come up behind you, push you forward over the desk, flat on your face. Then kick the chair away, and step between your legs." He moved closer to Alex so they were mere inches apart. "Unzip your ridiculously well-tailored trousers and push them right down to your thighs."

"Oh my God." Alex's words were no more than a strangled breath.

Tate ran a single finger down Alex's arm, and watched the goose bumps spring up in its wake. "Run my hands over your arse. Grip the cool, taut, flesh. Slowly, *slowly*, spread you open...."

Alex's pulse was fast, Tate could feel it at his wrist. Sweat had formed in the hollow of his throat. "How refreshingly spontaneous of you, Tate Somerton." Alex's voice was ragged. "I thought you didn't just act?"

"I thought I didn't, either. But there's something about the imaginary vision of your arse stretched out over that table that gives me ideas."

"Oh fuck."

Tate reached for Alex a second before Alex grabbed him, their mouths coming together with force and need. Tate had excited himself as well as Alex. So what was he playing at? Did he finally believe Alex? Had he forgiven him? Part of him was bloody angry at Alex spying on the business, confused at the sudden change in their positions. Part of him was horrified at the thought of one of his staff trying to destroy Bonfils. And part of him was excited in a whole different way about creeping around with Alex in the half light, working together to try to save the company more drama—and being alone with a determined, sexy Alex. Inappropriate, he knew. But totally irresistible. He tugged Alex even closer, their gasps of breath unusually loud in the deserted warehouse. One step back for Alex, and he'd be pushed against the desk. Jesus, if Tate didn't hang on to one shred of sense, he'd be tempted to act out his sexual fantasy right now, right *here*—

Alex pulled away, panting, but distracted. "What's that noise? Some kind of machinery?"

"Nothing should be left switched on. The

afternoon shift finishes at five on a Saturday, and Percy does the last run-through of the warehouse before he leaves." But now Alex had mentioned it, Tate could hear it too. It was a rhythmic hum, volume ebbing and flowing. It could have been mechanical, or maybe part of the fittings being moved back and forth. His breathing sped up, and he swung his head in the direction of the noise, listening for the source. "It's from bay twelve. Has someone broken in after all?"

Alex frowned. "Did you say Percy locked up?"

*What?* "No, Alex. Don't even think it! I'd trust Percy with my life, let alone the Angel's Breath."

"Don't jump down my throat! I wasn't implying Percy had anything to do with this. But if someone's breaking in after hours, they must be getting past security somehow."

"So let's find out, shall we?"

They crept around the edge of bay ten and eleven, their view obscured by the shadows thrown by the towering pallets. The noise increased in volume the nearer they got to the source. Tate grimaced and picked up a roll of plastic wrap from the end of the aisle. Alex raised his eyebrows at such a daft weapon, but if it was some kind of machinery gone rogue, or a group of mischief-makers who might even be armed, Tate felt happier with something in his hands.

Instead, in the middle of the aisle in bay twelve, they found one of the staff chairs. On the chair was Percy, eyes closed, arms folded. And he was snoring.

"Gracious," Alex said with some awe. "I never

knew snoring could be that loud."

As they watched, temporarily stunned, Percy started to slump sideways off the chair.

"Shit!" Tate darted forward to try to catch him, arms barely meeting around Percy's middle, but the older man fell like a dead weight. Tate tumbled backward onto his arse, losing his grasp, and Percy followed him, landing full stretch over Tate's legs.

There was a large, wet stain on the chest area of Percy's shirt.

"Oh Jesus. Has he been shot?" Alex had gone pale. "Is that blood?"

Tate sniffed—this close to Percy, he could smell something totally out of place. "No. It appears to be... chocolate?"

Alex started to laugh, then must have realised how inappropriate that was, and clamped his mouth shut. "What's going on?"

Tate wriggled out from under Percy, letting the old man's body down as carefully as he could. The snoring stopped as Percy rolled onto his side. "Hot chocolate's his favorite drink, it's like a guilty secret vice of his. He has a supply in his locker, and when he stays late, he mixes up a mug or three to keep warm."

Alex crouched down beside him quickly, eyes wide. "There's no more noise. Is he... he can't be dead, can he?"

"No." Tate answered automatically, but then surreptitiously touched his fingertips to Percy's neck, just to check. "He's just unconscious. He'll be okay, right? But you need to get an ambulance here, to check him out. It's not a normal sleep."

Alex scrambled to one side to call 999. Tate remained on his knees beside Percy. Why was Percy in so deep a sleep? He didn't seem to have been hit on the head, and he'd never been the kind of man to collapse in a faint. His breathing was low but quite steady and, to Tate's astonishment and helpless irritation, the snoring started up again. He stood up when Alex came back over.

"The ambulance is on its way. How is he?"

"He actually seems comfortable."

"Should we put a cushion under him?"

Tate shook his head. "Just leave him for the moment. We don't know what other damage there may have been, but if there's no threat to his breathing, we should let him rest."

Alex looked down at the prone man. "He's teased and challenged me since day one, you know."

"I know."

"But when it came down to it, he cared enough about my safety to discount my expensive smashing accident."

Tate took a deep breath. "Which we now think may not have been accidental."

Alex nodded. He'd gone a shade paler.

Tate remembered his horror when he thought Alex could have been seriously hurt. That feeling was as alive now as it had been then. Nothing had changed in his heart. "You're okay now," he said gently to Alex. "And Percy will be too. This isn't some gangster movie." But they needed to know what was going on, and fast, before things escalated further.

Alex still looked restless. "I wish the ambulance would hurry up, but they seemed to ease off with the urgency when I said the patient was breathing okay."

Tate glanced quickly around. "We should check if anyone actually is here."

"I did that while I made the call," Alex said. "No one in the bays, no one in the delivery area. If they were here, we scared them off." He looked down at Percy again. Tate had shifted him into the recovery position. "Tate, how do you always know what to do?"

Tate sighed ruefully. "I'm trained in basic first aid. All management is. But I've also got a house full of potential accidents, remember? The kids were always falling or crashing into stuff when they were younger."

"How dreadful. Not now?"

When Tate looked at him, Alex had an odd, fond little smile on his face. "No, things are less hazardous as they get older. But now I have Gran instead to worry about."

"Jesus. Family life, eh?" Alex laughed, but it was brittle, and he didn't meet Tate's eyes.

It was an hour before they were alone again, after the ambulance took Percy to hospital, and Tate called Percy's wife to explain and reassure. He walked slowly back to join Alex, sitting on a chair outside Tate's office.

"The paramedics think he's been drugged," Tate said.

"What the hell—? In his chocolate, you mean?"

Tate had come to the same conclusion. "Yes, probably. If he put his usual tot of whisky into it as well, he probably wouldn't have noticed anything odd about the taste. If we hadn't arrived tonight, probably Percy would just have woken with a crappy headache and thought he'd fallen asleep on his watch."

"So... you reckon someone came in after hours and drugged Percy so he could move around the warehouse without being watched."

Tate nodded, trying so hard not to find this depressing, but it was a losing battle. "Must have been desperate, because he'd know we could check who'd been here."

"Tonight may have just been opportunistic," Alex said musingly. "Perhaps things aren't going well for them. They'll make mistakes as a result. All the better to catch them out. Wait a minute, though!"

Tate turned to see Alex staring, dumbstruck. "What? What's the matter?"

"What did you mean, you could check who'd been in here?

"The security passes," Tate said slowly. "There's a log kept centrally at Head Office, with remote access from here. And at this time of night, when there shouldn't be any other staff around..."

"Exactly!" Alex looked ready to dive straight back into the office, but Tate caught his arm.

"The remote access isn't working," he said wretchedly. "It's being overhauled this weekend. And it's my fault."

"What the hell?"

"Remember we talked about what I'd change, what improvements I'd want? I'm already doing what I can. The remote access is run on a crappy old server that barely works at the best of times. I thought a quiet weekend would be a good time to schedule the transfer over to a new host. How fucking stupid was I, what a bizarre coincidence—"

"No!" Alex snapped. "No coincidence. Who else knew about the IT work? Someone knew they'd be clear to move in tonight."

"Jesus. Me. Percy, of course, probably Stuart as well. The finance department, the security firm itself." Tate couldn't believe they'd come to a halt because of his bloody zealousness. Now they'd have to wait until someone was back in Head Office on Monday to check it on their behalf—

"So... did you see?" Alex broke into Tate's misery. "By the secure storage? A sweet paper on the floor."

What was he on about? So?"

Alex shook his head impatiently. "*After* the cleaners have been. I know the schedule—I often chat with them at the beginning of their shift."

Tate had no time to worry what shock there'd be in the cleaning team when they discovered they'd been *chatting* with a Bonfils son, no less.

Alex rushed on, "So someone *was* here tonight. And why would they be here unless they were up to no good?"

Tate smiled ruefully. "You mean, like us?"

"Tate, will you give me a break?"

"I'm sorry. I just feel I've let you down, now we have to wait until Monday—"

"Why? We can see the log right away at Head Office." Alex all but bounced on the balls of his feet.

Tate frowned. "London from Bristol, remember? And it's the middle of the night, there'll be no one to let us in—"

"I can get us in, easily. Don't argue, Tate. Isn't it the most important thing to find out who the hell's doing this? The lost invoicing, the defaced labels, the forged customs documentation, and now potential theft. Believe me, I've known enough scams and tricks over the years to guess where all this is going. And we must protect our wine!"

Tate wondered if Alex was even aware of the way his voice had tightened, and his pronunciation smoothed. And his possessive use of the phrase "our wine."

"So let's go." Alex slipped his arm into Tate's. "Right now!"

"What?" Tate's head was spinning again.

"To Head Office. Were you listening? We can be there and back by tomorrow afternoon. It's Sunday, and the traffic will be light."

"Overnight? But the kids—"

"I'll sort it out," Alex said. "Gran's morning Zumba class has been cancelled—someone broke their hip last week—and there's a shepherd's pie I made in the fridge that Hugo and Hattie can heat up, so Gran only has to microwave the vegetables for lunch. Amy has a history test for Monday, but she's pretty secure on the Tudors, we can catch up on revision when I get back."

Tate went very quiet. What was happening here? When had Alex absorbed so much of the family routine?

"Too much?" Alex looked terrified he'd done wrong.

"No," Tate said slowly. "Thanks. I think."

Alex's hand tightened on Tate's arm. "This needs to be settled once and for all. We'll check the access logs. We'll find out who's been in and out this evening, maybe other evenings after hours, too."

"But... it's at least two hours to London."

"We'll stay over somewhere and be in the office first thing tomorrow morning. Then as soon as rush hour's over, we'll start back to Bristol."

"God's sake, Alex. We don't even have any transport—"

"And you're Mr. Negative Vibes even more than usual," Alex said, almost too brightly. "Leave all that to me!"

# CHAPTER 20

The Bonfils company had an account at a national car hire firm with 24-hour service, as Alex well knew. Papa often worked antisocial hours, and Alex himself had used it enough times coming back from a club. Funny how he wasn't missing that party life while he was in Bristol, and he rarely felt the energy to go out on the town. That was what looking after three kids and a boisterous grandmother did to you, presumably. He was taking a chance the car firm would have a local branch, and also an available car at this late hour, but he was lucky on both counts. He'd worry later if it flagged up on the account at Head Office, and his cover was finally blown. After all, he was about to uncover the villain, wasn't he?

They drove into the outskirts of central London around three in the morning. Tate was yawning widely when Alex parked outside a small but prestigious boutique hotel in Green Park. It was often mentioned in the fashionable press, and was newly added to the Bonfils facilities list, though Alex didn't tell Tate any of that. Luckily, Tate was so tired he left Alex to check in and allowed himself to be guided to a double room on the third floor. They had no luggage—neither had allowed themselves the time to pick up any bags from home—but Alex had a small shopping bag of toiletries they'd bought at a service station on the M4. With Tate's back turned, Alex managed to persuade the sleepy girl at reception that he didn't need the suite on the top floor that his father usually booked; she still insisted he take one of the premier rooms on the floor below.

Unfortunately, Tate's indifference didn't survive his first step into that room.

"Alex, what is this place?"

"Just a hotel I know. Somewhere for us to sleep tonight." He paused on his way to the generous bathroom. He could feel Tate's tension as if it were his own, prickling over his skin like nervous fingertips. No, that careless comment wasn't going to work. Slowly, he turned back to face Tate.

Tate was very still. He didn't even seem to be breathing. For a wild second, Alex thought Tate would step back into the corridor and leave, but he stayed in the doorway. Just very, *very* still. A bit pale, too.

"Are you okay?" Alex asked. "Do you want a drink? Go and sit on the sofa, it looks very comfortable. The minibar will be stocked, and there's a fruit bowl and pastries if you're hungry. I can call room service if that burger we had on the way wasn't enough. Take your shoes off if you want—"

"Alex. *Alex!* Just look at all this."

Alex tried to see the room as Tate would. Thick carpets and exquisite wallpaper. A selection of modern art prints on the wall. Excellent air-conditioning. A suite of lounge furniture around a large, wall-mounted TV, over a full media center. An open doorway to the bedroom, with a king-size bed dressed in bright white linens and a colourful throw, the air fragrant with the scent from a huge vase of fresh flowers. The door on the other side of the lounge area was ajar and led to the bathroom, there were plush matching bathrobes hanging on a nearby hook, and what looked like two baths, although Alex assumed one would be the Jacuzzi. He turned back to find Tate glaring at him, his face flushed.

"Who the fuck are you?"

Alex blanched. "I told you!"

"Yes. You did. But you didn't tell me about all *this*. You magic up a car from nowhere in the middle of the night, you sail through the center of London as familiarly as if it's your backyard, you book us into a five-star hotel without any question, in a room so luxurious it's bloody painful."

Alex wasn't sure what to say. His heartbeat had increased, and he suspected the lump in his throat was from fear. "It's a company perk, that's all."

"Not for me, it's not." Tate looked both distressed and angry. His shoulders were very tight, his voice rough. "This is something else."

"This...?"

Tate waved helplessly, his gesture encompassing the whole room. "This brings it all home. It's brutal, Alex."

Alex winced. "Will you close the door and come in? I don't want everyone hearing us."

Tate moved slowly, as if his limbs were tired, as

if he were nothing but a robot. But he did close the door behind him and sat down on the beautifully upholstered sofa.

Alex's breath caught and he held it, praying to a God he'd never before passed the time of day with that he had a hope with this proud, stubborn man.

"I suppose I just hoped...," Tate said hesitantly. He was struggling to talk through tiredness and confusion. His cheeks pinked. "When we...."

*Tell me.* Alex so wanted to be close to Tate for this conversation. He moved across the room, ready to jump back if Tate was angry again. But Tate just watched him as he approached and sat down on the other end of the sofa.

"I hoped we were becoming something, together. Something special," Tate whispered.

"Everything personal between us has been true," Alex said, also softly. "I swear to you. I would never lie about that."

Tate was about to reply when he was ambushed by a loud yawn. He gave a bitter little chuckle. "I'm not used to being up this late. What the hell time is it, anyway?"

"I don't know exactly. Small hours of the morning."

"You drove all this way. You need to sleep."

Alex searched Tate's face, trying to gauge his feelings. Yes, he did need to sleep, but was Tate sleeping with him? Or was he threatening to leave?

"What do *you* want to do, Tate?"

"I don't know," Tate said grumpily. "Maybe I should go home—leave you to it."

"Don't!" Alex said, too urgently.

Tate stood, stretching his tired limbs, and sighed. "Okay. I mean, it's too late tonight. Or this morning. I need sleep too." He shook his head. "But I need more time, Alex, to think about what you've told me."

Alex thanked that unknown deity for his reprieve, even if it was temporary. "Of course. Thank you." That was Tate all over. Always so keen to make sense of things, to be in control. He was a rock to Alex's more volatile nature. Oh God, please, don't let him lose Tate over this stupid, selfish, childish scheme of his!

They undressed in silence, too tired for more than a quick wash. Tate slid into the luxurious bed in just his boxers and rolled over so his back was to Alex. Alex tried not to take it to heart. "Do you want me to call Gran in the morning?" he said quietly, though he hated talking to nothing but his pillow. "Explain we may be home later than expected?"

"I'll do it. You'll wake me if I sleep through the alarm?"

"I promise." Another moment of quiet, but from the cadence of Tate's breath, he wasn't asleep yet. "Tate?"

"Yeah?"

"No more lies, I promise. No more games."

"Sure."

Was that a genuine "sure" or a cynical one? Alex's emotions were all at sea. "You know everything about me now."

It was a full thirty seconds before Tate replied, his voice muffled against his pillow. "Maybe."

Alex lay there worrying until he could tell Tate was asleep.

Had he messed up the best thing in his life, for good?

In the middle of the night, Tate reached for him. All he said was "Alex," and it wasn't a question. His voice was slow and sleepy, but his lips were damp and urgent against Alex's mouth and neck. Alex took what he was given with a deep, loving gratitude. Tate didn't speak any more, but he was unmistakably hungry for Alex, caressing his body, sliding his hand into Alex's briefs with a low, sexy growl. This was no sleepwalking episode.

Alex rejoiced in it. He arched, moaning, beneath Tate's hands. His cock hardened painfully and his thighs ached as he stretched them wide. Tate squirmed down the mattress until his head rested at Alex's groin, then his mouth went to work on Alex's balls.

The bedroom was dark and still, the activity of 24-hour London muted beyond the thick curtains. The superior linen was cool and fresh-smelling as it snagged underneath them. The only sounds were their gasps and the wet slap of Tate's tongue. Alex knew he wouldn't last long—the evening's emotional drama had already exhausted him. He tugged at Tate to come back up the bed so they could kiss, and Tate understood quickly what his clumsy fingers meant. Their kissing was slow and sloppy and totally delicious. Alex traced the hairs on Tate's chest, tweaking his nipple until he groaned.

"Hold us," he whispered, and once again, Tate understood. He curled his damp palm around his and Alex's cock, and began a lazy, firm stroke of them both. Alex stretched like Freddie having his belly scratched, like a lazy cat, like a man in total accord with his lover. All he could pray was that the action became the reality.

"I love you," he whispered. "In case you never give me another chance to say it."

Tate didn't reply, didn't even acknowledge having heard. His heartbeat was fast against Alex's chest and he nipped at Alex's lower lip. Alex knew by now that meant Tate was close to climax.

"Together," Alex gasped. He meant their cocks, their bodies, their kisses—their just about everything. Excitement was racing through his veins like a lava flow, and his groin ached to let go of the climax building there. "Do you hear?"

"Shh," was all Tate said, but Alex felt Tate's smile against his lips. He came, with Tate's happy moan in his ear, and Tate's comforting hand on his cheek as he joined Alex in climax.

First thing in the morning, Alex summoned a manager of the Bonfils Head Office, and marched into the building as if he owned the place. Which, Tate thought dryly, he more or less did. The manager tried to ingratiate himself with the boss's son, but to give Alex credit, he refused all the fawning and swore the man to secrecy on the pretence he was planning a birthday surprise for Mr. Henri. Then they were left alone in a small, private meeting room in Human Resources. Alex immediately turned to the coffee machine set up on a counter at the back wall, and Tate powered up the two powerful laptops on the desk.

"Do you have access to everything?" he asked Alex, and when Alex confirmed his password was all-reaching, Tate noted it down. "I'll start searching the access logs. Are your personnel records digitised?" When Alex stared at him blankly, Tate shook his head. "Well, I'll just log in and take a look. I need you to skim through the personnel records while I'm searching. Look for the application forms from warehouse staff and take copies of any handwritten pages."

"We...? Why?"

"Please, Alex," Tate said. "Just do it. I'll explain later."

"Yes, sir," Alex might have muttered under his breath, but he was smiling as he brought coffee over for them both and settled willingly enough behind the screen.

It took Tate a while to familiarise himself with the search functions. He was also hampered by the fact all Bonfils locations were in one database, and he didn't know the specific numeric code for the Bristol warehouse. Meanwhile, Alex was cursing beside him at the nearby filing cabinets, trying to find his way around the mass of necessary paper kept for every single staff member. The printer's chugging was the only other noise in the room.

Finally, Tate rolled through a digitised log and his breath caught in his chest. "Here's the other night."

"What? Show me." Alex skidded his chair across the floor and pushed up close behind Tate.

Tate tensed, he couldn't help himself. Was he about to uncover industrial espionage, or make the biggest mistake of his career? Shouldn't he just log out quickly and leave it to the auditors or, God forbid, the police?

"Don't you trust me?" Alex's voice was soft, a little offended. He was watching Tate's expression very closely, Tate must have let his confusion show on his face. Alex always stepped into Tate's personal space, like he thought he had the right to do, smelling of that tantalising cologne he wore, although Tate couldn't imagine when he'd found the time to freshen up, when they'd arrived at the hotel with no change of clothes or toiletries. And oh, but he smelled so good....

"I don't know," Tate said, as honest as he'd ever been. "I don't know what's what any more."

"It's my fault. But there's nothing more to upset you, I swear. You know everything about me now." Alex paused for the briefest second. "You have everything of me."

*Everything of me.* The moment felt like a tipping point not just for finding the saboteur, but for them as a couple. Tate was vividly aware of Alex, and his whole body shivered in response. What's more, his heart swelled with an astonishing, previously unheard of, joy. Yeah, Tate had been shocked by who Alex really was—but it was too late to withdraw, wasn't it? Not if he treasured his innate honesty. Their connection was already in place. Despite the confusion of the previous night, a joyful relief washed over him at being with Alex.

Oh, but it felt good to turn in Alex's arms and press his chin briefly against Alex's throat. To smell him, to hold him, to allow him close. He wasn't surrendering to it, he was embracing it. He couldn't help but worry about what would happen—how anyone could ever reconcile Tate's chaotic life on the breadline with that of the millionaire boss's son—but he knew what he already had was precious, even if it ended tomorrow.

Which he very much dreaded but could no longer control.

He should be angry with Alex. When really... he breathed in the man in his arms, Alex's body vibrating with his sexiness, his humour, his earnestness, his enthusiasm. *I love him.* So what the hell did anything else matter?

"So," Alex said a little nervously, perhaps afraid of losing this further step to reconciliation. "You found the log? Who visited the warehouse Saturday night?"

"There's Percy, there are the cleaners, the security man who did his round about nine o'clock. Then there's another pass that logged in at half nine."

"Just before *we* got there." Alex's worried eyes met Tate's. "Who the hell was it?"

"Stuart. It was Stuart." Tate felt nauseous. "Looks like he went into the store, as well!"

# CHAPTER 21

They left Head Office immediately after Tate found the access log, but it was already early afternoon by the time they got back to Bristol and drove to the warehouse. Everything was quiet in the parking lot, with only a few cars parked near the main entrance.

"Is it open?" Alex asked, peering through the windscreen at the shadowed doors. No one was visible in the foyer.

"There was an inventory check planned for this morning which may still be going on. But it'll only be a small selection of staff."

"Do you think Stuart will be here?"

"I don't know if he was on the rota for the inventory, but why not? He could have volunteered to be involved—it'd be an ideal opportunity for him to roam the warehouse with hardly anyone to watch him. He has no idea we're on to him. We haven't alerted Head Office yet, against my better judgment, and I don't know if Percy saw him in the store before he was drugged."

"I know I persuaded you not to report it immediately," Alex said grimly. "I want that confrontation. Don't you? I think he *will* suspect the game's up. After all, Percy's in hospital, and I bet the company grapevine knows by now that weird things are happening. So he'll either run for cover, or go for broke and try something again today. And that last, rash step will be his ultimate undoing."

Tate shook his head. "Where the hell did you pick up all this ludicrous vocabulary?"

"The Packaging girls." Alex grinned. "Let's go in. I'm staying here all day and night, until we catch him out, but I'd rather be somewhere indoors to do it."

They clambered out, only to see a familiar car hurtling across the parking lot, then screeching to a halt in the space beside them.

"Louise?" Tate hurried over to her as she leaped out of the car with a grim look on her face. His throat tightened. "Oh my God. Is everything okay at the house?"

"Hell, yeah." Louise dismissed his panic with an airy wave of her hand. "Kids all fed, then settled to homework, followed by the promise of Alex's shepherd's pie—did you know he puts baked beans in it? No wonder the kids love it—then a Disney movie on TV, with Gran working on her own homework from her latest tapestry making club. They can cope perfectly well without you now and then, you know."

Tate's mouth opened then shut abruptly. He couldn't think of a reply to that.

"And Percy?" Alex asked. Tate was touched he'd developed such a care for the old codger.

"He's fine too. They're keeping him in hospital for another night, but he should be back tomorrow."

"This is your Sunday too, so what are you doing here?" Tate felt he'd been outmaneuvered somewhere. Alex and Louise shared a significant look. "Alex, did you call her?"

"Yes, he did." Louise answered for Alex. "And he's told me all about it. Plus Penny's in there today on the inventory check, so I'm fully on board. Let's go get him, boys!"

"Louise, this isn't a day out at the seaside."

"Seaside?" Alex tilted his head and gave a childlike smile. "Excellent idea. Can we do that on our next date?"

"For God's sake." Tate despaired of them both and jogged toward the warehouse, assuming they'd follow.

They let themselves into the senior staff entrance with Tate's card, but everything looked just as usual, and very calm on the floor. They paused by Tate's office for a few moments, while Tate gazed out over the inventory work going on. A reduced number of staff moved around the shelves, checking pallets with electronic readers, making occasional notes on clipboards. He could hear the familiar rumble of a delivery van arriving at the warehouse's back door. Nothing amiss. No one where they shouldn't be, nothing being lifted out of place. Had it all been their paranoia?

"I'll go and guard the store room," Alex said. "Louise? With me."

She winked at Tate and followed Alex meekly but with obvious excitement.

Tate waved to a couple of the nearby staff. "Is

Stuart in today?" he asked.

"Yeah, he's in Packaging," one of them said. "They had a problem with the new boxes, so he's helping out. Been there since opening time."

Tate took a deep breath to steady his nerves. *Game on.* He'd grab a coffee then go over to Packaging, and face Stuart there. Keep it all nice and calm, no more drama in the warehouse itself—

"Hey!" Alex's cry came from across the room, where the secure store was. "What the hell do you think you're doing in there?"

All of Tate's *nice and calm* deserted him in a second. Had Stuart come back to the warehouse without Tate seeing? His office had a view of the main entrance, but no one had come or gone since he'd arrived. Perhaps someone had snuck in through the delivery bay at the back. The staff at the nearby bays had paused in their work, puzzled. There was the sound of running feet in the distance.

"Stop him!" came Alex's imperious tone. "He's been in the store, and he's taking a bottle of Angel's Breath to that van!"

Someone else shouted: there were raised voices, then a thump, as if a box had been dropped to the floor. *Not the Angel's Breath!* Tate prayed desperately. Louise came running around the end of bay six.

"He's coming down bay seven!" she yelled. She was panting, had never been very fit, but the determination on her face was epic. "Alex's trying to cut him off!"

Tate had a wild desire to giggle. It was all like some kind of Western. That was, until he realised the footsteps were coming his way instead—Stuart must have changed direction and was now powering down the aisle of bay five. Its exit lay diagonally across from Tate's office door.

Tate's blood was fired up in seconds. This bloody man had tried to destroy his livelihood, had assaulted Alex and also landed Percy in the hospital. He'd been causing trouble, and now stealing, probably passing their secret launch over to the competition.

*No more!*

A man rounded the corner of the aisle, staff scattering around him in shock.

"Tate!" Louise yelled from the other direction, and he thought he could see Alex racing toward him as well, but several yards behind her.

Tate pounced, but it didn't end as he planned. Despite years of school rugby, he seemed to have misjudged the tackle. He crashed into a body thinner than he expected, his grip slipped on the man's arms, and he staggered sideways. The man shoved back at him, and Tate crashed against the nearest shelf with an *oof* of shock. He was disoriented for a second, temporarily dazed, trying to regain his balance. How close was Alex? Was Stuart making his escape already?

The man had stopped, however, his hands on his knees, wheezing. He seemed scared and confused, unsure where to run. To Tate's shock, it wasn't Stuart.

"Jamie?" he gasped. He gripped the shelving

and righted himself. "What the hell are you doing here?"

"F-fuck off!" the young man growled at him. "Leave me alone. Wh-what's it got to do wiv you?"

"Jamie, are you the saboteur? The thief?" *Jesus.* Things started to slot into place. Jamie always in the same places as Stuart, always hanging around the delivery vans, always overeager to help load and unload. Jamie was just as able on the forklift, just as familiar with the warehouse routine. Jamie's passion for toffees, *Jamie's previous job at Fenchurch's.*

Jamie backed up against the opposite shelving unit, still wheezing, obviously even less fit than Lou. And he looked close to tears. "It's all gone wrong. I fucked up, I *fucked up*! What'll he do to me?" He looked around wildly, staff members gathered at the mouth of the bays, staring in amazement and confusion. "Fuck you all!" And he turned to make a dash for the warehouse exit.

Suddenly, a large, bulky object hurtled across in front of Tate like a charging rhino. Tate stepped back instinctively, only recognising Percy at the last minute, throwing himself in his own version of an aggressive tackle at the fleeing Jamie. They both fell to the ground with an alarming crash, Percy landing heavily across Jamie's torso. There was no way the skinny young man would get out of that.

Percy gripped Jamie by the collar and yanked up his head so their noses almost met. "What have you been doin', y' little sod? What's this all about?"

"I had to, I had to," Jamie squealed. "I owe

Tristram Fenchurch more'n a fousand pounds!"

"Fenchurch's snobby son 'n' heir?" Percy gripped harder. "At that bettin' shop he owns? What did he tell you to do?"

Jamie was in genuine tears now, though Tate wasn't sure it was from Percy's weight on top of him or from fear. "Get a job at Bonfils, he said, we'll pretend we let you go. Just mess fings up a bit, he said, and he'd waive half the debt. I had to do it, Percy! Just nick some paperwork, that was all he wanted. Mess up some deliveries. Ruin some labels. Cause 'em hassle, he said, while they're getting ready for the Awards."

"You stupid, stupid boy," Percy growled. "One for gamblin' in the first place, two for bitin' the hand that feeds y'."

"Take it easy, Percy." Tate was worried Percy would yank Jamie's head off, but he didn't feel like calling him off completely, not just yet.

Another set of running footsteps arrived at the group. "Where's my security card?" Stuart was blustering, anger and panic in his eyes. "That's the third time I've lost it this month, don't know what the hell makes me so bloody careless nowadays. I need it to get back into Packaging. Jamie, have you picked it up for me like the other times?" He stopped, staring with shock at Jamie on the floor. "What the hell's going on?"

"Y've been usin' Stuart's pass to get about, haven't you?" Percy gave Jamie an extra shake, as if to dislodge more words. "What else have y' done?"

Jamie wailed. "Let go! I only meant to put the

wind up 'im."

"What? Who?" Tate asked.

Jamie groaned. Percy was still sitting on him. "Tristram wasn't happy wiv what I did, see? It wasn't enough, he wanted more information. Wanted a look at the new bubbly! I shifted boxes around so I could get to the good stuff quickly, was gonna add a bottle to a usual delivery, then drop it off at Fenchurch's along the way. But Prince Harry was nosing around, like he knew what I was up to, what I'd done. I thought it'd scare him off if he had an accident."

Percy was very red-faced. "Did y' loosen the straps on the shelvin' that day? No other way that would've happened. Do y'know how bloody dangerous that could have been, boy?"

"Just to scare him!" Jamie repeated piteously. "I didn't think it'd fall like that, honest!"

"And today?" Alex barked at him. "What were you doing today?"

"Get Percy off me! I was only gonna take one bottle—"

"Just one would have been enough to cause Bonfils inestimable damage," came a deep voice from behind Tate.

Everyone spun around, and even Jamie turned his head toward the voice. A tall, handsome, mature man stood in the doorway of the warehouse, dressed incongruously in a beautifully tailored three-piece suit. Behind him stood Tina Archer, a look of fearful regret on her face.

"Mr. Charles?" Louise said, still gathering her breath after chasing Jamie down.

"Dammit. Papa." Alex whispered so quietly, probably only Tate could hear his weary resignation.

"It seems Tina returned from her holiday none too soon to bring me up to speed," Charles said grimly. "Please climb off the young man, Mr. Grove, and call the police at once."

Tate fussed over Percy in his office while they waited for the police to arrive, and Alex and his father watched over the now openly weeping Jamie.

"You're meant to be in hospital," Tate scolded him.

"I left," Percy said bluntly, his grimace showing his distaste at having been taken there in the first place. "There were things to attend to here. I'm fine, boy, don't fuss. It was just a bit of extra sleep, for which I'm truly and wholly ashamed."

"It wasn't your fault. Jamie had a tub of his mum's sleeping tablets in his pocket. I reckon he slipped a handful into your drink so he could have uninterrupted time to nose about in the warehouse."

"Yeah, I guessed that. I've been thinkin' things through while I was laid up. If I'd been quicker to go look for him, we wouldn't have had this farce today, but I stupidly—"

"—fell asleep on your way through the bays." Tate could have bitten his tongue at the stark look on Percy's face. "But like I say, it wasn't your fault.

245

And he put you on a chair. He obviously didn't want you to come to harm, lying on the floor where you dropped."

"Stupid boy," Percy still grumbled. Tate didn't know if he meant Jamie or Tate.

"I warned Edward Fenchurch that it would be a troublesome distraction if he let Tristram open his own disreputable business," Charles said from the doorway.

Tate tried not to yelp. Damned man kept creeping up on them!

"Not exactly a den of iniquity, Papa. Just a modest bookmakers shop, with a few fruit machines on the side," Alex said, appearing at his father's heels.

"Enough for *you* to have noticed?" Charles raised a single, aristocratic eyebrow. Perhaps that was where Percy had picked it up from.

"Enough to lead Jamie astray," Tate said, probably a little too sharply. "Idjit that he is."

"Mr. Charles, sir." Percy interrupted, red in the face again but maybe for different reasons. "I'll have my notice on Mr. Somerton's desk by the end of the day."

"*What?*" It was a chorus from both Tate and Alex.

"All my fault for lettin' this go on." Percy shook his head with every point made. "I employed the boy in the first place, told Tate I was sorry for him not fittin' in at Fenchurch's, when he was still workin' for them all along. I missed all the mischief he got up to. And then I let myself get distracted by..." He was obviously aghast at saying it but screwed up his courage. "A cup of hot chocolate."

Charles Bonfils looked amazed. And was that a smile teasing the edge of his mouth, one he was trying to suppress?

Before Charles could reply, Alex pushed in front of his father. "As Alexandre Bonfils, and a member of the family company, I refuse to accept this man's resignation. In fact, he's a damned hero, and should be promoted."

A ripple of voices rose behind the two Bonfils men, where the more persistently inquisitive staff had gathered outside the office. Tate winced. Alex's secret was truly out now—the warehouse rumor mill would start grinding in exactly five seconds flat.

"Thought as much," Percy muttered.

"What?" Startled, Tate stepped closer to him. "You knew who Alex was? When? How?"

"Don't y' ever read the bloody newsletters?" Percy grumbled. "I've known Mr. Charles since he took over this company from *his* father, and I can spot a son of his a mile off. Even with that cheap hair dye thing he's got goin'."

"Why didn't you tell me?"

"I reckoned there'd be a reason he was snoopin' around like an idjit boy," Percy said. "First I thought he was a spy for Head Office audit, which he kinda was, but not the way I dreaded. Then I thought it was a charity stunt. Or maybe one of those reality shows my missus watches all the time."

"I can't believe you didn't tell me." Tate shook

his head slowly, stunned.

"Well, then I could see the pair of y' getting cozy—"

"*Cozy?*"

Percy deliberately ignored him. "So, I thought I'd let y' get on with it. Y'd sort it out between y'selves sooner or later."

Tate didn't know whether to yell at Percy or hug him for his misplaced tact. "We did," he replied, his voice softening as he glanced at Alex. "We have." Alex and Charles had withdrawn to the doorway and were conversing in low, urgent tones. Tate hoped Alex wasn't being fired—again.

Mr. Charles stepped back into the office. "Mr. Grove," he began in his most serious tone. "As my son rather impetuously but honestly said, I will not accept your resignation. It is completely unwarranted. In fact, I will be promoting you to Assistant Manager of the warehouse from the first of next month."

For once, Percy was struck speechless.

"And Mr. Somerton?"

Tate straightened, determined to face his boss with courage and confidence in what he'd done. "Mr. Charles, sir. I'm really sorry about all this—"

"Why should you be?" Charles interrupted. "You've brought the perpetrator to justice. We've been lax with security, though none of us could have anticipated such a ramshackle campaign as this. I'll be speaking to Edward Fenchurch later today to let him know what his son has been up to. I suspect the betting shop will soon be removed from the Fenchurch portfolio. And I will be demanding assurances from Tristram's father that this pathetic attempt at industrial espionage was nothing more than a spoiled child's petulance."

"Kids, eh?" Alex said cheekily, then paled as his father turned to him.

"And *you.*" Charles glanced back over Alex's shoulder at the staff gathered outside the office. He didn't say a word but watched and waited until they all scurried away. Mobile phones were already in their hands, to spread the latest gossip.

"You, Alexandre, have been astonishing."

"In, you know... a good or bad way?" Alex asked.

"Did you think you could rummage around in the company records on a Sunday without someone alerting me? And no, it wasn't that poor manager you bullied on his day off, but someone who takes the time to examine Head Office movements on *her* day off."

"Bloody Tina," Alex muttered.

"Tell me, why on earth were you unofficially working in Bristol in the first place, and why didn't I know a thing about it?"

"Now wait a moment," Tate found himself saying. "Alex has been determined to protect this company from the very beginning." Charles's expression was inscrutable, Alex's was shocked, yet he stared at Tate with sparkling eyes. "He should be praised for what he's done. I reckon," he added quickly.

Charles nodded slowly, then turned again to his son. "You have a fine champion here, Alex. What do you say on your own behalf?"

"I wanted...." Alex paused, perhaps unable to

articulate that in front of his father.

"To be your own man, yet also a Bonfils man. To help the company. Yes, I understand that now." Charles hesitated for only a second, then put his hand on Alex's arm. "I think that we may discuss at the next board meeting a role for you going forward. Maybe in Human Resources, as you've proved so knowledgeable about staff motivation."

And to Tate's delight, it was Alex's turn to be speechless.

Tate and Alex travelled home together that night after work on the bus, Alex having returned the hire car. Tate had secretly hoped for a lift, especially as the bus was unusually crowded, but he supposed it was time to get back to reality.

"Why did you want to see the staff application forms?" Alex asked as they swayed side by side, squashed up in the wheelchair and baby buggy area. "When we were at Head Office? I still have the copies."

"I have the forged customs declaration form," Tate said. "I think we'll find Jamie's handwriting matches to that."

"Additional evidence. Good thinking." Alex nodded sagely as if he were masterminding the final Agatha Christie-type denouement of a crime. "In case Percy hadn't squashed him until he confessed wholeheartedly to his crimes."

"Alex," Tate warned him, though he couldn't

help smiling. The woman across from them had caught the bit about "crimes" and someone being squashed and looked very alarmed. Alex made an exaggerated zipping motion across his mouth—inevitably another thing he'd picked up from the Packaging staff—and was quiet for the rest of the journey.

The house seemed too quiet to Tate. Then he caught sight of Louise in the kitchen with the family and knew she'd told them the whole story. They all stared with awe at Alex as he followed Tate into the room.

"Okay, kids," Tate said firmly. "He's still the same bloke, we're all still the same. I don't want any weird or gushy behavior."

Hattie turned to Hugo and they both mouthed "gushy?" and rolled their eyes.

"It's time for Amy's bath, and has anyone taken Freddie out? Then I need help with supper and the laundry—"

"All done," Gran interrupted gleefully. Everyone nodded vigorously, even Freddie on the kitchen floor at Gran's feet.

Louise chipped in. "They wanted to get things done before you came home. Sausage and mash is in the oven, and all homework's finished. They want the whole story, Tatty!"

Tate blinked. He felt strangely disconcerted. "Okay. So I just need to get up to speed on what's happened while I was away."

Louise took his arm. She wore the studiedly patient expression she used for when someone elderly was feeling under the weather. "One night away, Tatty. That's all it was. You mustn't worry so much. The kids have been fine. Gran and I have looked after them. Amy washed her own hair for the first time last night, and we decided the twins will be in charge of laundry from now on. And maybe, with my help and a new chores rota, Gran can take time out for that holiday in Ibiza her bowling friends are planning."

"But wait a minute—"

"Tatty, what I'm trying to say is that, although they love you to bits, it's time for some *you* time, too. They don't need you worrying twenty-four hours of the day. They're growing up—"

"Regressing, in my case," Gran said airily.

"And they want you and Alex to have time to enjoy your relationship."

"What? Oh." Tate was truly touched, truly stunned, truly... scared. "But Alex won't be working at the warehouse any longer, he'll have a new job in London. He has his own place there, too."

Alex cleared his throat. "Way to answer for me, Tatty," he said with a frown that had more than a hint of mischief about it. "Maybe I want to stay in Bristol. I can handle my job at any location."

"You...?" Tate seemed to be losing the power of articulate speech.

"We want him to stay. We love Alex," Amy said, as firmly as if she'd brook no more discussion on the topic.

"Everyone loves him, Tate," Louise added. She leaned in to mutter in his ear, "Don't be a dick about this, BFF. Grab him while you can. What have I always said? You snooze, you lose."

"He loves you," Hattie said. "So he'll stay. He makes good crumpets. Much more butter than Gran lets us have."

Tate blinked hard and waited with bated breath for Hugo's response.

"So if he's the boss's son, he's got lots of money now, right?" Hugo said. "That's great. He can get me and Hattie new footballs."

"Only at Christmas," Alex said, with a wink at the H's.

"Sensible boy," Gran murmured by Tate's ear.

What could Tate do? It was all too much, too much love, too much hope, too much confusion and shock.

He turned and left the kitchen.

Gran came and found him in the living room. For once, she didn't immediately turn on the TV.

"Gran?" For the first time in a long while, he turned to her as his own parental figure. "What should I do? It's all been a shock. He's not the person I thought he was."

"Don't be stupid, boy," she snapped back. "That's *exactly* what he is. A real diamond. It's just the setting that's changed."

Tate couldn't disagree with that. "It wasn't real. He lied to me."

"He was playing a game, like one of Amy's ridiculous 3D puzzles. But, unlike her, he's a grown man and realises how stupid he was. He's seen the error of his ways."

Tate found himself smiling, unbidden. "How do you know? How can *I* know?"

"Tate, you have to let go."

"Of what?"

Gran's voice was soft. "Of your pride, your fear. Of a misplaced desire to be your parents. They would want us—*you*—to live your own life. We're a team now, and we're finding our own strengths."

"I miss them so much." Tate could barely whisper.

"I know. They've gone from life, my darling boy, I know that as well as you do, and I mourn it every day. But they're still in our hearts. And now you have a chance to bring a new heart into your life." She looked at him with fond, teary eyes and grabbed him in a huge, warm hug. Then slightly spoiled the sentimentality by hissing in his ear, "Don't fuck it up, boy!"

Alex had shamelessly embellished the tale of their intrepid adventure—about the speed he'd driven to and from London, the blinding moment they discovered Stuart's pass had been used, Tate's courage in tackling Jamie, and Percy's even more courageous one—in every retelling.

"When I believe Percy's never even played rugby!" Alex told the kids, having acted out the tackle. "Astonishing innate knowledge of back row strategy, I must say."

Now he and Tate were left alone in Tate's

room. No one had suggested setting out the sofa downstairs, though Gran had ostentatiously rushed the kids to bed before the issue arose. Tate and Alex undressed slowly, stopping to touch each other's hand now and then, to sneak a tired kiss by Tate's wardrobe as they hung up their shirts.

"What do we do now?" Tate said quietly.

"I was sort of hoping for reunion sex," Alex said frankly.

Tate chuckled. "Maybe soon. But I mean about you and me. How we make this work."

Alex swallowed hard. "Does that mean... you want to? Make it work, I mean?"

Tate let his grin grow. "Yes. God, yes!"

Alex grinned too. "I'm on the case, then. I've already appointed an agent to sell my London property. If you don't want me to stay here, I can buy somewhere in town instead. I also have Papa's PA working on a fully equipped office in Bristol, so I can work near you, if not with you."

"That's fast!"

"Tina is very good, I owe her a lot as a friend and colleague. Even if she ratted on me to Papa as soon as she got back from her holiday and discovered I wasn't anywhere to be found." He sat down on the bed and drew Tate down beside him. "If this is all too fast, tell me. But I'm not going away. Papa was right, I want to be my own man as well as a Bonfils one. And that means not letting go of the best thing I got out of this daft scheme of mine."

"You mean the dark hair?" Tate said slyly. When Alex laughed, he ran his hand through

Alex's silky hair, then leaned his head onto Alex's shoulder. Slowly, their breathing settled into a similar pace.

"You stood up to my father," Alex murmured in an awed tone. "For me."

"Yeah. I protect my own," Tate whispered and tugged Alex tighter.

Alex sucked in a breath. "Can you... possibly... bear the *money* thing? Because I want us all to enjoy it."

"No spoiling, though."

"Jesus, Tate. I understand that for the kids, but all I'm talking about is a Game of Thrones box set for Gran—"

Tate glared up, but Alex was wiggling his eyebrows and, dammit, Tate had to laugh. "Am I going to be some kind of kept man?"

Alex looked unusually serious. "I want to keep you, but not like that. Not like a bribe."

The time had come, Tate realised, to reassure the usually so assured Alex Bonfils. He shifted on the bed, took Alex's face in his hands, and kissed him firmly. "You don't need money. I love you already."

"I... what? You do?" Alex's eyes lit up. "So you don't have a wish list like the rest of the family?"

Tate couldn't have described how happy he felt when Alex said "the" family, rather than "your" family. Maybe Alex didn't even realise how he'd absorbed them—and been absorbed by them—so joyously. "Um. Wish list?"

"Box sets for Gran, like I said. Footballs and guitar lessons for the twins. A robot for Amy, preferably one with full AI, she says, but at the least a fully interactive vocabulary. And luckily Freddie can't write, or I suspect there'd be dog toys specified as well."

Tate laughed, and Alex hugged him closer.

"See? No Somerton jet planes, no holiday homes, no designer knickers. This family will keep our feet on the ground. Though now I can revert to being sickeningly rich, there will be a few things on my own behalf...."

"I can guess," Tate said. "A decent coffee machine at the warehouse. New socks every time there's a hole, so you can give up darning. A *car.*"

They laughed together now, long and hard, and that somehow morphed into deep kissing. When they broke for a breathless moment, Tate found Alex had a final question for the day.

"If I *could* bribe you, what would it take?"

Tate gave it serious thought. Who hadn't dreamed of winning the lottery, or inheriting a huge sum? "Contributions to local causes. A donation for the playground equipment. Better shower facilities at the warehouse for those who cycle to work. A range of quality but less expensive Bonfils wines, so the staff can drink as well as the management."

"Maybe monthly wine tastings. Excellent idea! I'll look into it as a staff perk." Alex's eyes gleamed with the advent of ideas. "Nothing for you, personally?"

Tate licked his lips and gathered up his courage. "Well.... You, staying here with me."

Alex's gaze held him for a long, long moment.

Then, "Consider it done," he said softly.

Tate's heart leaped. "And maybe one night," he added slyly, "I'd like us to smuggle ourselves back into the warehouse, turn off the CCTV, and meet in my office."

Alex flushed, very deeply, and very attractively.

"And you know what would happen next," Tate murmured into his ear, then nipped at Alex's ear lobe. "Let's start practicing that tonight!"

# EPILOGUE

Three months later

"So. Tell me what you think." Alex leaned over the carved white table on the tree-lined patio and gently tapped a fingernail on the glass of wine in Tate's hand.

"Give a guy time to think about it," Tate said with a cheeky smile. It was late afternoon and the air had settled into a peaceful stillness. They sat in the charming garden of the Fairweather Vineyard, after all the tourists and almost all the staff had gone home. This was where the grapes for Angel's Breath were grown, and Alex had confessed it was one of his favorite places to unwind.

Tate could understand that. The countryside around Bristol was lovely, but this was farther into Devon, nearer the coast, and further from any city influence. They'd arrived in the afternoon, and Alex had taken Tate on a tour of the site. The sky was clear of all but wispy cloud, and the smell of the countryside was sharp and sweet. Tate had seen pictures of all the vineyards that supplied Bonfils wine, but had never actually strolled among the vines, ambling on the rich grass between the rows, watching the leaves ripple in the breeze and the bunches of grapes hang pendulously on stalks that looked barely up to the job.

"They're almost ripe and ready for picking," Alex said. "That'll happen later in the summer. Maybe we could come and help out, like Henri and I used to do."

"I'd like that," Tate said.

"Now, back to the tasting." Alex gestured sternly at the small selection of glasses in front of Tate, each one half-full of sparkling white wine. "Don't make me wait for my dinner any longer. Do you know what powers of management I had to conjure up in organising time away from our darling family? Just so that we could have these few days together."

*Our family.* For Tate, that was never going to get old. "Hurts me to admit it, but I couldn't have done it as efficiently." It was the start of the summer holidays, when everybody would usually be at home full-time, but somehow Alex had arranged for the H's to stay at a friend's house for the week, Amy's acceptance on a science tutoring course much to her ecstatic delight, and Gran's delighted inclusion on a residential *Sounds of the 50s* trip at the local Butlins.

"That's because you don't delegate," Alex said promptly. "You run yourself ragged trying to juggle priorities, and you see any slip of control as a personal, potential failure."

Tate stared at him. A few months ago, if someone had said the same to him—and, in fact, Louise often had—Tate would have leaped to the defensive. Yet now he could see that he probably *had* been setting himself an impossible standard and ignored everything else he needed in life. Like time to be himself; to read a book all the way through; to pursue the sommelier course he'd recently been accepted for, and without any help from the Bonfils family themselves; and to be with Alex.

But right now, he didn't resent Alex for saying it. Alex was almost as bad on the self-sacrifice, after all. He'd sat up with Freddie the night the dog was ill. He was first along the landing to comfort Amy when she had occasional night terrors. And he attended many of the school meetings as the children's co-guardian when Tate had a late shift. In fact, rumor had it that the school were begging him to be a governor. Alex couldn't help charming people, Tate knew that as well as anyone. His frankness and enthusiasm were captivating. But only Tate had Alex to himself in the evenings, to wind down with and take to bed.

He took his time over the three wines. He looked first, admiring the shine of them, the clarity, the delicate yellow. Then he swirled them slowly inside the glass, watching how the droplets clung to the sides, judging the alcohol content.

"For God's sake," Alex muttered, though he was grinning. "You don't have to show off for me. I don't want to miss the entrees, remember? The crème fraiche is made on a nearby farm, and with smoked salmon it's heavenly."

Tate crinkled his nose, then smelled the wines slowly, one by one, savoring the light fizz under his nose.

"Sip the damned things," Alex said. His eyes were alight now with anticipation. "You're a bloody tease."

Tate sipped each slowly. He swallowed—he liked to do that, to feel the texture in his throat as well as his mouth—and took a mere sip of water between each one.

"Well? Well?"

"This one." Tate pointed at the third glass. "It's by far the best. Smooth, yet an exciting sparkle on the tongue. The grape flavor is richer, too, without adding to the weight of the bouquet."

"Yes!" Alex punched the air, then pulled his arm back down, embarrassed. "That's the Angel's Breath, you know."

"I guessed," Tate said with a smile. The sun here caught the highlights in Alex's blond hair, though darker strands still lingered. Tate liked them: it was a fitting illustration of the many layers to his lover's personality. "It's the very best taste. You know why?"

"Years of blending and experimentation? The English soil? The relentless rain at certain times of the year?"

"It's the taste of you," Tate said simply, and shockingly frankly. Alex had brought him happiness and friendship and adventure, alongside a freedom Tate had never thought he'd find again. One day he'd pluck up the courage and say all that aloud. In the meantime, he lifted his glass in a toast of love to Alex Bonfils. And from the besotted look on Alex's face, he didn't think he needed the words anyway.

After dinner, they sat back out on the patio, finishing a bottle of the esteemed Angel's Breath. Alex reached into the bag he'd left on the table.

"Whose is that videocam?" Tate asked.

Alex was swamped with sudden guilt. "You know, don't you?"

"What? That it's Hugo's? That you bought it for him? Of course I do."

"It wasn't too expensive," Alex rushed to justify himself. "He's got a really good eye for video composition, and it's good to have a record of all that's happened in the last few months—"

Tate's hand on his arm stopped him. Then Tate's mouth on his stopped him for even longer. "I know. I'm not angry. Hugo loves it. Though we may have to restrict usage—he filmed me yelling at the football on TV last week, then Freddie on Gran's lap the other evening, both of them slack-jawed and snoring. But do you really think I'm such a spoilsport I'd stop you treating the kids?"

"I know you're awkward about my money—"

"Only when it's wasted. Or you spoil the kids too *much*. And while we're on the subject, what about all the other gifts?"

"I'm sorry?" Alex had hoped for a greater impact, exposing the undercover boss thing, but unfortunately most people seemed to know all about it by the time he confessed, so there wasn't a lot to expose. But what he liked most of all in the

TV program was when the boss then rewarded people for their good service, so he'd thrown his full efforts into *that* bit.

"Percy has his promotion, but you still treated him and Mrs. Grove to a seaside holiday."

"We'll go and visit them there, too," Alex said eagerly. "There are apparently machines where you can slide pennies down a chute and they nudge novelty prizes over the edge. Hattie's going to show me the best technique."

"Then Stuart got an F1 experience, he hasn't stopped talking about it since. And Penny in Packaging has an all-expenses paid evening at the club of her choice—"

"But that's got a secondary motive, because it's for two—"

"And yes, she's going to take Louise." Tate grinned. "Then there are the staff showers you had installed. The secure bike racks. A day off for everyone on their birthday. Free cakes at break times. A staff children's Christmas party. And the kitchen you put in so that we can make our own hot lunches, plus have decent tea and coffee instead of vending machines."

"I mean, that's a Health and Safety issue, isn't it? Those plastic cups are a scalded lap waiting to happen."

Tate frowned slightly. "The only problem is when you try and make me wear ridiculously expensive clothes."

"God, but you looked good in London. I could hardly keep my hands off you." Alex found it difficult to speak steadily when he remembered

Tate at the Heritage Wine Awards, just a couple of nights ago. The way Tate had stood his own ground, proudly by Alex's side all evening, the way he'd answered boldly and knowledgeably to all that nonsensical industry small talk. Alex hadn't pulled any strings at all to get Tate accepted on a management fast track at Bonfils—with another pair of helping hands in the family, and the bliss Alex insisted he brought to Tate's life nowadays, Tate had taken that opportunity as soon as he could.

"Is that what you're watching now?" Tate asked, gesturing at the camera.

The UK Heritage Wine Awards ceremony had been too long, too stuffy, with warm wine and bland buffet food. But Alex was inordinately proud that Bonfils scooped the Gold Award for Angel's Breath, and also several other wine awards. Charles Bonfils had been seen to greet Edward Fenchurch with politeness, but a certain amount of coolness. Edward Fenchurch's son Tristram had not accompanied him.

However, Charles Bonfils's sons had. Henri and his wife were glowing with pride, and networked with the industry professionals in their usual, smooth, sophisticated way. And Alexandre had been unusually well behaved, and escorted by his new partner Tate Somerton, with a new sexy haircut and wearing a Hugo Boss suit that looked like it had been made for him—which it had, despite Tate's protests.

But both Alex and Tate had been glad to escape the venue at the earliest opportunity. They'd politely refused to attend any of the post-award parties, and instead they had a quiet steak meal with the family, who'd travelled to London with them. Then they stayed in a modest London hotel for the night—Alex had insisted on an overnight stay so the adults could all drink—and the next morning, Gran took the children home. He and Tate had a short break planned on their own. It had all been arranged in secret, partly to escape any media interest from them venturing out to this red-carpet event, but mainly because they needed some time alone.

"Let me see."

Alex snuggled up closer to Tate so they could share the screen.

They'd snuck out of the awards venue by the side entrance to meet up with everyone. Hugo's video started with an alarming close-up of Tate's face as the twins ran forward to meet him, accompanied by peals of laughter from Hattie behind the camera. Then Hugo had adjusted the zoom and taken a panoramic view of the group on their way to supper.

Gran wore a surprisingly sophisticated velvet skirt suit, though Alex assessed the style as around twenty years out of date, and her hair was an alarming shade of copper. Hattie was beside her now, grinning at the camera. The H's had worn matching trouser suits in a vividly bright tartan fabric, with the familiar—to Alex, at least—eclectic trademarks of a Vivienne Westwood design. After Alex's introduction to the designer, and their fittings at the studio, the twins had been fawned over by the whole Westwood team. Alex wondered, slightly nervously, how long it'd be before the H's were on the pages of celebrity magazines themselves. He and Tate would fight that as long as they could, and should.

The camera angle slid quickly sideways, back toward the door Tate and Alex had just stepped through.

"There's Papa," Alex murmured.

"I had no idea what he'd say," Tate said. "Whether we'd be in disgrace for creeping out early—"

"Which we weren't, as I told you, he's confessed in the past he'd like to do the same—"

"—and then Amy just marched up to him and asked to interview him for her school project on money. I think most of her class are writing and drawing different currencies of the world. *Amy* wants to do a report on the fallout of the banking crisis across retail industry." Tate winced at the memory, but Alex laughed.

They watched Amy in her best pink princess frock, but with a sturdy messenger bag over her shoulder, waylay Mr. Charles. They couldn't hear exactly what she said but saw her pull out a *Frozen* notebook and pen, and start listing her questions. Listening carefully, Mr. Charles was blinking hard.

"She's so bright," Tate sighed. "I'm so impossibly proud of her. But my God, I was mortified she ambushed him like that."

"She'd be a great journalist if she chose." Alex put one arm around Tate to hug him in sympathy and pointed with his free hand at the screen.

"Look. This is where Papa put on his sternest business face, told her he'd get his people to talk to her people, and made an exclusive appointment for her to visit our Head Office."

Amy had turned away, her little cheeks very flushed and a huge grin on her face. Alex had never loved his father more than in that moment. Though Papa might have to protect his company against a hostile takeover from the likes of Amy Somerton one day.

"And here's Papa wishing us the best."

Hugo had pointed the camera up to get a good angle on the tall Mr. Charles Bonfils as he bade the family goodbye for the evening, with a gracious handshake and, "Good night, Alexandre, Tate. Thank you for sharing this evening with us, and for all you've done to help bring us this award."

Alex watched his own startled expression as he went to shake Papa's hand but was drawn into a full body hug. He didn't think he'd ever seen Papa show so much emotion. *Well, well, well.* Maybe the family hadn't been as disturbed as Alex had feared when he suggested all the changes. Note to self—start discussions on subsidised staff healthcare at the next board meeting. The camera angle swung again, this time to Tate's face. Hugo's giggle was very loud, as he was nearest the microphone.

"Tate, why's your mouth open like a goldfish's?"

Alex chuckled, half under his breath. It never failed, whenever they met Papa. Tate was going to take a very long time to get used to Mr. Charles calling him by his first name.

The night was drawing in, and they'd all but finished the bottle. There'd be more shared drinks in the future, but this first taste of Angel's Breath felt special to Alex.

"It's gorgeous." Tate was still admiring it. "It's light but it has a full flavor. More citrusy than I'd expected."

"We should make the most of it while we're here. I doubt we'll be drinking it on a daily basis back home."

He didn't miss the way Tate tensed. Was it from the mention of home? "Do you miss them? The family?" Alex asked tentatively. "I mean, we can leave early if you want. I know there's always so much to do in the house. I'll admit I had promised to help Hugo with editing his film, and supervise Hattie sewing a beret to go with her suit. And I'm meant to sit with Gran soon and take her through the family trees for the first series of *Game of Thrones*." He'd booked out one of the exclusive summer house apartments on the estate for the whole week, but if Tate wanted to get back quickly—

"Are you kidding me?" Tate almost snorted the wine out of his nose. "This is the only holiday on my own I've had since a disastrous long weekend in Greece with school friends. I burned scarlet all over, got food poisoning, and bitten by a ray. Never touched ouzo again in my life, either." He caught Alex's hand, tightly. "Seriously, though. I do miss them, after all I live with them every day of the year. But this is... magic, being here with you, in this glorious place."

"With lots of time for sex, as noisy and as boisterous as we like." Alex didn't mind sharing Tate's room at the house, though he'd decided to keep on his London apartment for the time being. They could use it as an overnight escape if they needed. And his office in Bristol had a luxurious couch in it, ostensibly for visitors, but also useful for the frequent making out sessions with Tate, when they both had overlapping break times.

Tate's grip sent goose bumps all up his arm; Tate's smile made his heart soar; Tate's wicked sense of abandon had him coming harder than he ever had in his life, whenever they let loose in bed....

No, that was never going to get old.

He touched his glass to Tate's and together they sipped the sparkling wine. "You know we could afford to move to a bigger place?" he said softly to Tate.

"*You* could. I can't."

"Tate...."

Tate smiled and touched his fingertips to Alex's lips. "No, it's my turn to tease now. I know what you mean, and I'm on board with that. Maybe one day. But at the moment, I don't want to disturb—"

"The family. Yes, I get it."

Tate's answering smile turned Alex's stomach upside down and curled his toes. "You do, don't you?"

Alex wanted to hold Tate closer than ever, until they were one body. Doubtless Amy and her fantasy robot would be working on such a future innovation in years to come. "They're a treasure to me. They're mine, if that's not too forward of me to say."

"You? Forward?" Tate gave a soft snort. "And when would that *not* be?"

Alex traced Tate's lips with his forefinger, wiping the dampness still lingering, loving the way Tate leaned into him. "Are you happy, Tate?"

Tate looked puzzled, then his eyes softened. "You're not the big, bold, arrogant sod you once were, Alex Bonfils. But that's our secret, right? I'm happy, yes. Very happy, exactly where I am right now."

That was what mattered to Alex, more than anything else. "This co-guardian thing with the children?"

Tate went still. "It's too much for you? I can understand that—"

"No. Never." Alex swallowed hard. He felt as nervous as if he were back in front of his school housemaster again after another prank gone wrong, or Papa, after another scandalous tabloid exposé. But thankfully that wasn't his life any longer, was it? "I would like to make it formal."

"Formal...?"

"You and me, Tate. As an official couple, looking after the family."

Tate's expression would have been comical if it wasn't so stricken. "Are you proposing to me?"

*Oh, God.* "Okay. Sorry. I mean, one day." Alex

felt so mortified, his skin heated all over. He was a bloody idiot; he'd been horribly clumsy with his words, too hasty with his intentions. "I mean, I know it's come out of the blue for you, but I think it'd be good for the kids, and make it much easier when we need to take turns at the official parenting jobs—"

"Just for the kids, eh?" Tate's voice was strangely flat.

*Fuck.* He'd done it again. What was it about this relationship with Tate, that he could put his foot in his mouth so spectacularly, so often? "I didn't mean that. I meant, because I want to be with you for the long term. Because this, this life with you, is what I want. *All* that I want." Tate was still staring at him and his lips were pursed tight. "I love you. Properly, sincerely, deeply. It's not just a whim, or a fashion. And I love the kids, and the things we all do together, and being part of your family, and I love you—did I say that already?— well, it always bears saying again, and I love—"

"Hush." Tate put his fingers on Alex's lips. "You don't give me any chance to answer. Must be because you've always been so certain of getting your own way."

"That's not—!"

"I know, you idjit. I love you too. And it's a yes."

"It is?"

Tate was laughing now. "Yes. Definitely yes. What you said, about loving the things we do together, Mr. Bonfils...."

Alex's hand lingered on Tate's thigh, tracing the pattern of the trouser fabric, and Tate's muscles beneath. "What exactly are you insinuating, Mr. Somerton?" But he didn't give Tate a chance to reply to *this* question. He slid his hand around the back of Tate's neck and brought him in for a long, sexy kiss with a lot of tongue. One of the candles on the table flickered gently, then finally snuffed out. Slowly, Alex drew back, and they sat there for a few moments more, silent and with their foreheads touching, their breath evening out in tandem.

"I don't think either of us needs much more practice in this," Tate whispered.

"You reckon?"

"But far be it from me to stop you."

Alex chuckled. With the dusk air cooling around them, the fresh smell of vines and hedgerows in the wind, and the taste of Angel's Breath still on Tate's lips, Alex grinned as he lifted Tate's chin and initiated another kiss.

This was the taste of a real fortune.

.

READ ON...

For excerpts from other Romancing the... books.

## ROMANCING THE ROUGH DIAMOND

BLURB:

Where trust is the most precious jewel of all.

When Mayfair jewellers Starsmith Stones wins the commission for a British gay royal wedding, CEO Joel Sterling is recommended to the brilliant young designer Matt Barth—only to discover Matt's the man with whom he shared an anonymous and passionate kiss on the celebration night.

Disenchanted with the commercial jewellery industry, Matt nowadays prefers muddy archaeological digs to designing. Openly resentful of Starsmith's hostile takeover of his family's firm, he is horrified at the realisation he'll be working with the man who engineered that deal—but the opportunity to create something fabulous and unique for the royal couple is too tempting to refuse.

Working as a team reignites the spark between Joel and Matt. But when betrayal from within Starsmith threatens both the project and Joel's confidence, will they have built enough trust to keep their newfound love as precious as the royal jewels?

## CHAPTER ONE

Joel Sterling's phone was going to burn a hole in the pocket of his suit trousers.

At the very least, it was causing havoc with the beautifully tailored fabric as his hand turned it over nervously every thirty seconds. It needed to ring, and it needed to ring *soon*. He'd been on tenterhooks all evening, ever since he was told the Royal Household would make a decision before the end of today.

And a boring industry awards dinner wasn't the best place to be when his mind was anticipating probably the most influential contract of his career. Tonight he'd smiled so often his cheeks felt numb, listened to small talk and dispensed plenty of his own, and shaken a hundred hands— or so it felt, at this late stage of the evening. He didn't often attend these jewellery trade events. As CEO of Starsmith Stones, he had a marketing and sales team to be the public face of the company, and he preferred to manage everything from the office. But there'd been a clash of diary dates, and he'd offered to cover tonight personally. Starsmith had a prestigious and long-standing reputation to maintain. It didn't occupy one of the prime sites on London's Mayfair by accident. So the occasional—if, yes, boring—awards dinner was probably covered within his job description.

But his phone needed to ring.

Claridge's historic London hotel was as glamourous as expected, and the catering had been superb. The Jewellers Guild always hired the best for their events. He'd been served by professionally alert and beautifully dressed staff, and the 1930s design of marble and mirrors made the setting the epitome of luxury and taste. He'd also attracted his fair share of curiosity and attention from his peers, whether with awe, admiration, or antagonism. It came with the job, he assumed, along with the additional novelty that he was young—still in his late twenties—and not from the usual moneyed or aristocratic background.

His reputation obviously preceded him, but he wasn't intimidated by that attitude. He knew he was exactly what Starsmith had been looking for when they headhunted him from his previous employer two years ago, straight into his senior position. He was a tough negotiator but could also charm in any boardroom. The network of international goldsmiths based in London also liked to deal with him. Admittedly, some of the old guard wanted to challenge him, to see how much he would bend under the weight of their "superior" experience. They'd been disappointed in that, to date. And some of the younger traders were just shit scared of him—he knew that too, even if it hadn't been whispered none too quietly behind his back on many occasions.

That was all fine. He'd fought hard for this role. He'd devoted all of his working adult life to the jewellery industry, to getting to this point. Starsmith Stones, under his leadership, was going to be one of the best players in the world. He'd make sure of that. Their profitability grew by the quarter, and the team he had around him was second to none. He was loving the life of a tough businessman—at the office, at least.

But tonight? Tonight that bloody phone needed to ring. The next call could change his whole career, maybe even his life. And Joel Sterling, cool negotiator, level-headed executive, and strategic planner, certainly wasn't one to make melodramatic statements like that—

Someone rudely nudged his elbow. "Don't usually see you out and about, socialising with us minions, Sterling. Have you had a chance to think about our European contract yet?"

The blunt question was from a salesman at Marchant's, a London silver merchant Starsmith had dealt with in the past. But Starsmith's premier pieces were traditionally struck in gold, and at the moment, Joel didn't have any need for more silver.

"Dan." He nodded, barely polite. He didn't like the man, though he knew he was on duty, whatever the setting. Business deals could be forged as easily in social situations as in the boardroom. "It's on my desk. You understand, Starsmith is not currently looking at producing another silver collection. But I have time scheduled tomorrow to go through the details."

The salesman, Dan Llewellyn, young and good-looking but with sweat on his brow either from nerves or too much drink, blustered, "No need. You can trust me, it's—"

"I will go through the details," Joel interrupted firmly, though without raising his voice, "in my own time. Then I will let you know if we have any interest."

"Is it the price?" Dan frowned. "I'm already down to the wire on margin. You guys are only interested in the bottom line, I know so—"

"I'm interested in the best product at a competitive cost."

"As long as it's lower than anyone else's in the market," Dan snapped back.

"I'm sorry?" Joel said, more sharply now. He was irritated because what Dan implied wasn't, in fact, true. Starsmith paid fair prices, but only for the highest quality product. It appeared Marchant's had far lower standards, and he'd heard their business practices weren't always above board. "I believe I just said that I'll let you know."

"Jesus." Dan looked angry and even more flustered. "You're a tough bastard, Sterling."

"I'm a thorough bastard." Joel sounded calmer than he felt. Was that vibration on his hip from a received text? His fingers itched to reach for it. "That's what Starsmith pays me for. Now please excuse me. I have other people to see."

He dodged swiftly out of the ballroom, leaving more than a couple of startled faces in his wake and darted into one of the more intimate, private bars. He was greeted with more stylish, 1930s-inspired décor, dark wood and red velvet furnishings, and an immediately reduced noise level. With relief, he saw it was barely occupied, apart from a middle-aged couple sitting in one of the small, snug booths, a young man at the horseshoe-shaped marble counter nursing a beer, and a bartender who was struggling to hide a yawn behind his hand. The night was drawing to a close, the attendees at the trade event would soon be moving on to clubs and restaurants in central London, and it looked like Claridge's residents were elsewhere too.

Joel paused at one of the empty booths, flipped open the button of his Tom Ford suit jacket, and pulled his phone from his pocket. He had a message to call the office. At last! He hit speed dial quickly. "Teresa? Are you still at work?"

"Finishing paperwork in peace and quiet," his PA, Teresa Manners, half whispered. "No one here but me and the cleaner, and he's at the other end of the corridor. Can you talk?"

After a quick glance around, Joel slipped into the booth, where he could rest on the stiffly upholstered seat and the high sides would shelter his voice. "Yes. What news?"

"I'm too old for this 007 stuff." Teresa chuckled. He knew she'd be shaking her immaculately coiffured head at his eagerness. "But don't worry, I fully understand the need for secrecy at this stage. Brace yourself."

For good news or bad? It was like waiting on school exam results all over again. "Tell me!"

She took pity on his impatience. "My unofficial contact at the palace called me as soon as they finished for the day. The commission is as good as ours. The palace will contact Starsmith tomorrow, and it'll be announced officially in next month's trade press."

"Three weeks' time!" Joel took a deep breath to try and calm his speeding pulse. The aroma in the bar was a rich mixture of wood polish, expensive fragrances, and good liquor. Joel thought he'd remember that smell forever as defining one of the best moments of his life. He realised he was grinning like a fool.

This news was life changing! For six long months, Starsmith had been in negotiations for a commission from the British Royal Family, the first in their company's history. Joel had initially heard about it from a casual comment at one of the networking lunches Starsmith hosted, where the guest list included celebrity friends of the aristocracy. The first gay wedding involving a member of the British Royal Family in direct line to the throne was seeking a London firm to provide jewellery for the grooms. Prince "Artie" Arthur, currently eighth in terms of succession— young, handsome, and with a twinkle in his eye to match his older brothers', William and Harry— was marrying his long-time boyfriend, the opera star and independently wealthy Paolo Astra. They were a gorgeous and eminently newsworthy couple, and the media was already wetting its pants at the thought of the coverage.

Joel's overwhelming desire had been to make that deal for Starsmith. The wedding date was still another six months away. But within twenty-four hours of the marriage announcement, he'd made a presentation to palace representatives, and knew it had gone well. He'd put his whole heart into it! Starsmith had already been informed they'd made the very short, select, and confidential list of approved firms.

And now Teresa's message was wonderfully welcome. Starsmith had won.

"Joel? Are you still there?" Teresa sounded wary. "While I have your attention, I've been asked to alert you about one of the acquisition deals on this month's schedule. It's Barth Gems, a small, independent jewellers that has been in financial trouble for some time. Our business development team identified them for potential takeover months ago, and we're due to sign tomorrow. But the owner is still wrangling a couple of the conditions. He's facing retirement, and it's a family business—there's a son involved, it seems. An awkward young man who isn't actually an acting member of the company, but who keeps throwing up obstacles to the final contract."

Joel tried to concentrate on business as usual, but his mind was racing ahead. "The team can handle it."

"I know. They just wanted you to know."

Joel didn't want to hear about obstacles. He wanted to cheer, dance, shout aloud with excitement. He was amazed the very air hadn't changed around him somehow, charged with his emotions. "Tell them to agree to the conditions," he said, in a moment of rashness. "I can't remember the specifics of the deal, though I'm sure it's not big enough to cause us serious financial grief. But we don't want any bad publicity for the company at this time. Not now we've got—"

"Hush, it's still a secret, remember," Teresa broke in with caution but then spoiled it by giving a very unbusinesslike yelp of delight. "Won't it be marvellous?"

"Yes. And thanks for staying on late to take the call. I would say take tomorrow off in return—"

"But that's when the work will start in earnest, right?" Teresa chuckled again. "No problem. You owe me plenty already. I'll just add it to your slate. And I'll be in at seven to start making calls to the team."

"Give my apologies to Dylan."

She snorted. "He's used to it by now."

Teresa had a loving husband, Dylan, and three kids. For a fleeting moment, Joel imagined having someone close to tell his news to. He couldn't remember the last time he'd gone home to anyone at all. Then he realised Teresa was still talking.

"—and I can't wait until it's common knowledge and I can tell the kids. They're mad for anything about the Royal Family."

Joel thanked her again and finished the call but stayed sitting in the booth for a while longer. He couldn't wait either, but mainly to get away from here and think through everything the royal commission would mean. It wasn't just the grooms' rings, but gifts for the whole wedding party, including VIP guests. So far, he hadn't dared bring anyone except Teresa and his head of design on board. He'd been scared of jinxing the deal. But although Starsmith's work to date had earned them notice, he knew this commission would demand something even better—a blend of modern style and traditional sophistication. His in-house design team was excellent, but maybe he should hire a freelancer to bring fresh inspiration. It would have to be someone both innovative and talented enough. *Project Palace*. Yes, that's what they'd call it. God! If they were successful, this could make Starsmith's the first choice of royal families across the world—

"You look like you need a drink. May I get you one?"

Joel looked up to face the man from the bar, who'd wandered over. He had a beer in each hand now, one of them held out toward Joel. His smile was quizzical, a little nervous. It was a very attractive smile. Joel found himself irresistibly drawn to it, to the underlying self-deprecation he saw, mixed with an undeniable hint of mischief. He was about as tall as Joel and of a similar age, with chestnut-coloured hair cut short at the sides and wavy on top, the hint of a dark beard, and sharp blue eyes. *Lovely, lively eyes.* He wore a dark suit that was smart but probably a few seasons old, and the heavy body under his white shirt hinted of strength and fitness. A man who worked outdoors, maybe. Joel hadn't seen him in the ballroom, though the suit implied he was on business of some kind. No tie, no identity lanyard, no slick, acquisitive arrogance in his manner. Joel was startled at how relieved he felt about that.

"Couldn't help seeing you smile," the stranger said bluntly. "After your phone call. Like some kind of private joke."

"I'm sorry?"

"Shit." The man frowned and shook his head. "Dammit, I'm the one who's sorry. My conversation is usually a lot more civil. I just meant... it was good to see someone so cheerful tonight. I'm not asking about the call—that's your business."

"Yes. It is."

The man looked irritated now. His expressions changed within seconds. Everything he thought seemed to show on his face. He apparently had no professional detachment. It wasn't the restrained behaviour Joel was used to, and he regretted there was no hint of the original, sexy grin.

"Just thought you may like to celebrate, whatever the hell it was," the guy said. "But you don't want a clumsy arse like me butting in." He put the beer down on the table in front of Joel and took a step back. "I'll leave you to it."

"Wait." The word escaped Joel without any further thought. He didn't know whether this was a pickup—wasn't sure whether he minded. He had plenty of advances when he did socialise in London, and he knew his position and power were attractive. He wasn't bad-looking either, though he didn't think he was particularly vain. But this guy apparently had no idea who Joel was, had just approached him with a simple expression of companionship. This guy who had a refreshingly blunt way of speaking that Joel hadn't found in the corporate behaviour so far this evening, who had thought to buy Joel a drink, when Joel could have drunk himself stupid several times over on Starsmith's account, and who... was hot.

What else did Joel have to look forward to when he got home, apart from plans for the workday ahead? And yes, dammit, even if he couldn't tell anyone why, he *did* want to celebrate.

"Join me," he said, smiling and gesturing at the cushioned seat beside him.

# ROMANCING THE UGLY DUCKLING

## BLURB:

Is this the makeover of a lifetime?

Ambitious fashionista Perry Goodwood lands the project of his dreams—track down a celebrity family's missing brother in the Scottish Highlands and bring him back to London for a TV reality show. But first he must transform the rugged loner into a glamourous sophisticate.

Greg Ventura has no use for high fashion. He lives on the isolated island of North Uist to escape the reminder that he's nowhere near as handsome as his gorgeous brothers and avoid the painful childhood memories of being bullied.

Greg wants nothing to do with city life, and Perry's never been outside London. When Perry is stranded on North Uist, this conflict seems insurmountable. But Greg is captivated by the vivacious Perry, and Perry by both the island and his host. However, Perry's one heartfelt wish remains: that ugly duckling Greg fulfill his potential as a swan.

## CHAPTER ONE

Somewhere along the line, at some distant, unremembered stage of a previous life, Perry Goodwood must have done something *really* good. His too small but tastefully decorated office in the Latham Agency, London, was currently full of men. Tall, dark-haired, dancing-eyed, perfectly groomed, shirt-straining-torso'd men. Four of them. *Brothers*, no less.

He hadn't seen such a fine selection of male gorgeousness since he was a young gay teenager with copies of *Men's Health* secreted under his mattress. And even then, the gorgeousness had been static, easily creased, and with eyes only for the camera. Today's exhibition was nothing remotely like that titillating but ultimately unsatisfying experience of his youth. This was, quite honestly, a lusty heaven come to life—and it was all happening in *his* office! Perry Goodwood, lowly assistant fashion designer, occasional actor/model, and makeover consultant to several TV stars. Well, B-list ones, at least. Admittedly, Perry's personal client portfolio—and any further plans for developing worldwide domination—was still a work in progress.

But someone, somewhere, had recommended his services to this astonishing group of Adonises. If Perry hadn't known that person was his rather creepy boss, Eddy Latham, he'd have offered to love them forever.

"So, Mr. Goodwood, can you help us?"

Perry blinked hard. Someone was talking to him. One of the gorgeous *brothers* was talking to him. The one who seemed older and in charge of the group. He was staring at Perry with earnest dark eyes. An errant curl teased his forehead, and the beautifully trimmed beard brushed his strong, manly jaw like a caress.

Perry's lower lip wobbled with excitement.

"It's a matter of total discretion, of course," the man continued. "My family can trust you on that, I'm sure."

Perry hadn't matched all the other names to the faces, partly because they all began with the initial G, and partly because his brain had shorted out after the third firm, warm, crushing handshake. But he recognised this hero at least. Geoffrey Ventura, Premier League footballer for the last ten years, with a hallowed place in the England squad for the last five, though Perry would've been hard-pressed to name the tournaments as he never watched football, just the footballers. But Geoff Ventura was also a darling of the press, one of the wittiest and most quoted sports celebrities in the media, and eldest sibling of a family notable for its testosterone-fuelled sportsmen and their glamourous social partners.

Perry had suffered crushes on many a straight man in his time, but he didn't dare admit that, in his teens, he'd had a picture of rising star Geoff Ventura under his bed. And now the man himself was here. In Perry's office.

*Heavens, you already know all this. Get a grip, Perry!*

"Of course you can trust me," Perry said. "We pride ourselves at the Latham Agency in delivering what our client wants in a professional and discreet way." God, he sounded like he was reading from the glossy brochure.

"Mr. Latham told us we could rely on you," Geoff said. "I'm so reassured."

That was amazing in itself. Perry couldn't remember the last time Eddy Latham, the owner of the PR agency, had been that positive about Perry's career prospects. Eddy wasn't the world's best at staff motivation. But for the moment, Perry's cynicism was squashed by the glow from Greg Ventura's praise. "I'll certainly do my best for you. What is it exactly you need?"

"It's not us who needs it," said another brother at Geoff's shoulder.

Perry had placed all the other Venturas by now. This slightly more scowly one was Gerry, ex-university rower and now something Big in City Finance. He'd married a supermodel who was purportedly related to the ill-fated Russian royal family, if *Who's Doing Who?* was to be believed. It was the magazine of choice in the agency staff room, bought and pored over religiously every week by Perry's friend and colleague, Antony.

"Gerry's right," Geoff said. He looked slightly uncomfortable. "We need your help for our brother Greg."

Perry didn't remember a fifth brother in any of

the celebrity interviews. "There's another one like you?"

Gerry Ventura snorted.

"Gerry, please," Geoff said warningly.

"Greg didn't want to be part of the family, Geoff. He's the one who scarpered off as soon as he was old enough, didn't he? Don't see why we're chasing after him now."

"He ran off?" Perry was having trouble keeping up, let alone understanding what it had to do with him.

"Greg lives elsewhere," Geoff said smoothly.

"Fucking middle of nowhere," Gerry muttered.

"But he's still family," contributed one of the remaining two brothers. They looked a few years younger than the others, just as well-dressed but considerably livelier, and more alike in the flesh than in photos, which was to be expected as they were the twins, George and Gareth. They'd both had short-lived but controversial careers in movies, and now had investments in a long list of London nightclubs. Lived most of their lives in those establishments too, as Perry recalled from media gossip.

"And that's the point, isn't it?" said the other twin. The two of them rocked back on their heels, crossing their arms and presenting a brace of smug, mirror-image grins.

Perry looked to Geoff for guidance. "The point...?" He only had two seats in his office, which he'd offered to Geoff and Gerry at the start, then taken Gerry's seat himself because Gerry hadn't seemed to want to settle. He now stood with the twins, all of them ranged behind Geoff like an imperial guard protecting their emperor.

Geoff leaned forward in his chair, reaching out a beautifully manicured hand to grasp Perry's, as if they were the only people in the world. The one thing that saved Perry's head from being turned by this personal attention—and it threatened to set him spinning more than that poor girl in *The Exorcist*—was that he remembered seeing Geoff use this tactic before in a TV interviewer.

"You see, Perry," Geoff said in his smooth, very persuasive way, "we have a commitment. A media contract."

"A potential contract," Gerry snapped.

Geoff's shoulders tensed but otherwise he ignored his brother, his gaze still fixed on Perry. "Yes, it's still potential at this delicate stage of the negotiations. And it's contingent on the whole family being involved—all the brothers. We all need to be available, and together."

Perry nodded slowly. Things were becoming clearer. "And your brother Greg isn't with you?"

Gerry snorted again. "Not in any bloody way."

Geoff bit his lip as if restraining his temper with difficulty. "Certainly not in terms of location. And not... well, not in his lifestyle choices either. That's why we've come to Latham's Agency. Greg needs to be back here in London with us—and looking his very best—by the end of next month to sign the deal."

"It's all or nothing," said Twin #1.

"All for one and one for all!" added Twin #2 gleefully. He turned to Twin #1, and they high-fived each other.

"Bloody kids," Gerry muttered.

Perry was still floundering a bit, but before he could ask any more questions, his boss stuck his head around the door. "Everything going well?" he asked with loud, blustering, and rather insincere jollity.

Perry resisted rolling his eyes. At times like this, Eddy Latham was the worst kind of boss, in that he wanted to be in on all the projects but was never prepared to do any of the work. "Everything's fine, Mr. Latham."

Unfortunately that wasn't enough incentive for Eddy to withdraw. Instead he eased himself into the room with the other five men, taking up a position beside Perry's chair. Eddy was only five foot six, but about the same measurements around the middle. As the Venturas took several steps to the side to accommodate him, Perry couldn't help comparing it to a rush-hour commuter jumping onto the train just as it pulled away and squeezing everyone else along inside the carriage.

"As I suggested, Peregrine's your man," Eddy said confidently. He was the only person who ever used Perry's full name. "He launched Mandy Price, the glamour model turned TV presenter. And Professor Ignatius Froome, that academic who never brushed his hair or cleaned his teeth before Peregrine took him in hand. I'm sure you remember them both? The makeovers were impressive. My agency's credentials speak for themselves."

Unfortunately, Perry remembered both of those obstreperous clients with nothing less than horror. He'd long suspected Eddy passed all the lost causes to Perry so that if Perry succeeded, the agency would benefit, but if he failed to deliver the makeover—well, it'd be Perry's fault alone. This wasn't going to be one of *those* jobs, was it?

Geoff Ventura glanced at Perry. "This is far more than a cosmetic job."

"I can do far more than a cosmetic job," Perry said smartly.

A small smile twitched at the edge of Geoff's lips. "Yes, I'm sure you can."

"Geoff, you're not serious?" Gerry snapped. "This can't work."

Geoff frowned at his brother. "We have no other choice."

"Rubbish! I say we negotiate without Greg."

Geoff shook his head. "They won't agree to that. I've tried. It's all or none of us."

"No fucking way." Gerry's face grew darker. "They won't go with the Howells instead of us. They wouldn't be that stupid. A bunch of ponced-up shop boys and girls without an ounce of genuine talent between them? With us, they have real celebrity. We've all succeeded in our own field. We have true credibility. The public loves us."

Perry's ears pricked up. The Howells were another celebrity family from south London, and always in the popular media. They consisted of three wannabe supermodels, a loud-mouthed matriarch, and several young men with impossibly white teeth, and Perry followed their exploits avidly. Well, he *was* gay. And only human. In fact, it had been his mischief that renamed them in the office as the Howlers.

Geoff shrugged, but his expression had hardened. "The public loves them too. It's what the media does, Gerry. Chooses what makes the best TV, regardless of merit."

Perry leaned surreptitiously toward the twins, speaking half under his breath. "Are we talking about a TV deal here?"

Twin#1—possibly George—nodded vigorously. "A reality show series. You know, like the Kardashians? It'd be really big. The production company wants to feature a London family."

Gareth joined in. "They approached both us and the Howells, and they're filming simultaneous pilot episodes next month."

"A day in the life," George said breathlessly.

"Warts and all!" Gareth followed with a deep chuckle, though only he and George seemed to be finding this whole thing funny.

In fact, Gerry's face was like thunder as he leaned over to hiss at Geoff. "We need this show, you hear me?"

"Things not so rosy in the financial garden? I hear you've been overtrading in some of your more bullish deals," Geoff said snidely.

"Don't get high and mighty with me. *I* hear you haven't been chosen for the first team squad this season, so you'll be needing another income as well."

"For God's sake—!"

"Gentlemen, please!" Eddy cried, flapping his hands as if to cool them all down.

"I'm just saying that this is an opportunity we don't want to miss," Gerry growled, still glaring at Geoff. "And it's critical we all look good—that we all look *civilised*. We've got a reputation to maintain."

"Even Greg?" Geoff said tightly.

"Especially Greg," Gerry snapped.

The room fell silent for a moment. Geoff looked weary, Gerry still glared, and the twins tried, unsuccessfully in Perry's opinion, to look innocent of everything.

Perry asked tentatively, "About your brother Greg. Can you give me any idea what I'd be working with?"

"Go on," Gerry said to Geoff. "Show him."

With a low sigh, Geoff pulled out a photo from his jacket's inner pocket and handed it to Perry.

The first surprise was that the photo was of a teenage boy rather than a man. Wasn't Greg Ventura an adult like his brothers? It looked like an old photograph too: something about the fuzzy quality of the print. The boy was in the foreground, leaning back against a wooden fence in a field, scowling at the camera as if he wanted to attack it with the heavy spade he gripped in one hand. Perry could see his resemblance to the other Ventura brothers in his square jaw and smouldering eyes, but the similarity ended there. He had none of their rugged, elegantly styled good looks. He was tall and broad, but his limbs looked too large for his body, obvious in the clumsy way he slouched against the fence. His dark hair was all over the place, badly cut with lank tangles brushing his shoulders and hanging over his forehead. The clothes didn't do much to help, either. His jeans were patched in several places, and worn and stained over the knees. And in Perry's opinion, a faded flannel shirt was rarely a good look on such a young man. Was that dirt on the rolled-up sleeve, or something worse? Perry gave a private shudder.

The worst thing was the acne. Poor kid was covered with it, from chin to forehead, what Perry could see of his skin under the thatch of hair. No wonder he tried to hide his face. His nose was big in proportion to his cheeks, his eyes very widely spaced. That generous mouth might have been attractive in a smile, but instead it was twisted in a weirdly uneven and unpleasant scowl.

"Um. What is he... twelve? Thirteen?" Perry asked.

"Twenty-five at the moment," George said with a grin.

"Nearly twenty-six," Gareth added. "His birthday is in two months' time."

"But this photo—"

"It's the only one I could find," Geoff said shortly. For a brief moment, he looked pained. "That's him at our uncle's farm in Hampshire. We used to spend school holidays there."

"Ghastly place," Gerry muttered. "Wild animals and filth everywhere."

"Greg loved it!" George retorted.

"You're a snob, Gerry," Gareth added. The

twins didn't seem to have any shame in insulting their elders.

"He never liked having his photo taken," Geoff said, his gaze on the image.

"Not bloody surprised." That was Gerry again. "Look at the state of him! A grubby, lopsided, goblin-faced lump. I always said he was some kind of throwback. Nothing like the rest of us. No wonder we called him the Ventura Ugly Duckling."

"You mean you did," Geoff said quietly.

"No one ever contradicted me," Gerry said smugly, as if this was a familiar argument.

Geoff and the twins all flushed.

Perry took another look at the photo. He'd rarely seen a man's looks he couldn't improve with careful dressing and a good hairstylist, but he was struggling to decide where to start with Greg Ventura.

"Peregrine?" Eddy was giving Perry what he called a *pointed look*. "What's your plan of action?"

*My—what the hell?* Perry drew a deep breath. "Where is Greg now?"

"The Western Isles," Geoff said.

Perry had no idea where that was. He'd never been anywhere but London in his whole life.

Geoff continued, "We'll pay for everything, of course."

Perry could imagine Eddy's eyes lighting up with pound signs. The deal was already done, he could see, insurmountable challenge or not. "Okay. Well, if you'd like to bring him in to the agency, I can assess what needs to be done."

Gerry laughed. "Oh he won't come here."

"I'm sorry?"

Geoff bit back what looked like a long-suffering sigh. "I've rung him several times, but his phone never seems to be charged up."

"Or he's ignoring you," George muttered, then winked at Gareth.

"I sent him a letter in the end," Geoff said carefully, as if he was afraid of angrier words spilling out against his will, "explaining it all, and that it was time he came back to London. His reply was... well, brusque in the extreme."

"One creased postcard," Gareth said, with some glee. "Didn't even put enough postage on it. Geoff had to pay the excess on delivery."

"It said—" George added.

"I'm here to stay!" the twins chorused together.

Geoff sighed and stood, straightening his cuffs as if preparing to leave. "It appears he won't leave the Isles. At least, not at the moment. You'll have to go to him."

Perry blinked hard, scrambling to his feet in Geoff Ventura's wake. "Go where?"

Geoff peered at him as if he were mentally challenged. "To Scotland. We'll make the arrangements. Then you can do your magic with Greg right there, and bring him back in good time for the filming."

"Remember," Gerry added darkly. "He has to come willingly. He has to take part in the show with us all. And he has to look as *good* as us all. He can't show us up. The media will rip us to shreds if he appears in his ugly duckling mode."

"Go to Scotland?" Perry's attention was still fixed on that shocking nugget of news. He swung around to face Eddy, but Eddy wasn't meeting his gaze. "I can't do that!"

"Peregrine. It's only for a week or so. We'll talk about it later. Not now, please."

"I mean," Perry gabbled on, aware that the Venturas were looking at him with varying degrees of sympathy, amusement, and vindictiveness. "I have other clients. I have a flat, a social life. Weekly lunch with my mother."

Eddy turned to the Venturas and gestured to the door with his plump hand, albeit the space only allowed for single file exit from the room. "It'll be fine," he said pointedly.

Perry stood, watching them all walk across the office floor on their way out, where all he could hear was the floating thread of Eddy's voice, declaring gaily, "We'll be in touch!"

# ROMANCING THE WRONG TWIN

## BLURB:

How tangled can a romantic web get?

When gruff arctic explorer Dominic Hartington-George seeks sponsorship for his latest expedition, his London PA insists on a more media-friendly profile—like dating celebrity supermodel Zeb Z.

Zeb can't make the date, so he asks his identical twin, Aidan, to stand in for just one evening. Aidan, a struggling playwright, shuns the limelight to the extent people don't even know Zeb has a sibling, but he reluctantly agrees.

When the deception has to continue beyond the first date, Aidan struggles to keep up the pretence. Dominic likes his sassy, intelligent companion, and Aidan starts falling for the forthright explorer. But how long can Aidan's conscience cope as confusion abounds? Will coming clean as "the other twin" destroy the trust they've built?

## CHAPTER ONE

Dominic Hartington-George poured four sachets of sugar into the indistinguishable hot liquid they served in these premier London-address offices and sighed to himself. Sitting on his own in the luxuriously carpeted foyer, he wondered if he could work the Tardis-clone vending machine enough to get a chocolate bar as well.

On the pretext of needing a piss, he'd escaped from the meeting currently going on between his agent, Tanya Richards, and his PR company representatives. Well, he hadn't said that exactly, as Tanya had already briefed him about his language needing to be more socially acceptable. Apparently he wasn't on the top of a snowcapped mountain at the moment, where no one cared how he expressed his bodily needs except for the odd passing llama.

Dominic wondered idly why a llama's company felt infinitely more attractive compared to the meeting. And as an experienced mountaineer, he'd met a few llamas in his time. But he couldn't do anything about today, could he? He couldn't run away like he usually did—or as Tanya and his mother accused him of doing— to some mountain range to hide himself in another wild adventure.

CLARE LONDON

Because he was broke.

Not only that, but he was hawking his begging bowl around London in the hope of a sponsorship deal. He had to endure long meetings, cheesy smiles that set off a cramp in his jaw, and daily spreadsheet reminders of just how much money was involved in climbing the Eiger. It all just emphasised the size of the shit pile he was in. What was more, he struggled to cope with negotiation at the best of times. In fact, he was beginning to think he'd be better suited to standing outside on the street and offering copies of the *Big Issue*. He was no bloody good at bowing and scraping. Wasn't that what he employed Tanya for, anyway?

"It's a necessary evil," she'd told him firmly. He'd just announced his next expedition, and *she'd* announced a resounding, financial no-can-do. "You may have an aristocratic name and impeccable pedigree, but—"

"Bugger-all money?" he'd interrupted almost gleefully. For centuries his family was famous for being adventurers—and infamous for gambling away every treasure they ever owned. Great-Grandad had wasted the final thousands of the family fortune on a rangy horse in the Epsom Derby that, rather than romping home at 200-1, had fallen over its own feet in the first fifteen yards and had to be put out to grass. After that, the surviving Hartington-Georges moved to their more modest London properties and lived on the erratic income from opening their ancestral home to the public. Dom suspected his elegant sophisticate of a mother had never got over the shock of a stranger approaching her one afternoon and asking to be escorted to the baby-changing facilities.

Tanya had continued, "So if you want to continue your mountaineering projects—"

"No question!" he'd snapped.

Tanya had just inclined her head, unfazed. She hadn't worked for Dom for two years without learning "his ways". "So we must look at ways to raise the funds. And one of those is through sponsorship deals. Take that disgusted look off your face, Dom. A lot of sportsmen and explorers do that nowadays."

"Climb mountains with a big yellow M emblazoned on my forehead?"

Tanya let a smile tease the corners of her mouth. "I think it'd be more suitable if it were in the outdoor clothing and survival equipment market. I have contacts I can approach."

Tanya always had contacts. Dom had to admire that in her. Also her ability to manage her insolent runt of an assistant, Eric—oh, and her ability to cope with Dom in full grumpy mode. There weren't many people who managed to do that. His own mother only dropped into his Ladbroke Grove house a few times a year. Otherwise, they were both happy to keep correspondence to the occasional phone call or bumping into each other at family friends' events.

"You need to come out of your shell," Tanya had said to him. That was an hour before she employed the PR company. "And that doesn't include dancing on a pub table to karaoke."

*Bloody hell.* If having a night out with his climbing mates wasn't coming out of his shell, Dom didn't know what was. At the end of a training week in North Wales, he'd needed to unwind. A visit to a familiar and discreet London pub around the back of Kentish Town, where the licensing hours were applied loosely, if at all, had been just the thing. The food was plain, plentiful, and delicious, though the karaoke machine was a new addition. Dom had tolerated it only because it promised a set of old rock classics. He'd been halfway through a roaring-drunk rendition of "We Are the Champions" when he'd been snapped by one of those damned paparazzi, passing by on the off chance of a story. And yes, he had been standing on the table at the time, but the landlord didn't care, so why should anyone else?

But apparently that wasn't the right *kind* of shell-emerging. "Other options?"

Tanya had looked him in the eye and said wryly, "Get a job. You know, like the rest of us mortals."

Dom had felt physically sick. Not at the thought of hard graft, he was used to that and was no coward when it came to rolling up his sleeves. But the thought of sitting in an office in a suit and tie, shackled to a computer for eight hours a day, and answering to *someone else*....

He'd shuddered.

So here he was now, in the plush offices paid for by poor saps like himself and the companies who branded them, trying to rebrand Dominic

Hartington-George.

It was time to face the music again.

Dom had hoped to sneak back into the conference room with his coffee (tea? rat's pee?), but everyone turned to face him as he took his seat again. Tanya frowned at him, and Eric had that habitual smirk on his face, as if Dom were the greatest entertainment since schoolboys painted glue on the teacher's chalk. Of course, Dom thought rather glumly, that might be true, even if chalk had given way to an iPad stylus.

Two virtually interchangeable, slick-looking blondes in brightly coloured, tightly fitted skirt suits and matching pearl earrings represented the PR company. One of them blushed every time she looked at him.

She was the first to speak. "Tanya says you're looking for a makeover. You know, like they do on the TV? *10 Years Younger, Look Good Naked,* that kind of thing?"

What was this modern habit of talking in questions all the time? Dom stared at her steadily until she blushed again. "I have no idea what you're talking about," he said bluntly.

"I mean... obviously you don't need help with your looks," she stammered.

*Ah.* That explained some of the blushing. He often got that with younger women. If he turned his head, he would catch sight of Tanya's frown moving to a whole new level of disapproval. It was almost enough to cheer him up.

"Just the presentation," the other girl said, more sharply. The young one looked at her with naked gratitude. "We'll get someone on his wardrobe. Ellie, look into a suitable hairstylist too."

"Hairstylist?" Dom switched his glare to her. Polly, he thought her name was. He reassessed her as more assertive than just slick. Was that why his death glare didn't work as well on her as on other people?

Polly raised an eyebrow at him as if she could hear exactly what he was thinking right then, and she was far from intimidated. "And let's now address the, shall we say, *thorny* issue of social image."

"What the hell does that mean?"

Polly didn't even flinch. She was obviously used to stroppy clients.

Tanya touched his arm. "Dom. Please. You want your funding, don't you?"

"But why does it matter what I look like?" He could hear the plaintive note in his voice; he sounded like a petulant child. But he didn't want to be bothered with this. "I climb rocks and mountains, ladies. I wear bulky, padded clothes and thick-soled boots. My face is usually covered with goggles or a mask against the sun and dust. I grunt and curse and fart. I see no reason for social chitchat, I eat like a hungry horse, and I don't—repeat, don't—*moisturise*."

To his surprise Polly laughed. "I hear you, Mr. Hartington-George."

"Call me Dom," he said grudgingly.

"You're a fine man, Dom. Handsome and assertive and brave. We know all that."

*They do?*

"We're just looking for a way to brand you so that other brands want to match up with you. They'll pay for that privilege, you see. And that means making you look even more attractive."

"And more amenable," Tanya said half under her breath.

Dom couldn't say he hated Polly's style of flattery, but he was still wary. And he supposed he hadn't spent much time or money on his looks for a few years now.

"What about a girlfriend?" Ellie asked timidly.

Dom started.

"If the client were seen with a suitable partner... someone already media-friendly...."

"The intrepid adventurer captured and tamed by homespun beauty? Great idea. It'd certainly build a marketable strapline." Polly nodded and started scribbling on her notepad. "We have Alisha W already on the books. And I believe Suzie de Luca is in London for a shoot."

"No thanks." Dom's deep voice sounded very clear in the room.

Beside him, Tanya closed her eyes.

"Well, if not them, there are plenty of other ladies who'd love to be seen with you," Polly continued, unconcerned. "It'd be just another assignment, of course..."

"Of course," Tanya echoed, her voice rather faint and her eyes still closed tight.

"...although we would expect you, Dom, to look

happy with the arrangement on photoshoots and at public events. Meanwhile, it'll be excellent publicity for both of you, and you may even build a little romance, while persuading the media that the Daredevil Man in the wild can also be the Doting Man at home."

"No thanks," Dom repeated slowly. "Maybe that would be fine if you hadn't missed the whole point. The point that, even if I had time for dating, I don't date women."

Tanya leaned forward over the conference table and sank her head into her hands.

Eric snorted. Dom hoped it was because of nerves and not ridicule, else he'd thrash the kid when they got out of here. Eric was in his early twenties, overkeen, too bold, and completely unfazed by Don's gravitas. And he had the most disrespectful sense of humour Dom had ever known—albeit it made him laugh.

Ellie's eyes opened very wide. "You mean you're gay?"

"You're choosing *now* to come out?" Tanya muttered.

"It's not a matter of coming out!" Dom snapped back. What bloody century did these people live in? These city types were meant to be alert to the whole modern-world thing. "I've never been *in*. I just don't choose to expose my love life to every bloody person on the planet."

"If you had one to expose," Eric mumbled.

Dom glared at the kid, but Eric returned the stare without fear. *Bugger.* Dom should never have invited Eric on that mates' night out, or confessed in his cups just how bloody long it'd been since he, Dom, had dated anyone—man, woman, or llama. Meanwhile, the rest of the room was deathly silent.

Then Polly laughed again.

*Laughed?* "Something amusing you?" Dom asked icily. He pushed his chair back, ready to leave.

Tanya made a small sound of distress, but Dom was just thankful this would be the end of the whole stupid, misguided campaign—

"That's perfect!" Polly smiled broadly. "I've already had interest in your expedition from We Will Survive, who supply climbing gear to most of the London exhibitions and stores. They have a contract for next year's ascent on Everest too. And we all know how they embrace equality on all levels, don't we? This really will launch you as a man of the moment."

"Do we? Will it?"

Tanya surreptitiously pinched Dom in his side.

Polly rushed on regardless. "They have a major presence in the LGBTQ community and are linked to many gay climbing clubs and events. They'll be thrilled to have representation from another openly gay celebrity." She was already directing Ellie to look up a contact number.

"Another?"

"They used the famous gay model Zeb Z for that swimwear campaign last year."

"Famous for what? Being gay?" Dom was still irritated, especially as things didn't seem to be going the way he expected. "There's no way you're promoting me for my sexuality rather than my work."

"No, no!" Polly's smile never wavered. "That's not what I meant. Just that I know now where to start pitching the campaign. You and Zeb Z.

This is a *great* idea!"

# OTHER CLARE LONDON TITLES

**Novels**
Sweet Summer Sweat
Freeman
Romancing the Wrong Twin
Romancing the Ugly Duckling
Romancing the Undercover Millionaire
Romancing the Rough Diamond
72 Hours
Branded
True Colours
Flying Colours
Compulsion

*

Flashbulb
Dear Alex
Hidden Hearts
Just-You Eyes
Dancing Days
The Tourist
Blinded by Our Eyes
Goldilocks and the Bear
Telltale (Gothic horror)

# ABOUT CLARE LONDON

Clare took the pen name London from the city where she lives, loves, and writes. A lone, brave female in a frenetic, testosterone-fuelled family home, she juggles her writing with the weekly wash, waiting for the far distant day when she can afford to give up her day job as an accountant. She's written in many genres and across many settings, with novels and short stories published both online and in print. Most of her work features male/male romance and drama with a healthy serving of physical passion, as she enjoys both reading and writing about strong, sympathetic and sexy characters.

Clare currently has several novels sulking at that tricky chapter 3 stage and plenty of other projects in mind . . . she just has to find out where she left them in that frenetic, testosterone-fuelled family home.

All the details and free fiction are available at her website. Visit her today and say hello!

Website + blog: http://www.clarelondon.com
Newsletter: http://bit.ly/2WpHlyK
Facebook: clarelondonauthor
Twitter: clare_london
Goodreads: http://bit.ly/2lNSfC2
Amazon: author/clarelondon
Bookbub: profile/clare-london
Instagram: clarelondon11

Printed in Great Britain
by Amazon